T.H.U.G. L.I.F.E.

Also by Sanyika Shakur

Monster: The Autobiography of an L.A. Gang Member

T.H.U.G. L.I.F.E.

a novel by
SANYIKA SHAKUR

Grove Press
New York

Published simultaneously in Canada
Printed in the United States of America

ISBN-13: 978-0-8021-4424-9

Grove Press
an imprint of Grove/Atlantic, Inc.
841 Broadway
New York, NY 10003

Distributed by Publishers Group West

www.groveatlantic.com

09 10 11 12 10 9 8 7 6 5 4 3 2 1

For Samir, Kim, Kendis, Kerwin, and Kershaun

It's a family affair

T.H.U.G.
L.I.F.E.

Inconspicuously, Anyhow opened the window and raised the venetian blinds slowly, careful not to allow the individual blades to announce his presence. He scanned the partially illuminated den with a trained eye, looking hard at corners and door frames leading to other parts of the spacious town house, which could conceal an occupant lying in wait. Seeing no hint of movement or shadow, Anyhow held fast to the lower seal and with one swift motion hefted himself up and through the window. He landed with learned precision like a stalking cat—smooth and gracious, eyes alert, ears tuned like scanners for inordinate sounds. After a moment on toes and fingertips, confident that his entrance had gone unnoticed, Anyhow lifted his short muscular frame quickly and eased to the darkest part of the room. From this point he stood as still as any inanimate object.

From his immediate left his eyes took in the room. A fifty-three-inch Mitsubishi television set stood diagonally in the corner, resembling in the dimness an Easter Island statue head. Its wide, spoon-shaped screen reflected the hall to his right from where the night light shone. He'd use it as a cautionary reflector. Atop the big screen sat two eight-by-ten photographs in chestnut-mahogany frames. Although they were not entirely visible from this distance, he could make out the fact that one was a graduation photo and the other a family photo. A raggedy car rolled by on the street in front of the house, its engine knocking badly, begging for oil and a ring job. Anyhow cursed himself for not having closed the window. They had warned him about this. *Damn,* he thought to himself. One photo, the graduation cap and gown one, was the most visible—visible enough, that is, to reveal the person to be an Amerikan. Something he sensed anyway by the cold temperature of the room. "They," he'd been told once, "are like polar bears." Next to the big screen on the left side stood a two-and-a-half-foot Sanyo speaker and on its top a vase with tacky ornamental designs painted on it. A door leading two steps up to what must be a kitchen, he thought, and then the window from whence he came. Under it, but slightly leftward, was a love seat made of black calfskin. On it a child's notebook was laid open with a pencil across the page. A picture of an oceanscape dominated the wall above it. To the left of the love seat stood the matching Sanyo speaker. On its top was a Holy Bible encased in glass, a long-since-dead rose stem protruded from its middle. The cold temperature of the room caused Anyhow to raise the collar of his Fila sweat jacket and clench his teeth. A longneck, mushroom-topped Tiffany lamp stood erect catty-corner to his position. Next to it was an immobile wet bar with a child's crayon drawing haphazardly taped to it. The drawing was of stick people. Behind the ebony-oak bar was a full stereo set inserted into the wall. Its reel to reel, however, stood out on a shelf made especially for it. That portion of the room was deep brown paneling, grooved expensively with wedge-end chip stone. Two Norman Rockwell drawings adorned the paneling and led to a plethora of photographs framed in different sizes, all of which covered the expanse of the entire wall. Sitting out from the wall, on an awkward-looking end table, was an antique lamp of considerable expense—a Gregorian—imported from England.

The door with the light shining through its hall broke the wall and to his immediate right stood a six-shelf bookstand densely packed with leather-bound medical texts. *Where is it?* Anyhow thought, feeling his blood begin to boil, which was a comforting thing against the backdrop of the icy den. They said it would be in the den. He pondered, looking slowly around the walls for something he might have missed, squenching his eyes like Steve Austin, but where in the damn . . . his thoughts were cut short by a framed medical doctorate degree above his head to the right. Hmmm. He positioned himself in front of the certificate and raised his gloved hands toward it. But something furtive caught his eye to the left, and in one learned, fluid motion he reached for his Glock, drew, and fired. The room in a second's time was awash with light, gunfire, and assertive shouts. Instead of feeling secure as he had in the past when his Glock barked, Anyhow was knocked back into a ball of confusion, fear, and pain. Briefly there was light, and then came the darkness.

* * *

WESTSIDE NIGHT BANDIT CAPTURED! the headlines screamed the following morning. The paper slid across the Formica table, knocking two packs of Sweet 'n Low into the lap of Detective Sweeney. He ignored them and stared unblinking at the newspaper. He read, moving his lips without sound.

John Sweeney was a bald Irishman who'd grown up in the San Fernando Valley and lived in a state of constant fear all of his life. First he feared his domineering father, who'd taken great pains to let him never forget he was of "Fighting Irish" descent. He'd often demonstrate this fighting spirit by routinely finding something to jump on John about. Of course back in the 1970s this was not, as it is today, considered child abuse. Joseph Sweeney was also an alcoholic who'd find fault with John for the most trivial things and then use that as an excuse for history lessons through brutality. John feared and resented his father. His mother had learned her history lesson early and had long since graduated in divorce court. Because she was deathly afraid of Joseph, she didn't pursue a custody battle and John was left to his dad. As an overweight, pimple-faced boy, John caught the eye and brutish attention of the local stoners; thus, they were his second lesson in fear education. And in the late seventies, his school district began to bus in New Afrikans from South Central L.A. With a short right hook, which knocked out his two front teeth, John Sweeney met his first Crip and there started his third fear. When Career Day was held at his school, El Camino Real High, he sat at two booths and planned his future. One was the USMC booth and the other was an LAPD recruitment booth. After fearfully completing his senior year—taking all the bumps and bruises his dad, the locals, and the Crips (who were in no short supply being bused from South Central) could give him—John Sweeney joined the marines. After four years he was honorably discharged and went directly into the LAPD, assigned to the 77th division in South Central L.A. Within the 77th Division he was designated to the Community Resources Against Street Hoodlums unit, better known by its acronym, CRASH—the gang detail—and Sweeney was in nirvana. Ten years with CRASH, two fatal shootings, and countless arrests later, John Sweeney made detective, assigned to the homicide unit.

John Sweeney learned every dirty trick in the book. All the years of being bullied, beaten, and ridiculed were repaid in spades over the years of his tour of duty in L.A. ghettos and ganglands. He wasn't, by any stretch of the imagination, a good cop. He was, however, a great prison warden. He was the senior dick and thus the primary in all cases given to this team. He'd been a gold shield for four years now. "Oh, shit," Sweeney chuckled between sips of his steaming coffee, "Alvin Harper is the Westside Night Bandit."

"Yeah, it says as much right there," said Jesse Mendoza, Sweeney's partner. As if Sweeney were stupid.

"No, I know that, but what I'm saying is—"

"Yeah, yeah. Don't tell me," interrupted Mendoza. "He's another shithead gang banger you knew from CRASH, right?"

"Yep, but more than that he's a suspect in some one-eighty-sevens I've not been able to make any headway on. Maybe with these twenty-two burgs over his head and him hinging on three strikes he may want to cut a deal."

"Oh, yeah, a deal," retorted Mendoza cynically. "As if we haven't bargained the city's safety away by allowing dead bang slime to walk scott fuckin' free." At that, he tipped and drained his Styrofoam cup, crushing it noisily in his hand.

"We've no more bargained this city's safety away than the government is controlled by the president. Now, what do you say we get down to County General and see ol' Anyhow before he gets sent to Central and put in the Blood Module. After he's there, his homies will fuse him with subcultural strength and he'll probably never tell." Sweeney finished off his coffee laced with Sweet 'n Low, stood, struggled into his knit blazer, and rubbed tiredly on his shaved head.

"Well, I think it'll be a dry run," responded Mendoza, giving his tailored suit the once-over.

"Yeah, your optimism is too bright, Jess." Sweeney left a dollar tip and pushed out into the early L.A. sunlight. Mendoza followed, mumbling something about the dollar being too much of a tip. They stood next to the navy blue Chevy Lumina and removed their coats, which they'd just put on not fifty yards prior. Both wore white starched button-down collared shirts. Mendoza's was long sleeved and Sweeney's was short, exposing his Steve Garvey–like arms and USMC tattoo. Although their vehicle was supposed to be unmarked, it stood out like a woman in a men's communal shower. If the fact that it had no hubcaps over its black rims, dressed in traditional black wall police tires was not enough, then certainly the license plate prefixed with "e" was a dead giveaway. The mounted antenna was an altogether different thing. Unmarked indeed. Mendoza maneuvered the turbo-charged Chevy out onto Manchester Avenue and caught the moderate flow of commuter traffic. Instinctively his left hand began to tug lightly at the left side of his Pancho Villa mustache, a habit since high school when he'd first shown signs of facial hair. It earned him the nickname Lefty. He never used it because nicknames, he felt, were precursors to being gang affiliated, nor would anyone openly refer to him as such. So, à la

Benjamin Siegel, no one faced him with "Lefty." But that's what his peers knew him as.

Jesse Mendoza was a thirty-nine-year-old Chicano with deep-seeded machismo beliefs. Born and raised in the Estrada Courts housing project in East L.A., he managed through some tightwire maneuvering to escape the drag-iron recruitment net of the local gangs. In his project were the VNE, or Varrio Nuevo Estrada. Most of his childhood friends had cliqued, grown up hard in the *varrio,* and eventually died young or went to prison. He used his education as a means, indeed as a weapon, to fight his way out of the poverty-stricken labyrinth of Estrada Courts. Joining the LAPD was but one of four ways to actually escape the *varrio.* The other options, of course, generally available to most youth in the ghettos, were entertainer, athlete, or U.S. Armed Forces recruit. By joining the LAPD he did, in fact, join the U.S. Armed Forces. Five-foot-ten and thin as a rail, with sunken facial features, he looked like a mustached Detective Munch on the popular television show *Homicide.* He'd worn glasses up until his tour of duty began, then he was turned on to Lenscrafters and was fitted with Bausch and Lomb contact lenses. Married and the father of twin girls, he loathed being called Mexican. "Mexicans," he'd quickly say, correcting anyone who had the unfortunate luck of being so ignorant, "were born and lived in Mexico. I am a Chicano, born in Aztlán, in what you call the United States but is really Aztec land, the Chicano Nation."

Jesse Mendoza was, perhaps more than anything, a stubborn cynic. This he'd taken above and beyond the trained cynicism doled out at the academy and mixed it with a touch of machismo, pessimism, and prejudice to come up with a less than sociable personality that no one other than police officers could tolerate. Mendoza was, above all, a straight arrow. He pushed the line of law and order as it was written. He was no vigilante. He hated racism and still, while upholding the written laws of the land, knew that poor people were at a vast disadvantage in most situations in the face of the state.

The police radio squawked some coded feedback, which Sweeney instinctively turned down. The Lumina bore forward toward the on-ramp of the Harbor Freeway. Mendoza deliberately blocked off a blue custom dully truck, lowered on some gold Dayton wire rims, and shot onto the freeway accelerating constantly until he'd reached in excess of seventy mph and caught the flow of traffic as if they'd been in it since Long Beach. Both officers hated County General Hospital. The often nonlucid staff made every trip there a tedious one. The highway patrol vehicle flew past on the inner lane next to the divider. The Crown Victoria floated easily at ninety-seven mph. The only difference between the marked and unmarked CHP vehicles were row lights on top and color-reàl stealth.

"Good morning L.A.," Mendoza said sarcastically, tugging on his mustache.

Lapeace was disturbed from a pleasant dream by the dancing pager vibrating noisily on the nightstand. It had been vibing for some time but in his dream it had been his twelve-inch tubs subbing the bass line of Tupac's newest single "Hit 'Em Up." Panty-clad women danced around his 3600 Chevy Suburban as he puffed on a blunt the size of a small child. The atmosphere was too cool, but the subbing had persisted long after the song had gone off and he frowned (even in his sleep) because that meant he was getting feedback through his lines, which was a sign of sloppy instalation. In his dream, he lifted up on a cloud of indo smoke and rode it like a Jet-Ski toward the back of the block-long truck to check his amp modulation. The feedback continued until finally his REM was broken and he realized that the sound was not in his head but coming from his pager.

Slowly he opened his eyes and peered suspiciously around the room. *Where the fuck am I?* he thought to himself, seeing no familiar furnishings. The pager danced again, breaking his thought. He grabbed it like a screaming child with his hand over its mouth in an attempt to shut it up and pushed the received button. 29 910 459-83. He stared at the cryptic message and fell back onto his pillow as if a great load had been lifted from his chest. He closed his eyes and clenched the silent Intel pager in his massive hand and tried with no success to recapture the sight of the panty-clad women. "Shit," he muttered under his breath and looked for the first time at the woman lying sound asleep beside him. Her hourglass shape caused the deep blue triple-goose comforter to rise and lower like the mountainous contour of the Rockies. Her Brandy-like braids, strewn in thirty different directions over the fluffy pillow, were pulled back from her face exposing her beautifully sculpted features. She was evidently young, as her face glowed radiantly with young skin. *What's her name?* Lapeace thought to himself. Tamika? Talibah? Tayari? What? He'd done this countless times. Met a woman at a club, macked up on her, and left the club with her for a steamy sexual roll, only to forget her name the next day—or even the same night. He always said he'd do better, but things only got worse. Now here he was again with an unknown body. *And where was he this time?* he wondered. *And my truck*—this thought caused him to leap up from the bed and head for the window. Nearly tripping over a clump of clothes on the floor, his foot got momentarily caught up in a Karl Kani belt. He shook it loose, reached the windowpane and the string on the miniblinds. Through a dirty pane of glass and a barrage of bars he could make out the top of Lucky—his green Lexus 3600 Suburban XLT. Across the top of Lucky, which was parked in the driveway, Lapeace could see two Mexican men painting the trim on the adjacent house. They spoke in rapid Spanish between gulps of Corona and strokes of the paintbrush. Before lowering the blinds he tried to look up the drive to see just where he was, but the bedroom was too far back and his view was obscured by the house next door. He thought about venturing out of the room but decided against it because if she was as young as she looked she might just be living with her parents.

"Good morning, Lapeace," said a crisp, young singsong voice. Startled by the break in silence, he let go of the drawstring and the blinds crashed onto the window seal noisily.

"Damn, don't do that," he said, trying to remember her name. "You ain't right."

"Aw, you ain't gotta be all jumpy. I only said good morning," she replied cooing as if talking to a child who'd been frightened. She'd gotten up and propped her head in her hand supported by her elbow on the bed. The comforter fell slightly away revealing her naked breasts.

"Naw, I was just thinking about something. I ain't trippin'. Eh, where . . ." and suddenly he realized that he was naked. He looked down at himself and quickly over to the clump of clothes, none of which she missed. His body tensed, obviously aware of his audience, as he tried to suck in his gut and push out his chest, not that he had much of either. She looked on in amusement as he held his breath in an attempt to look mannish. *Men are just as vain as they accuse women of being,* she thought to herself.

"Um . . . are . . . we . . . I mean, is this . . ." but his train of thought would not connect accordingly, and his shyness splattered all over the room, revealing beyond the phat truck, expensive jewelry, and designer clothes a shy man-child stripped to his essence.

"Come here, baby," she beckoned and held open her arms allowing her supple breasts to swing freely with her movement. Hesitantly, Lapeace stepped forward, trying to make it to the bed quickly and shield his nakedness, but still his heavy dick hit and slapped both thighs as he walked. Instead of embracing him or letting him get under the comforter with her, she held him at arm's distance and stared up into his dark, handsome face. He looked down questioningly, tracing the length of her fine thin arms to her beautifully manicured hands, which rested firm on both of his thighs.

"Lapeace, you are a fine brotha. You ain't got nothing to be ashamed about baby. Nothing." And with that she took him into her warm mouth and sucked him to an erection. Lapeace groaned, moaned, and leaned into her bobbing head with one hand in her braids and the other twisting and manipulating his own nipple. Feeling the coming explosion, and not wanting the sensation to end, he withdrew from her and yanked back the comforter, revealing one of her fingers working furiously on her clit. He lifted her hand and sucked the nectar from her fingers. Licking every digit individually until her fingers were covered with saliva, he guided her hand to his extended dick and she began to stroke it gently while he busied himself with her wetness below. Before long she was moaning his name as he licked and lapped at her hot pussy. Lying on her back, arched into a bridgelike overpass, she ground her pelvis rhythmically into his face. Her firm breasts were held lovingly in each hand and her pretty toes were pointed toward the ceiling. "Do it Lapeace, eat that pussy baby. Ohh, yes, do it you sexy mothafucka, do it!" she hissed through pants and moans. And Lapeace smacked cheerfully on as her juices ran freely into his mouth. Satisfied that she had come, Lapeace got on his knees and gently entered her temple, allowing her to feel every raised vein in his shaft. When he'd buried the length, he slowly pulled out the engorged head and pushed with one even stroke until he'd buried it again and then proceeded to make passionate love to the woman whose name he still couldn't remember. After an hour of multiple positions, they were both drained and exhausted, laid out breathing soulfully in satisfied gestures. They said nothing, just listened to the Mexican painters' lively exchange next door. Their peaceful time was interrupted by the buzzing of the doorbell. Lapeace looked over at her blissful face and nudged her lightly.

"Eh," he started, hoping she wouldn't notice he hadn't said her name once this morning. "Ain't you gonna answer the door?" He got no reply. Just a low breathing sound similar to a baby's snore. He nudged her again, this time a bit harder. "Say, somebody's at yo' door, ain't you gonna answer it?" *Bzzz, Bzzz.* She then began to stir, slowly scooting to the end of the bed, pulling the comforter with her as she went. "Uh-uhn," said Lapeace, snatching and gathering up the comforter. "You ain't got nothing to be ashamed of—you fine," he said, mimicking her words playfully.

"Now you learning," she said, with a backward mischievous glance, and strutted naked as the day she was born toward the bedroom door. Lapeace sat up straight, holding the balled-up comforter over his genitals, eyes transfixed on her lovely muscular ass. *Damn,* he thought to himself, *she is fine!* When she got to the bedroom door, knowing he was looking, she put both of her tiny feet together, which served only to accent her bow legs, and bent full at the waist, bringing her face down to rest fully on her knees. Through her bow she could see his mouth fall slack. *Bzzz, Bzzz.* She lifted up and exited the room.

"Damn," Lapeace said aloud to himself. "She's straight." For the first time he really scoped out the room. Hip-hop posters canvased every wall. Tupac was prominently displayed, going back three albums. Kausion, Kam, MC Lyte, the Poetess, Ice Cube, Bahamadia, and the 5th Ward Boyz. One whole wall was nothing but CDs—there must have been two thousand. Alphabetically cataloged. Atop a cute pink thirteen-inch Zenith television sat a row of small photos of her and some hip-hop artists: Too Short, Spice 1, MC Eiht, Mopreme from Thug Life, and Sheena Lester, editor in chief of *Rap Pages* magazine. He moved over to the nightstand on her side and read a list of things to do, one of which included: "Meet Spike at Georgia's." *Was that Spike Lee? And was Georgia's Denzel Washington's place on Melrose? What was her damn name?* he thought to himself angrily now. Over the headboard was a giant poster advertising Sankofa, and it was framed. He heard her padding down what must be the hall and tumbled onto the bed.

"UPS is so stupid," she came in complaining. "They know I got an account with them but wouldn't leave my package without my receipt book." Lapeace, knowing nothing about UPS or receipt books, gestured helplessly with his hands and eyebrows. He lay there pretending to be contemplating her dilemma while lusting at her sexy stance. *Damn, she is fine.* Just then her phone rang and she plopped onto the bed with her back facing him. Her braids hung lightly down her back and he couldn't help but reach out and rub her silky skin. In circular motions his big dark hands caressed her bare back. He eased them up to her shoulders and began to massage her tension-filled traps.

"Uhmm, yes . . . that's it . . ." she said softly. "No, no, not you Mr. Duke, excuse me. No this is a good time. Okay, are you ready? Tashima Mustafa . . . 5428 Hillcrest Drive. L.A. California, 90043, 213-296-2871. And my pager number is 213-412-3880. Yes, I overstand. I'll be looking forward to it. Thank you. Bye."

Mustafa? Hillcrest Drive? Two things hit him at once. One, she was Tashima Mustafa, CEO of RapLife Music—the phattest hip-hop company on the West Coast and no doubt one of the biggest after Death Row Records. And two, he was in Rollin' Sixty neighborhood. His worst enemies. He had to disguise both his excitement at having hit Tashima Mustafa as well as his dismay at being caught in the Sixties during daylight hours. When she'd finished her call she asked was he hungry, to which he replied he was. He thought she was going to make them breakfast but instead suggested they go to Roscoe's Chicken & Waffles. She left the room after breaking his lustful embrace and began to shower, humming an indistinguishable tune that sounded like the old Teddy Pendergrass song, "Close the Door." Lapeace's pager vibrated and at its sudden life he hollered through the bathroom door and asked Tashima if he could use the phone.

"It's about time you answered that damn pager. Someone's been blowing you up all morning," she shouted over the stream of shower water, surprising him that she'd been up the first time it had gone off. He said nothing and went to the phone. After he dialed the number he walked over to the side window and watched two Mexican kids playing happily in the next yard. On the fourth ring the phone was picked up by a service, which began with some lyrics from Tupac:

Gimme my money in stacks,
And lace my bitches with dime figures.

Real niggas fingas on nickel-plated nine triggers
Must see my enemies defeated,
Catch 'em while they coked up and weeded
Open fire now them niggas bleeding.

"West up, this is Sekou, I ain't in right now, but leave a message and I'll hit you back. Out."

Beeeeeeeeep. "Sekou, it's me, L.P. Pick up da phone, nigga."

"Hello?"

"Man, why you keep that fucking service on like you ain't there when you always there?"

"Aw, I be just screening my calls and shit. You feel me?"

"Yeah, I feel you, homie," muttered Lapeace. Sliding open Tashima's nightstand drawer and seeing a large-caliber weapon under a quarter ounce of pot—indo, no doubt the chronic.

"Why you didn't hit me back earlier, Peace?"

"Huh? Oh, shit, 'cause I got the message and I ain't had nuttin to say. Shit, fuck that nigga."

"You know he stubo, huh? They fin' to stretch that fool."

"Fuck him," said Lapeace, fiddling around in the drawer seeing a fresh pack of Philly Blunts, two extra clips for the weapon, and a battery for a Motorola cellular phone. He was trying to distract himself from the news of Anyhow's capture and what seemed to be an imminent life term. He'd felt queasy really since he'd gotten the coded message this morning.

29 910 459-83

29 was the code given to Anyhow, Lapeace's set, to monitor his movements and to be able to talk over cordless lines without fear of conspiracy charges. 9-10 is the alphabetical numerical

sequence for "I-J," meaning "in jail." 459 is the penal code for burglary and 83 was the street number for Lapeace's neighborhood, Eighty-third Street.

"Hello? Peace, you there?" asked Sekou, wondering where his homie had gone and why there was an eerie silence.

"Yeah, yeah, I'm here."

"That's your boy still, ain't it, Peace?"

"Nigga, you mad? Hell naw! Fuck that slob ass fool. Eh, cuz, I'm fin' to take a shower and grub, I'll hit you on the hip later on."

"Wait, I—"

"I'm out." Click. Lapeace broke the connection and immediately the phone rang. Lapeace knew it was Sekou who'd hit him back with Star 69. He sat there by the phone until it stopped ringing and then moved to collect his clothes from the middle of the floor. He hoped his things hadn't gotten too wrinkled. As he smoothed over the fabric on his black Kani jeans, he thought of some connections he could tap into, which could draw on more particulars involving the case with Anyhow. He had a sista friend who worked at the L.A. *Sentinel* that he could call who'd probably know more from a pig's perspective than he'd learned from Sekou's street version. *Burglary?* he thought. *Anyhow?* Unless it was an industrial burglary, involving a gang of money or jewelry, he couldn't see it. He'd lain his clothes out neatly on the unmade bed when Tashima came into the room wrapped in a black fluffy towel, smelling of fresh strawberries.

"Your turn, lover man," she said, bowing gracefully.

"Right on, then," said Lapeace evenly and sauntered past her, but not before she'd grabbed a handful of his ass. He tensed quickly to her touch and she complimented him on his glutes. He blushed and kept his pace. The hot shower did him well, and soon he was dressed and lacing his black Kani boots. Standing in front of the mirror, he checked his appearance. Triple zero baldhead, two half-karat diamond studs in his left ear, one gold loop in his right. Thick eyebrows. Strong nose leading down to a thick dark mustache clipped neatly over full lips. He had a strong chin and jawline to match. His neck was still thick and muscular from being a jock in high school. He wore one two-inch herringbone necklace out over his Kani hoody, black Kani pants blushed up over his black Kani boots. Hopefully they could get in and out of Roscoe's before the sun started to heat things up and he'd look ridiculous in the same gear, which was the bomb last night. "Can we take your car, Tashima?" he asked, hoping she wouldn't inquire as to why.

"My car ain't here. It was hit by a Mexican and now it's being painted. Is something wrong with your truck?" she asked suspiciously.

"Naw, the truck is straight. It's just that it's hella dirty, you know?"

"Dirty?" she asked incredulously. "Dirty how? As in real dirt and grime? Dirty as in you got some heat in it, or meanin' that you've done some dirt in it? The first two I can stand, but I can't fade the latter. So, come on now, holler at me," she said with her head tilted slightly leftward supporting the weight of her question.

"Not the third, fo' sho'. It's just a film of dust over it. Nothing we can't stand. I wouldn't jeopardize you, Tashima," Lapeace countered, stepping up to her five-foot-two frame of young beauty, allowing his six-two height to tower over her persuasively.

"I sure hope not, 'cause I ain't in no gettin'-shot-at mood this morning."

"I feel you on that," Lapeace responded, wanting to add, "'cause I know you be dumpin' back." But he didn't want to reveal the fact that he'd been snooping in her drawer. She moved over toward the nightstand that held her weapon. Her Pelle Pelle jeans were beige, hip-hop baggy, and fresh. Her braids, which he learned were not extensions, were pulled back and fastened in a ponytail by a black hair tie. Some black Ray-Ban baby locs sat atop her head and her black T-shirt bore the faces of Suga-T, B-Legit, D-Shot, and E-40 on the front and on the back was simply "The Click, Game Related." Her Norflake three-quarter-top boots were unlaced with the tongue hanging out.

"Lapeace," she said, stopping before she reached the drawer. "You got heat in the truck, right?"

Reluctantly, after a few seconds, Lapeace said, "Fo' sho'—in my lap at all times."

"Awright, volume ten," she said with a bright laugh and opened the drawer, retrieved the box of blunts and the pot, hesitated, then closed the drawer. She wore only eyeliner that accentuated her almond-shaped, amber-brown eyes and her lips were culturally atavistic works of art. Sculpted, seemingly, from the bloodline of New Afrika's finest.

"Let's bounce," she said, walking two steps ahead of Lapeace, who snatched up his pager, keys, and Chapstick on the way out. At the kitchen they stopped briefly, as Tashima went to the service area and poured what sounded like dog food in a bowl. When she returned she explained that she had a rottweiler named Kody that was just getting over Parvo, and she felt very bad for him. She looked depressed. They walked up the dark hallway past two other bedrooms and into a spacious dining area, then an equally large living room furnished with low black-lacquered tables and leather. The walls reflected platinum everywhere.

Before exiting the house, Tashima punched in a code for her alarm. From the porch, Lapeace hit his alarm but no sound returned, just a red light on his remote signaling his alarm had been disarmed. He pushed a second green button and Lucky roared to life. Tashima stopped momentarily and gazed at the truck and then quickly at his hand, raising an eyebrow. "That's pretty phat, man," she said, smiling, watching as his fingers touched a third button that unlocked the doors. They entered the air-conditioned confines of the plush Suburban, sat momentarily, and then backed out of the driveway slowly.

Lapeace took Hillcrest, down past 57th to Slauson, turned right, and didn't play any music until he'd crossed Dean. He grabbed up his remote, pressed 5-4 and Sean Levert's "Put Your Body Where Your Mouth Is" came out heavy and strong—flooding the interior of the truck with highs and lows, perfectly pitched, rapping them up in real soulful R&B—without the nasal twang. The Suburban pushed up Slauson, effortlessly gliding like a big ship over calm waters. Tashima nestled back into the big seat and relaxed. Neither spoke a word, just let Sean do his thing. South Central faded past as the small, hobbled-together storefront businesses gave way to more commercialized and less relevant to New Afrikan peoples stores. At La Cienega, Lapeace turned right and headed north toward Washington Boulevard. Lapeace circumvented the Rollin' Sixties neighborhood as well as several smaller sets, some hostile toward his sand, some not. He just wasn't in the mind-set to be dumping or chitchatting with bangers. Not that he was such an active force in the zones (as he'd been a few years back), but still he'd gotten his rep the old-fashioned way. He'd killed for it.

They arrived at Roscoe's quicker than Tashima expected. The big truck floated so smoothly, coupled with the relaxing music, she'd almost dozed off. Lapeace guided her inside protectively, choosing a seat in the rear where he could sit with a bird's-eye view of all who came and went, Malcolm X–style. The place was, as usual, hustling with people, mostly young, game-related folk. A few elders sprinkled here and there. Across from them diagonally sat a brotha who kept staring at Tashima, but because her back was to him she was unaware of his persistent gaze. He sat with a woman who looked very familiar in a wholesome, nonthreatening way. He couldn't put his finger on just where he'd seen her before.

The waitress brought them menus and without looking they both ordered chicken, waffles, and orange juice. "Tashima, do you . . ." he started but didn't finish.

"Lapeace, everyone just calls me Shima. I'd feel more comfortable if you used it too," she said, her hand reaching across to sit on his.

"Awright," he began again. "Shima, do you know ol' boy behind you to your left? Don't look over too obvious. Just do it casually," he said, instructing her like a spy master. Shima was enjoying his little protective ways. She felt comfortable with him, and it hadn't escaped her notice that he'd taken the long way there.

"Maybe," she whispered across the table, "I should act like I'm going to the ladies' room?"

"Naw," he whispered back, lowering his voice to her level, "I don't think it's that serious."

"Oh," she said, surprised, leaning back in her booth. "I thought we were being clocked by jackers or somethin'." Lapeace just stared across at her without saying a word. His expression said it all: *Don't be playing like that.* She overstood. The couple were preparing to leave, gathering up their black leather appointment books, pens, and magazines when Shima turned slightly toward them. The man was muscularly thin, athletically so, like a track and field competitor. Dark-skinned, with tight, almost Asiatic-shaped eyes. His hair was cropped low on top, wavy in an "S"-curl fashion and faded to a one on the sides. His smile revealed splendid white teeth and he had no facial hair. He was dressed in black jack boots, stone-washed jeans, and a short-sleeved blue thermal shirt. The woman was quite short, but definitely packing. Close-cut hair, perhaps a two, waved from constant brushing. Her short hair accentuated her natural beauty. She wore no makeup. Didn't need to. The woman was fine. Her jeans were darker, loose fitting, and comfortably holed in key spots. The T-shirt she was wearing was white with a silkscreen photo of Jimi Hendrix across the front with the words "The Beginning" under him. They stood to leave. "Antoine, what is up, my brotha?" said Shima excitedly, scooting across and out of her booth to greet him.

"Hey Shima," said the brotha. "I thought that was you but I wasn't sure. Hey," he continued, "you know Me'shell Ndegeocello, don't you?"

"No, but I've always wanted to meet you," Shima answered warmly.

"The feeling is definitely mutual."

They'd all but forgotten about Lapeace sitting there looking sullen. He'd heard it all. And while he didn't know who Antoine was, he'd definitely heard of Me'shell Ndegeocello. He had her *Plantation Lullabies* CD in Lucky's CD changer. He made a mental note to play it on their way back.

"Oh," bubbled Shima, bouncing on her toes, "I'm so sorry. This is my friend Lapeace."

"Lapeace, good to meet you brotha," said Antoine, extending his hand for a power clench shake.

"Righteous," replied Lapeace, standing cordially to receive his hand, then shaking it strongly.

"Hey, Lapeace, how you doing?" greeted Me'shell, stepping up for a hug.

"I'm straight, and it's certainly a pleasure to meet you." His whole language pattern changed for the greeting. Shima, as usual, noted it. Lapeace stood a bit outside the circle while they chatted on about industry things. Antoine Fuqua was a major video director for Propaganda Films who'd been hired to shoot Me'shell's new video, plus it stemmed from the conversation that she'd be doing the score for an upcoming film Antoine was directing. They talked a minute more before final salutations were exchanged, then the pair left. The steamy hot chicken and waffles were the bomb, as always, and went down quickly. On the ride back, Lapeace began Me'shell's CD with his favorite, "Souls on Ice," and Shima listened attentively, agreeing off and on with traditional "I know that's right" and "Fo' sho'." The Suburban pushed on down Washington to Arlington and panned right. At the corner of Adams and Arlington they were caught by the light. They both sat staring across at the Elegant Manor, the huge house used by the Universal Negro Improvement Association, Marcus Garvey's organization, which was still in existence. A black-and-white patrol car eased up in the turning lane, its tomato-faced occupants staring hard at Lapeace's truck. The green Lexus paint, covered by its thirteen coats of lacquer and accented by gold Daytons wrapped in 50-series low-profile Perellis, screamed *drug dealer* to the police. They sat and looked piggish, and Lapeace eased the music down. He wasn't worried about anything legitimate they could sweat him for, 'cause all that was covered—license, registration, and proof of insurance.

Even his heat was stashed so well they'd never find it. The light turned green and the truck churped out and got some rubber from its posey traction. The police turned right.

Lapeace took the double hill on Arlington slow, careful not to scrape the bottom of his bumpers against the asphalt, a precaution he'd been given when he'd had his coils cut. The vibration on his hip alerted him to a page. He lowered Me'shell's "If That's Your Boyfriend" and lifted up the cellular from its holder, keyed in the number, and pressed send. A moment later, a male voice came on the line.

"Hello."

"This is Lapeace."

"Please hold, sir," said the proper voice on the other end. A moment passed before a familiar voice came on.

"Lapeace, how are you this morning?" queried the voice in a colonized accent.

"I'm straight. What's up?"

"Well," began the voice cautiously, "it appears that she is willing to fight you in a custody battle. Now, we have more than enough grounds to win this case, but I don't know if you want your business in the court of law."

Lapeace looked pensive, outwardly disturbed at the news. "Well, let me get back to you this afternoon. Right now I'm in traffic and holding."

"Oh, I see," answered the voice. "Very well then. Call me back at the office, say, around three. Is that fine for you?"

"That's straight. Oh, and dig this: 29 910 459," said Lapeace, rattling off the numbers given to him earlier by Sekou. "Can you check into this for me?"

"Sure, Lapeace. At three, I'll have something for you."

"Awright, I'm out." The connection was broken and so was his laid-back mood. *Shit,* he thought to himself. *If it wasn't one thing it's another.* In midstride he flicked the CD from Me'shell Ndegeocello to Tupac and "You wonder why we call you bitch" came blaring out. So loud was it that Shima had to tap his leg for attention and signal for him to please turn it down. Reluctantly he did so, but only slightly. She tapped again, looking questionably at his cloudy face. He put the song on pause.

"Lapeace, what's wrong? Is it me or what?" she asked pointedly, trying to figure out his sudden mood change. Certainly she'd heard nothing on his end of the situation to warrant such a shift. *Perhaps,* she thought, *it was her and this was his sign of saying the date's over.*

"Naw, Shima, it ain't you," he said, coming to a stop behind a waste-management truck on Arlington and Vernon Avenue. "It's my ex-girl, really my ex-wife. She doesn't want me to have custody of my children. She wants to fight it out in court." He looked, for the first time, weak and frightened.

"You've been married and have children?" she asked in a nonbelieving tone.

"Yeah, I got caught up with a woman older than me and became dependent on her. It's a long story." He trailed off his discourse.

"I ain't mad at cha. It's just a trip to find a brotha your age who's been married these days. So, you ain't afraid of commitment, huh?" she asked, which was more rhetorical than an outright question.

"Naw, it ain't commitment that scares me, it's scandalous bitches that fuck me up." He'd grown angry, and it reflected in his language, tone, and driving. He was pushing Lucky with recklessness up Vernon Avenue. At Crenshaw he punched it through a yellow light and took Santa Rosalia up into the hills.

"Lapeace, can you please slow down a bit?" She'd grown afraid of his driving, and Lucky no longer seemed luxurious and comfortable, but more like a rolling coffin. When they got to Shima's house, he sat in the truck and wouldn't get out. She came around to his side and rested her elbows on his window. "Listen," she began, "I feel you, Lapeace. I see that you are a qualitative brotha. I don't know much about you, but from what I've seen I can dig you. But if you let some . . . some . . . ol' scandalous bitch drive you mad, you're as weak as any other fool out here." He shot her an eyebrow-connected glare, but she continued. "Now, what I suggest you do is," opening the door to the truck, "come on in here and blow a blunt with me and calm down."

"I gotta bounce," he responded, closing back his door, "but let's get together later, awright?"

"You ain't gonna get with me later, Lapeace."

"I will if that's what you want."

"You know it is . . ." She looked off thoughtfully.

"What," he said in a clowning voice, "I gotcha open?"

"Wide, baby," she said looking at him and holding his brown eyes to hers, "but I can close if I feel the catch is foul. So don't bug out on me, War."

"War? Where you get that from?" His mind had already fallen off of his ex-wife.

"Lapeace," she said slowly, "'La' is Swahili for no, isn't it?"

"Yeah."

"And 'peace'—no peace. Which means if there is no peace, it's only war. But which war are you fighting, soldier?" she asked seriously.

"The good fight," he answered and Lucky rumbled to life. "I'll hit you off later," he said, backing out of Shima's yard, never unlocking eyes with her. He was back in control of his mood and flicked the remote to reflect it. Out of his system came MC Lyte: "B boy, I've been lookin' for your ass since a quarter past . . ." Tashima smiled, waved, and he rolled off subbing down the block, hidden behind the dark tent of Lucky's windows.

2

Anyhow lay still in a morphine drift, too medicated to feel what he looked like. His torso resembled an early colonial map of Afrika drawn by marauding pirates. He'd been shot four times. Twice in the chest, once in the stomach, and once through the right biceps. A translucent tube ran from an extraction pump on the left side of his bed, up through his nose, and down into his stomach. A drainage tube had been inserted on his left side to pump fluid from his lungs, one of which had collapsed. Two ribs were fractured and a hairline fracture scarred his sternum. An incision had been made from under his armpit around his right breast and stopped just under center mass. Another ran vertically from his solar plexus to his pubis. His right arm had already begun to atrophy. His mouth was agape and his eyes were closed peacefully. An IV was taped to his left forearm and a catheter had been inserted, along with a colostomy bag for body waste.

He was on the thirteenth floor of the L.A. County Hospital, chained by the ankle to the bed, barely alive. "We tried to kill the nigger," said one detective the night he was brought in unconscious, "but them fuckers die harder than Bruce Willis." Anyhow was rigged to several machines that monitored his life: heart, respiratory, brain waves, etc. His condition was critical, and he looked every bit of it.

"I'm sorry," said the nurse, "but he is in no condition to be interviewed. His every conscious minute without medication is unbearably painful."

"All the more reason we'd like to speak with him now," said Sweeney, peering through icy blue eyes at the nurse with a you-know-the-rules look.

"I'm sorry, Detective . . . uh . . ."

"Sweeney," he interjected.

"Sweeney, of course, but doctor's orders."

"When," asked Mendoza, through smacks of ranch-flavored CornNuts, "will Mr. How, I mean Harper, be well enough for an interview?"

"I'm not sure. He's in pretty bad shape. You know, perhaps a week or two at the least," she said, hunching her bony shoulders helplessly.

"That bad, huh?" jestered Sweeney.

"Real bad."

"Thank you, uh, Nurse . . ." turning his head sideways.

"Richter," she said.

"We'll definitely be back." At that, the detectives turned and left the floor. Anyhow slept on, oblivious to it all.

Two weeks from that day they were back, and Nurse Richter gleefully prepared Anyhow for a bedside interview. He still experienced some pain but had gone from morphine to codeine and his condition had been downgraded from critical to stable. He was in the room with two other prisoner-patients: a Mexican who'd been shot in the head by the Lennox division of the L.A. Sheriff's Department as he exited a bank after robbing it and another brother who'd been mauled by an LAPD K-9 Unit. His face and neck were so bruised, scarred, and swollen that from the shoulders up there seemed to be one great mass of bloody flesh. His moans permeated the room. The low hum of the equipment, coupled with the periodical groan of the head-shot victim and ever-present sobs of the K-9 patient, created an eerie soundtrack of gloom, over which were laid the sights to these sounds. The atmosphere was utter despair and pain.

Anyhow had been out of the ICU for three days when he was informed that he had visitors. He was not delighted in the least when in through the double doors walked Sweeney and Mendoza. He just looked at them pathetically. They pulled up chairs and took off their coats. As usual, Sweeney's forearms were exposed, revealing a devil dog tattoo, with *Semper Fi* under it and *U.S.M.C.* over it. Mendoza's long-sleeved shirt was impeccably starched. He had in his hand a leather notepad, an accessory from Moca Max. He opened it and wrote:

Alvin Harper
6 Duce Brim
24 years old
Black male
Homicide suspect
August 27, 1996

"Alvin," began Sweeney in a jovial tone. "How goes it, fella?"

Anyhow ignored him and turned his head. The head-shot victim stared across at them from behind his head and neck brace.

"Oh, don't tell me you're not talking to us, Any. What's up with that, homeboy?" Sweeney called himself using the "native dialect," just like his settler forefathers. Silence. Low hum of technical equipment and the K-9 victim's sobs. "Yeah, well, what if I did . . . this."

"Ahh! Nurse! Nurse!" screamed Anyhow as a piercing bolt of pain shot through his arm. Sweeney had taken his thumb and pressed it hard into Anyhow's wound.

"Oh, don't worry about the nurse. She's one of us," replied Mendoza and wrote

Suspect responsive but belligerent:

in his notepad. "Now, we are going to begin again," instructed Sweeney. "How are you, Alvin?"

"Fuck you, pig," answered Anyhow defiantly.

"Oh yeah. Fuck me, huh?"

"Ahh! Ahh! Ahh! Ahh!" Anyhow cried until he began to cough up blood. The Mexican looked on in terror and the K-9 victim's sobs got louder.

"Don't feel too good, does it, Anynigger? Huh?"

"Noooo," answered Anyhow through the excruciating pain and curdling blood. Mendoza wrote

Suspect assaultive, might have to restrain:

"Now that we've got your attention, you little shit, we'd like to talk to you about a couple of hot ones that your name keeps coming up on. Do you hear me?" asked Sweeney, leaning into the ear of Anyhow, breathing heavily.

"Do you feel like talking, Alvin?" asked Mendoza, as if he had just run into him at a shopping mall.

"Hey!" Sweeney shouted, reaching with that bloody thumb. "My partner's talking to you."

"I hear him, man. Shit. You just watch that fuckin' thumb," grumbled Anyhow angrily, looking with injurious intent at Sweeney. The look was not lost on Sweeney, who responded with a feigned backhand that caused Anyhow to turn his head.

"Answer him then," demanded Sweeney.

"What, man? Whatcha wanna talk about? I don't know nothing 'bout no hot ones. Nothing."

"Well, we think a bit different. Now, we'll lead and you follow. If what you say doesn't jibe with what we already know, you get the thumb. You got that?"

"Man, I told you that I . . . Ahh! Ahh! Awright, man, awright!!"

Mendoza wrote:

Suspect has agreed to talk openly with myself,
Det. J Mendoza #68201. And Det. J Sweeney
#532307-Hom. Unit 77th Div.

Sweeney wiped the blood from his thumb on Anyhow's bed clothes and leaned over the bed rail.

"Where you wanna start with this?" asked Anyhow, willingly, not wanting again to feel Sweeney's thumb penetrating his wounded arm. It had gone in clear to the muscle. He looked across the room and saw in the Mexican's eye terror and hate. In the K-9 victim's slits—'cause his eyes were but that—there came a stream of tears.

"From the beginning, Any. From the fucking start."

Anyhow and Lapeace had grown up together. Their parents had migrated from the South at approximately the same time. It was the early 1960s and South Central was predominantly Amerikan (white), especially in the area that Ansil and Evelyn Harper moved into. They lived on 64th Street and Normandie Avenue. They were the second New Afrikan family on the block. Evelyn worked downtown in the garment district, sewing fabrics for clothing designers. Ansil worked as a television repairman. Together their wages allowed them to move out of the Jordan Downs housing projects quickly and reside comfortably on L.A.'s Westside, although not too far west. They were both twenty years old and energetic; the future, they felt, looked bright for them. They considered themselves "good Negroes," for they didn't involve themselves in freedom marches, sit-ins, or integration protests. They openly opposed the civil rights movement and Rev. King. Said he was a troublemaker. Their flight from the South was more akin to the fable of the Pilgrims fleeing England than anything else. Though, of course, they'd passed it off as good fortune. In '67—two years after "that terrible riot in Watts," as Evelyn called it—they had their first child. She was named Gloria after Ansil's grandmother. In '72—the year those "dreadful terrorists murdered all those nice Jewish athletes," as Evelyn had said—they had Alvin. By this time the complexion of the neighborhood had turned dark. White flight had rendered the area an economic disaster zone. Cheerfully the Harpers endured twelve years of disdainful stares, hostile gestures, mysterious house fires, sugar in their gas tank, and epithets scrawled across the front door without once wanting to leave their home. And even though they despised Rev. King and the civil rights movement, they gingerly enjoyed the fruits of the struggle, complaining the whole time. In '73 they moved into Baldwin Hills and joined the ranks of the petty bourgeoisie. Ansil, by this time, owned the second-largest appliance chain in L.A. and Evelyn, of course, had long since been domesticated. Alvin complained about every elementary school he was made to attend, until finally, in the fourth grade, he was sent to Raymond Avenue on 76th and Normandie. He and Lapeace met over a lunch pail, which belonged to neither one of them. It was from this point that the competition began and grew steadily like a festering cyst, infectious and malignant.

Septima and Latimer Jackson arrived from Tuscaloosa, Alabama, under very different circumstances than the Harpers. Unlike the Harpers, Septima and Latimer were both community activists in their town. At their local high school, they formed NAACP awareness groups and counseled fellow students on the importance of voter registration. Their parents were founding members of the Deacons for Defense, a community self-defense organization that protected people from Klan terror. Septima met Latimer during a debate over the relevance of the Nation of Islam's position on nonviolence. They were the only two out of the entire auditorium who'd agreed with Malcolm X's position on selective retaliatory violence. At lunch, they talked and found they had other things in common. Later, they learned that their parents were both in the same organizations. They were married fresh out of high school and continued their fieldwork with the NAACP.

When the Klan bombed the 16th Street Baptist Church in Alabama, Septima and Latimer were incensed with rage. Ignoring their parents' advice for patience and collective struggle, Septima and Latimer secretly attacked two known Klan residences. One was the home of the local exalted Cyclops, which they dynamited, killing the Cyclops and his wife. The other was the Klan Kleagle house, which they torched, waiting until the residents came running out, then opening up with shotguns. It was under these circumstances that they came to Los Angeles. They moved in with Septima's Aunt Pearl, a militant in her own right. Pearl was a member of a secret society of revolutionaries called the House of Umoja. She sent Septima and Latimer underground for nine months and, when they surfaced, they were Asali and Tafuta Shakur, Black Panther Party members. On August 21, 1971, the day George Jackson was murdered in San Quentin during a Cointelpro-orchestrated escape attempt, Lapeace was born. It was this event that had inspired the name No-Peace. Asali died from complications at child birth, a blow that sent Tafuta spiraling out of control. He threw himself into the movement's most active section, the Black Liberation Army, and honored every order coming from the central committee. In 1974 Tafuta, along with his entire unit, were captured for killing two Los Angeles police officers and became prisoners of war. Tafuta died of cancer in solitary confinement in 1978. Lapeace was seven at the time, raised thereafter solely by his great-aunt Pearl. The genetic fire of his parents did not go out in him. Instead, it was a double infusion, and his DNA was laced with an explosive dose of courage and perseverance. Though untrained, it went awry and was used for less than admirable deeds.

The stolen lunch pail was but the beginning of a crime-ridden development that rolled back years of social growth, most of which Lapeace was ignorant of. They both developed evenly for a while, but in the fifth grade Lapeace shot up like a bean stalk. He was the tallest in his class. When they went out for Pop Warner football, both vying for the quarterback position, Lapeace won out. They both liked the same girl, Felencia Robinson—light-complexioned, bowlegged, and "pretty as a Georgia peach," the teacher had once said. They brought her lunch, carried her books, and even threatened the king of the school for her. Anyhow even went so far as to have his parents offer to pick her up from school, but she declined. When the candy drive came, Anyhow used all of his piggy-bank allowance money to purchase her whole box. When she came out to the school yard with her Girl Scout cookies, he bought those too. Lapeace sulked at his own destitution. Anyhow won her heart through his piggy bank. During a field trip to the L.A. Zoo, Lapeace dared Anyhow to climb the fence into the polar bear area. He said he would if Lapeace slapped Darcell Whitman on the back of the neck. Darcell's brother Sandman was a killer. He'd killed another boy while out hunting on a high school expedition and never did a day in jail. Darcell never let anyone forget this, and the teachers confirmed his story. Anyhow, challenged in the presence of his classmates, couldn't back down. So when Mrs. Shepard wasn't looking he scaled the wrought-iron gate, eased down into the moat, climbed up the other side, and stood defiantly on the polar bear's side. At that moment Lapeace reared back and slapped the hell out of Darcell Whitman's fat neck. It was the sudden smack and yelp of Darcell that caused Mrs. Shepard to see Anyhow in the polar bear area. Her panning head caught him in her peripheral vision and she forgot about Darcell and began to scream for the zoo attendant to rescue Anyhow. He couldn't overstand the commotion. He climbed out just as he'd climbed in. They'd both ended up suspended. Anyhow could not go on any more field trips and Lapeace's house was pelted with rocks for two nights straight.

By the sixth grade the stakes had been raised. After school, Anyhow would go down to the house of a woman named Martha who lived on his old block. His father would retrieve him around 6:30 daily, depending on how the prostitute he picked up on Century and Prairie looked. Sometimes he didn't pick up the boy until 7:30. Martha would always smile and beam with pride when she'd see Mr. Harper's Townhouse Lincoln roll up in front of her house. For she remembered when he was a young pup riding the bus back and forth. Anyhow ran complete circles around old Martha. She'd instruct him to stay in the backyard and he'd wander out front. She'd yell through the front screen door for him to stay in front of the house. He'd wind up down the street. She'd hold her hands on her girdled hips and holler for him not to leave the block, and he'd be gone. It was she who'd named him Anyhow. Because "whatever you said to him, no matter what it was, he was going to do his thing Anyhow," she said to Mr. Harper. Any started hanging out at Harvard Park, a stronghold of the Brim gang, the oldest Blood gang in L.A. As an occupational orphan, he hit the streets in search of surrogates. He ran into Bruno and Kurt Dog, two young riders. They put him to work burglarizing houses for guns, which they used to wage war on Crips. Simultaneously, Lapeace found his surrogates in the Eight Tray Gangsters. The competition continued. In the middle of the school year they were bringing guns to school.

"Nigga," Anyhow said while leaning up against the school's chain-link fence, "I got guns! Man, I got enough guns to kill all you fools." He finished by gesturing wildly with his hands as if talking to his loyal subjects. The other children just looked on quietly, not overstanding the significance of what Any was saying. On the other side of the yard, Lapeace stood towering over his peers.

"You got a gun on you now?" asked Darryl Long, looking up at Lapeace challengingly.

"I'm a gangsta. I keep a gun," he answered coolly.

"Let me see then."

And Lapeace raised up his sweatshirt and revealed the butt of a .22 Ruger.

"Damn, that nigga really gotta gun!" The crowd oohed and ahhed accordingly, and Lapeace stood in the thick of them like the king of the jungle. It was the crowd's fault that the respective bragging turned into a lunchtime shoot-out. Each group had loyalty to their leader, though none were bangers, as such. Why, it was the first time in Raymond Avenue's history that they had two kings of the school. Lapeace and Anyhow fought three times, twice at school and once in the Mobil station lot. All three battles resulted in draws. They'd fought to an exhausted standstill thrice. They wore their battle scars, lumps, and bruises like medals of valor. Not one smirk had been heard about them either. Now, however, the loyalist camps cried for an escalation in the two-year-old competition. *Certainly,* reasoned the groups, *a shoot-out couldn't possibly end in a draw.*

So Darcell Whitman, who'd of course joined ranks with Anyhow's group (it was Any who'd shown Darcell where Lapeace lived), went over to Darryl Long, who was standing next to the ball box writing NANCY GREEN IS A BITCH in permanent marker, and said, "Eh, man, I heard that Lapeace gotta gun. Is it true?"

"Yeah, man, he gotta gat . . . hold up," said Darryl, trying to remember how *bitch* was spelled. "I hate that ho Nancy, man."

"Yeah, I see," said Darcell, sweating furiously from the noontime heat, his blubber gut heaving like pistons.

"Eh, do Anyhoe gotta gat too?"

"You bet not let him hear dat . . ."

"Yeah, yeah," said Darryl, shaking off Darcell's warning. "Betcha Any can outshoot La Freak."

"In yo' dreams, boy. My nigga 'Peace is straighter'n a mother-fucka, fool."

"How you know, nigga?" asked Darcell.

"'Cause, nigga . . . I know."

"Fool," said Darcell, "Anyhow will bust a cap anywhere. Right here, if he want."

"Now you trippin' fatty . . ."

"Don't call me that, nigga."

"So what'cha saying?" challenged Darryl, stepping up on Darcell.

"Nigga, my brotha—"

"Yo' brotha's a shermhead, nigga. Now what?"

"We'll see," said Darcell sullenly and ambled off. The die had been cast. Once back in their respective groups, the snow job kicked in.

"Aw, Lapeace," began Darryl, shaking his head from side to side slowly, pathetically, "that nigga fatboy Dar just told me that Anyhoe talking 'bout cappin on you at lunchtime. You should bail up now and just go home."

"Whaaaat?" asked Lapeace, not believing what he'd heard. "Go home?" he asked incredulously.

"Yeah, Lapeace. Don't let him shoot you down. Go on and leave, man." At that he put his hand on Lapeace's shoulder and walked off.

"Where he at?" insisted Lapeace and stalked off toward the cafeteria, hand under his sweatshirt.

Across the yard, standing near the tetherball court, Darcell was doing his thing on Anyhow. "Eh, is it true your father is a fag?"

"What!?" answered Anyhow.

"Well, La Freak said yo' father be getting fucked and stuff . . . You know . . . that's what he telling people."

"Where he at?"

"He over there by the cafeteria, but be careful, Any, 'cause he got a big-ass forty-four on him. Talkin' 'bout killin' niggas today. So watch out."

"Man, fuck you. I'm fin to cap this nigga." And Any stalked off toward the lunch area. The crowd gathered like cumulus clouds before a storm, approaching from both the north and the south. The end result could be nothing but thunder. Lapeace walked head and shoulders above his peers, looking determined and pensive, hand under his sweatshirt. His strides were sure, his attitude fearless. Arriving under the canopy from the north was Anyhow and his motley crew. Any was barely distinguishable in their midst. He had no outstanding qualities, beyond ignorance and courage, that set him apart from his peers. But as they approached, the crowd flanking him gave way and there he stood—short, dark, and clouded. They drew their weapons simultaneously and the shooting started thereafter. The screaming children moved like hunted wildebeests, or, better yet, a school of fish in terrified sync. The gunfire from Anyhow's weapon was deafening under the canopy. He was firing a four-inch .357, standing perfectly still, legs apart. Lapeace's .22 barked like a Chihuahua in defense. Amazingly, no one was shot, as bullets pinged and ponged off metal Formica and Plexiglas recklessly. Lapeace lost the gunfight, not because he was wounded or had run but because his weapon was not loud enough. So the day after that school had been recessed due to security concerns, and when the students filed back into their classrooms Anyhow was clearly the man. Anyhow and Lapeace were arrested and spent the weekend in Los Padrinos juvenile hall. They both had scheduled court dates and had been expelled from the L.A. Unified School District.

3

Before Lapeace could even exit his car, he saw the marshal stepping across the street. The man's gait was cowboyish in a manner that Lapeace couldn't put into coherent thought. Perhaps it was attributed to his marshal status? Then again, it was physical too . . . *forget it,* he thought. "Yeah," said Lapeace, sighing.

"This here is your notice to appear in court on eight–thirty–ninety-six. You have been served."

Lapeace took the subpoena and threw it on the seat. Then, after a second thought, he picked it up and took it with him. He climbed the stairs to his second-story apartment, unlocked the door, moved in quickly, and whistled once. Out ran Ramona smiling joyfully, tongue hanging out of her mouth, tail wagging wildly. She was a pitch-black pit bull, fully groomed and trained to his voice command. He'd given her his ex-wife's middle name. Ramona jumped up on his legs, and her muscular hind quarters flexed and bulged as she licked, lapped, and smiled.

"Yeah," jostled Lapeace, doing a little dance with her. "That's my girl, yeah. And you look just like her." Ramona caught the ill intent in his voice and stopped smiling. She, after all, had her pride. He put her down and went to check his messages. *Beep* . . .

"Lapeace this is Joi. Call me when you can, please?" *Beep* . . .

"Yo, what up, nig-ga? Dis Young Game. Reach at a muthafucka when you can ridah." Click. *Beep* . . .

"Lapeace, this is Ted from Kawasaki of L.A. Your bike is ready. We'll be open all day and until seven tomorrow. Goodbye." Click. *Beep* . . .

"29-915-50-187-83." Click. Lapeace knew the voice and what the series of numbers meant, but his mind refused to process them. He didn't want to process them. Click . . . rewind . . . *Beep* . . . "29-915-50-187-83." *Good Lawd!* he thought to himself, rubbing his tension-filled forehead. He tried to carry on. *Beep* . . .

"Hey Lapeace. I just wanted to leave this message and tell you how much I enjoyed you last night and this morning. You are special. Hope to see you tonight. You got me open. In the p.m., I'm out." Click. Not even Shima's candy rain voice could stir him under the pressure mounting after the numerical message. He moved rapidly to the one room of his apartment that he'd converted into an office and grabbed up the paper extending itself out from the fax machine. He read eagerly, tapping his foot, scanning over inconsequential transmissions until finally he came across what he needed. A small, one-line transmission amid the thick of a whole paragraph. Ongea Uso. He ripped the paper from the machine and shredded it. He retrieved the confettied strips and took half to the bathroom and flushed them. The other half he stuffed into the garbage disposal. Against the background whirl of the disposal machine, he fed Ramona the remainder of a top sirloin steak he'd left in the fridge. He cut it up into big chunks, microwaved it for ten seconds, and mixed it with some Gravy Train, doused with a generous splash of Hennessy. Ramona loved her food that way. He stopped, frozen, in an oblivious-to-everything sort of thought-lock, when Ramona barked and broke it. She wanted her food and he was holding it, stuck standing there like a statue. Her sudden high-pitched bark quickly snapped him out of it.

"Awright, girl. Awright, here you go. You just like that other bitch." Ramona growled. He flicked off the disposal machine, opened the cabinet above the Frigidaire, and retrieved two one-gallon bottles. Christian Brothers and Alizé. Mixed him a drink and walked into the living room. Atop the Kenwood speaker, next to the black leather La-Z-Boy recliner, he had half an indo blunt in a Baccarat ashtray. Sitting back in the recliner he put a fire to the blunt, drew in a chest full of its arousing mint-flavored aroma, coughed once, and closed his eyes. *Shit's falling apart,* he thought to himself. He blew out a heavy stream of smoke, reached for his remote, and recited one of his favorite lines from Tupac.

I smoke a blunt to take the pain out
And if I wasn't high I'd prob'ly try to blow my brains out,
Lord knows . . .

The indo was doing its thing and the tension began to subside slowly, receding like the ebb of the ocean. He needed some thought-provoking, pain-made music. He aimed the remote toward the system, mentally scanning the collection in the CD holder, which held up to a hundred discs, and chose the Goodie Mob. They came out just as he needed them to.

His connection to such music had always amazed even him. Lapeace sat back and drifted, remembering how he'd gone through so many phases in his musical development and appreciation that it was a wonder his interest in business hadn't come to rest upon it. Rhythm and blues was his constant diet as a child. His Aunt Pearl (who was trapped in a time warp, having not fully overstood the collapse and eradication of the movement) played nothing but Motown, Stax, and the Atlantic sound around the house. So he was rooted. Later on an older brotha had turned him on to the blues, and he could feel the pain from which they'd been made. Jimmy Reed, John Lee Hooker, and Buddy Guy were his favorites. When a Jamaican sista introduced him to reggae with Black Uhuru's "Guess Who's Coming to Dinner" he began a personal crusade toward the acquisition of everything they'd made. When their first female artist, Puma, died of cancer, he'd tried to attend her funeral but found it too complicated to get accurate information on its whereabouts. Peter "Steppin Razor" Tosh, Mutabaruka, and Bob Marley were his staples outside of Black Uhuru.

Lapeace hadn't entered the hip-hop nation with Run DMC like most West Coast youth. In fact, he found it too harsh, silly, and musically repetitive. From '84 to '88 he'd been deep in the sticks in rural Mississippi with family. When he returned to L.A. the first hip-hop he heard was "Black Steel in the Hour of Chaos" by Public Enemy, and he was a head from that point forward. As the hip-hop nation evolved so, too, did Lapeace. He wore the medallions, the beads, and the fades with P.E., Native Tongues, and Kid 'n Play. Sported the Raiders gear, the fatigues, and the ankhs with NWA, the SIWs, and X Clan. He lived for hip-hop. Even played for a moment with being an artist himself. That is, until his homeboy Sekou laced him about an idea he had to "come up." He visualized it as if it were yesterday and not four whole years ago.

"What you talkin' 'bout, Sekou?" asked Lapeace over a steaming hot basket of chili cheese fries.

"Listen," began Sekou, talking more with his hands than his mouth. "This is some foolproof shit, and it don't involve us doing nothing but gettin' a scanner and burnin' some gas."

"Yeah?" asked Lapeace, eyebrow raised in an attentive manner. "But what you talkin' 'bout?"

"Hold on, nigga, damn . . ."

"Well, I only got thirty minutes fo' lunch, nigga, damn," persisted Lapeace, his fingertips a mess of chili and cheese. The fries were long gone.

"Awright, check it. We roll around the city and listen for high-speed chases that involve GTA suspects and—"

"I'm gon', you done flipped yo' fuckin' wig," said Lapeace, licking his fingers and standing to leave.

"Naw, hold up, homie, check this out."

"Hurry up, Sekou," said Lapeace impatiently.

"Awright, what do niggas do when one time on 'em? Huh?"

"Run, shit."

"What if they in a G and got D or straps?"

"Toss that shit and bone out."

"Right!" said Sekou sharply, slapping his palms and startling the couple next to them.

"You talkin' 'bout helpin' them and they kick us down?"

"Nigga whaaat? Help, fool, I'm talkin' 'bout gettin' anything they throw and lockin' on that shit."

"Where you get this idea at, Sekou?" Lapeace asked, more interested now that he'd heard the plan.

"I dreamed it, homie," he responded, expecting Lapeace to ridicule him about dreaming. But he didn't. After they got off work that afternoon, they bought a Motorola scanner and listened for three days. On the fourth day, they rolled around the hood listening to dispatches, trying to catch the numerical codes and word codes for alphabets that the police used for license plates. After a month of dry runs, they came across what began as a routine traffic stop and escalated into a low-speed pursuit with the "suspect discarding what appears to be narcotics from the vehicle," an agitated voice cracked over the scanner.

"That's us, that's our shit!" Sekou said excitedly as Lapeace bore down on the accelerator, trying to reach 62nd and Van Ness Avenue. Sure enough, the chase had begun there because people were lined up getting bags and bundles out of the street. Some had burst on impact and cocaine was all over the street.

"Awright, phase two," said Lapeace, slamming on the brakes and skidding to a stop. The people looked up startled and Sekou and Lapeace jumped out with authority. "*Freeze,* you motherfuckers, you are under arrest. Get over here, *Now!*"

The people, arms full of kilos of cocaine and pounds of weed, stood wide-eyed for a moment, not sure of themselves, or Sekou and Lapeace, until the scanner cracked off a litany of codes aloud. At that, the people—mostly young brothas and sistas—dropped everything and ran for their lives. "One time!" they hollered as they ran for safety. Sekou and Lapeace quickly gathered up the unbusted kilos and pounds and burned rubber out of there. Neither held a tax-paying job from that point forward.

Lapeace was awakened by the agitated barking of Ramona as she stood in the attack-defense position facing the front door. Groggy and half-conscious, Lapeace struggled to his feet.

Ramona barked on, looked back once as if to say "Don't worry, I've got it," and kept on barking.

"Shhh," he said, fully aware now that someone was working the key, the knob moving from right to left. "Easy, girl, easy." The music had stopped for goodness knows how long and the only noise now was the squeaking knob and the tumblers in the lock missing their connections. He crept to the door and flipped on the light switch next to it, but instead of a light coming on a small inlaid panel opened just below the switch. He reached in it and grabbed the handle of a nickel-plated .380 automatic. By then, the door was slowly opening. The next few seconds were a blur. Swift motion, wrestling, tumbling, and then subduing. Lapeace was on top, gun down in the face of the intruder. Heavy breathing permeated the room and Ramona stood ready, teeth bared.

"Lapi, it's me, baby. It's me," pleaded a feminine voice. Lapeace released his grip on the dog's collar and let his body sag with relief.

"Aunt Pearl, what are you doing here?"

"Well, I needed to get indoors, 'cause it seemed someone was following me," she said, brushing off her clothes as if she'd been tumbling on the ground outdoors. Lapeace commanded Ramona to her room, replaced the heat in its stash, and turned on the lights. Aunt Pearl looked a mess. Her hair was disheveled and her overcoat was dirty and soiled. The heavy wool dress she wore, which peeked slightly from under her sullen topcoat, used to be pink; now it was a brownish color with light spots. She wore no stockings and her legs, from her knees down to her ankles, were the same size. It looked as if her feet were painfully stuffed into her shoes, which were ran over and neglected.

"Aunt Pearl, why didn't you ring the buzzer downstairs?"

"Oh, that old buzzer gives me the runaround. Besides, it has so many complicated numbers and stuff," she said dismissively, looking around the room.

"Yeah, but you could have been hurt, Aunt Pearl."

"Lapi," she said, ignoring his spiel altogether and walking aimlessly toward the kitchen, "do you have anything to drink? I'm awfully thirsty."

"Yeah, um, it's . . ."

"I've got it baby," she responded, grabbing the neck of the Christian Brothers and pouring herself a healthy shot. He told her to make herself at home and went into his room. Once inside, he leaned against the door and sighed heavily. His room, like the rest of the apartment, reflected his lifestyle. Lapeace was a thug and he lived a thug life. He wasn't a criminal, as he'd once been, because he took nothing from anyone, except, when the opportunity presented itself, a federally insured Bank of Brinks truck. He sold no dope and hustled no women. His hustle: venture capital and the stock market. And even at that he played the field through a designated hitter: his CPA. He'd begun, of course, like most rich people—the Kennedys, the Rockefellers, the Rothchilds—as a criminal and then legitimized his money through investments. He was ghetto rich, which, compared to the bourgeois rich, was but a drop in the bucket. Lapeace had never moved out of his hood, for he'd seen, in too many instances, where cats had grown wealthy and egotistical, left the safety net, and got jacked quick. In most cases, they'd been killed. He wasn't going out like that. And for his loyalty, his homies, old and young, loved and protected him. He'd been thugging for a lifetime. And even before Tupac and his group Thug Life articulated the lifestyle to the world, Lapeace was living it. By circumstances, stemming from destitution and desperation, Lapeace thugged as a way to survive. And now that he'd gotten a grip on economics and survival, he thugged as a custom, as a way of life. It was all he knew. Lapeace's science, which he'd proudly developed around the acronym T.H.U.G. L.I.F.E., was this: The Homies Undergo Generational Life in Five Episodes.

1. They develop a sense of consciousness for their neighborhood friends and feel a need to join in on their protection.
2. They pool their human resources into a familial clique or group.
3. They take full responsibility for individual and collective awareness through signs, propaganda, and group identification.
4. They peak in their activity in this regard and look out over the horizon, and either overstand that their time is now and catch the wave to the next episode or die there on the peak.
5. The Fifth Episode is one's descent from criminality and its hazardous lifestyle to a leveled living of peace.

To Lapeace, Thug Life meant an altogether different thing from what Webster said it was, or what elders used to call him as a child. His apartment reflected his various episodes, indeed his generational development. He threw nothing away, ever. He still had his first pair of karate sticks made from a broom handle and a six-inch piece of chain he'd bought from Holland's Hardware on Normandie. He had them, along with his first pair of brownies, hung on his bedroom wall. The first group picture of the homies, when everyone was still alive, out of jail and sane, he'd had blown up into a huge poster and framed nicely in black ebony on the wall in the hallway. Around it were smaller photos of various stages of his growth and development. His first Schwinn Apple Crate show bike, complete with knee action, disc brakes, and five speeds. His first real girlfriend stood with him in front of Hamburger Henry's on Normandie and 79th, where he'd gotten his first job. And his favorite photo, which he'd gotten blown up, displayed his most notorious G's in their prime—full-blown killers at large: Crazy De, Legs Diamons, Tray Stone, Mad Bone, Monster Kody, Tray Ball, Joker, Sidewinder, and Lil' Spike. It was, above all, a collector's item. Homies had offered to buy it on several occasions but Lapeace would not sell it, nor would he make a copy. On the photo they stood erect, proud, and a beaming testament to the indomitable thug spirit. Outlaw immortals. There were photos of him and Scarface; him and Spice I; he and Gangsta Nip; and others.

Just as he had G's he'd looked up to, he was, in his rite, a G with youngsters looking up to him. It never stopped. "Too black," Aunt Pearl had once said about his apartment. "You need some other colors in here, Lapi." But he'd shined her on. He loved low-built, highly glossed black furniture. He'd gone to Ikea and went black crazy. He had the old beige carpet, which came with the apartment, pulled up and in went some triple-padded Dacron high-low shag in midnight black. When you stepped on it you sunk and felt like you were walking on pillows. He had artifacts of authenticity as well. A Masai spear, an Ibo mask, and a Zulu mallet (which he called a head knocker) hung on a living room wall between an Asiatic fan and a painting of Queen Nzinga. Two beautiful pictures he'd gotten from Aunt Pearl, which had already been made into poster form, showed a collage of faces: Geronimo ji Jaga, Mutulu Shakur, Jalil Muntaqim, Sekou

Odinga, Sundiata Acoli, Herman Bell, Nuh Washington, Jihad Mumit, and Richard Mafundi Lake. Its title was FREE ALL NEW AFRIKAN PRISONERS OF WAR. The other was of a woman that Aunt Pearl described as "the matriarch of the Shakur tribe." Her face was smooth and her skin was cocoa brown. She wore an infectious smile with a gap in the center of her sparkling white teeth. Afrikan symbols hung from each ear and her hair was in small dreads. "She's a warrior queen, the living soul of our sistahood," Aunt Pearl had said when she'd given him the photo, "Overstand that your blood flows through this source, Lapi." Her name was boldly imprinted diagonally across the bottom: ASSATA SHAKUR. He never left home without looking at her picture. She was a beautiful woman, who in some ways reminded him of the way his relatives said his mother looked. His apartment was sparse—three bedrooms and cozy. His office contained his means of electronic communication with the world. A fax, computer, copier, printer, and two phones.

Lapeace stood in front of the double-mirrored closet doors and began to shed his Kani gear. He needed to hurry in order to make his three o'clock meeting—a face to face with his attorney. The message was clear. He regretted having to go. Once stripped to his heavy cotton Stafford boxers, he stood for a moment and studied his long frame. He needed to start back weight training, he reasoned. And for good measure he did one hundred push-ups, one hundred crunches, and one hundred jumping jacks. To shield his sound, he programmed a disc from the front room, by satellite remote—Mystikal's "I Ain't the Nigga to Fuck Wit" flooded the room densely. He opened up his closet and chose his gear. Fresh Stackhouse threes, blue Ben Davis jeans, and a Tommy Hilfiger long-sleeve T-shirt. He discarded the Herrinbone and donned an OG fourteen karat

S-chain with a north star emblem on it. North Star Car Club was a lowrider club that he and his homies began on the north side of their neighborhood. Every hood had a car club. He greased his head with Three Flowers, sprayed on some Cool Water, snapped on his Rollie, and looked at his image in the mirror. *I need some rest,* he said to himself, noticing the bags being formed underneath his eyes. "But still," he said aloud, "I ain't the nigga to fuck with." He cut the music and went into the bathroom. He flossed, brushed his teeth, and rinsed his mouth out with Plax. Popped in some ginseng gum and headed up the hall.

Aunt Pearl had drunk herself into an alcohol coma and lay wide-legged in the puffy recliner. He signaled for Ramona, who came quickly. He wanted to let her know he was leaving Aunt Pearl here. Ramona looked as if to say, "My sense of smell is one hundred times keener than yours." At the top of the stairs he started Lucky and went to retrieve his mail—nothing but junk. He took Florence Avenue to the Harbor Freeway and then changed over to the Santa Monica. Pat Metheny was bangin' on the system as he drove westbound smoothly. At La Brea he exited north and took it to Melrose Avenue. The area was Jewish—West Los Angeles. Jewish people, perhaps Hasids, he wasn't sure, walked easily up and down the streets in their black gear, hats to match. Stores, synagogues, and businesses announced their legends in Hebrew, not English. People looked oddly at him as Lucky rolled by subbing the bass line from "California Love," setting off car alarms. At Melrose Avenue Lapeace turned left and parked on the corner of Mansfield Street. Used his barcoded meter key and set the time for two hours. He entered the law office from the rear. Inside, at a heavily polished oakwood reception desk sat Erma—Safi's receptionist for twenty-two years—broad and alert. When she saw Lapeace stepping through the double glass doors, her face radiated a genuine smile and she played with straightening her desk.

"Hello Erma," greeted Lapeace, bending over the desk to hug her affectionately. "How've you been?"

"Well it's been going all right, I'd say. How've you been Lapeace? Seriously?"

"I've been okay," he said, indicating that today may be an end to that, "but we'll see how things develop."

"Oh, you'll be fine, brotha," she answered with assurance. "You'll be just fine."

"Right on," said Lapeace, feeling no real comfort in her words. Safi didn't tell her too much and he certainly didn't talk over phones. So her well wishes were founded in maternalism toward Lapeace, not facts. *Act like you know,* he told himself and smiled along with her. "Is he in?"

"Yep, and he's waiting for you," she added waving her dark firm arm toward the door leading to Safi's office. Lapeace walked to the door, knocked softly, and opened it. Safi Baraka, an orthodox Muslim in the thick of Jewish West L.A., stood in front of a humongous shelf of law books bound in calfskin leather, reading a brief.

"Assalaam Alaikum, Lapeace," greeted Safi with a smile and an extended hand.

"Walaikum Assalaam, Safi," he responded and took the soft, well-manicured hand.

"Sit, my brotha, sit. I'll only be a minute here, just going over some things. How was your drive here?"

"Cool, it was awright."

"Good, good," said Safi and continued to read on quietly. His office had that Muslim smell, that incense sort of aroma that gave off a clean smell. The room was awash in Arabic script framed in wood and glass. Over the top of his chair, behind his massive desk, was an awesome aerial photo of the Hajj, which looked to involve over a million people moving across the desert toward Mecca. On his desk was an Islamic flag. "Lapeace," Safi quipped, startling Lapeace out of his concentration, "we've got a potential problem. Of course, I'll need more time to evaluate the situation and assess the damage, but it doesn't seem good for us. This character, Anyhow, how long have you known him?"

"Since the seventies. About eighteen years," answered Lapeace, hands gripping the chair arms tightly. Lapeace's jaw had begun to quiver and tighten, his bushy eyebrows connecting in a pensive bridge of contemplation. He needed a blunt. The dreaded numbers came up on his mental screen: 29-915-20-187-83: Anyhow is telling about some murders involving the Eight Trays.

"Let's talk about some things, brother," Safi said, coming around the desk and sitting down.

4

Lapeace sat hunched over, elbows on his knees, face in his hands. He was trying to recollect with clarity when all this had begun. It went back further than what Anyhow was supposedly telling the police. The beginning was somewhere on the school yard, for sure. It was a contentious antagonism from the outset, no doubt. The repetitive competition, the thin line between peace and war, love and hate . . . Damn the shit had gotten thick. From the gunfight and the court case, which landed them both on probation, there began the brief show bike competition, which Lapeace felt he'd won because his music was louder, his truck lights were designed better—with them all working and he had knee action. Next they went on to lowriders. This was crucial because they'd also sworn their allegiance to their respective hoods and they were lowriding not as a sport or hobby but as a means to promote their neighborhood.

Lapeace had the advantage because he and Sekou had gotten their break on the dope. They sold it pound for pound, key for key. They rationalized that to sell it this way would yield less of a profit but ultimately would be much safer. Because they really didn't know whose dope it was or who it was connected to. They'd gotten five kilos of cocaine and four pounds of stress marijuana. They dumped each key for thirteen-five and each pound for seven-fifty. They came up almost overnight. Lapeace found himself cruising the streets of Granada Hills, Tujunga Canyon, Palmdale, Glendale, and other Amerikan enclaves looking for an elder Amerikan with an intact late-model Chevrolet. It took three weeks to find what he wanted and then another week of phone calls and personal visits to convince the couple that he'd take care of "Ethyl." He gave them $3,500 for the sky-blue 1962 Chevrolet. It was original and had 87,000 miles on it. He couldn't believe his luck. He took it from the Hoffmeisters' house straight to the hydraulic shop and got it cut with a C-frame step down so it would lay bumper to bumper. He had them install eight-inch strokes in the front and tens in the back. He picked it up the next day equipped with sixteen switches and a remote. From there he drove it to the sound shop and had them install beat-monster sounds. He paid extra for a stash spot to be cut under the seat for his weapon. While he waited for his sounds to be installed, he walked across the street and bought a pair of chrome Zenith rims on five twenty-inch tires, including a spare. He put them in the backseat and drove to Noble's Paint Shop on Florence and Hoover. Got his upholstery done in charcoal gray with black pinstripes. The car he had painted jet black with gray microsecrums covered with twenty coats of lacquer.

Had all the chrome redipped, including the emblems, and in two weeks from the day he'd bought Ethyl he had her on the 'Shaw with her ass in the air flossing. Couldn't no one fade him. He was hitting thirty-six inches on his second crank. The duce was hot. To ensure his safety against carjackers, he'd begun the North Star Car Club—all Eight Trays. Anyhow, of course, got the word on Lapeace's duce and at first couldn't believe it.

"Yeah," the lookie lous told him, "I saw that nigga on the 'Shaw last Sunday clownin' mothafuckas. Sounds, fresh paint, hydraulics, the whole shit."

"That ain't that nigga car," Anyhow protested.

"Shiiiit, I seen a North Star plaque on the back window," insisted the lookie lou. Anyhow was mad. And that night he himself caught a glimpse of Lapeace dipping down Gage Avenue locked up stagecoach style. He'd been left at the previous stage of the competition and he knew Lapeace knew he was back there. Anyhow tried to regain some clout by busting with a '63 Chevy on some gold Daytons, but by that time Lapeace had grown tired of lowriding and had aquired a black SS Monte Carlo.

Then, out of the night like a meteorite bringing light to the darkness, there erupted the gun battle that changed the competition. Like the natural order of developing opposites, increasingly becoming antagonistic, Lapeace and Anyhow were headed for a climactic collision since they set the stage for the next round of the struggle. The only way ever to end the struggle is the elimination of one of the opponents. But, like nature itself, doing its thing regardless of what else is going on, the changes thrust themselves upon the contenders without either of them really being prepared for it.

In Los Angeles on Sunday evenings, the young and in-crowd folks cruised Crenshaw Boulevard. Crenshaw, a main thoroughfare running north and south, is a wide, four-lane street fronted on both sides by commercial businesses, assorted apartment complexes, and foreign-owned motels. On the weekdays the 'Shaw is a bustling boulevard of business, tranquillity, and common sense. Working class folks used the vast artery as a way to cut through South Central. However, on the weekends—though especially on Sundays—the youth fell out on the 'Shaw en masse.

The whole atmosphere of the 'Shaw changed literally overnight. Parking lots normally reserved for patrons of the various commercial businesses were flooded with rowdy youth who'd come out to socialize and watch the cars. There'd be lowrider hopping contests to see which car could bounce the highest with the use of hydraulics. Muscle cars would pair off for street-racing matches. Most squeezed nitrous oxide—watered-down rocket fuel—to boost their speed.

The 'Shaw usually saw its fair amount of violence. Most of those who actually cruised the boulevard were not bangers at all. They lived in hoods, but only as residences and not as members of any gangs. Civilians still traversed the thoroughfare while the street scene raged. An odd mix of culture, sometimes manifested on the 'Shaw as civilian motorists simply using the street as a means to an end, were caught in a slow-moving parade of lolos or trucks on display. This would normally lead to a horn-blowing match and not more than a little bit of road rage.

The Burger King at Jefferson and Crenshaw was the best spot to post up at. The parking lot was huge. It was enclosed by a cyclone fence. The lot fronted the corner across Jefferson from the AM/PM station. The whole four-corner intersection was visible from the Burger King lot. Car and truck clubs jockeyed for the spot. But not on this night.

Cool was the night, a Sunday evening, and Crenshaw Boulevard was packed with lolos, trucks, motorcycles, and expensive foreign cars. Music flooded the street from every passing car. The 'Shaw was a montage of sounds—subbing bass lines threatening to shatter rear windows and high tweeters wreaking havoc on passengers' nerve endings. An almost bumper to bumper roll from Adams to Florence could be detailed by rear and front headlights in both directions. Beautifully made-up women sat perched in sublime vehicles as if they were queens being paraded through the streets of their village. Finger waves, braids, perms, and elaborately sculptured feathers were en vogue and on display as sistas rode alongside their men in vintage cars remade to fit this weekly ritual called flossin'. The men operating the cars wore baseball caps with team insignias on the front, set names stenciled on the sides. Some had braids, parted in big blocks, one on each side, one in the back, one on top, and one hanging down in their face. Bald heads, jheri curls, and cornrows were out as well. Car clubs moved slowly along the densely parked street like tribal floats in ceremonial regalia. Mafia IV Life, Individuals, Majestics, Street Life, Stylistics, South Side, North Star, and Du-Low placques hung prominently in their rear windows as they crept past. Rag tops, hard tops, t-tops, moon roofs, and chop tops were represented. Hip-hop and oldies bellowed from everywhere and indo smoke created an endless stream of mint aroma up and down the 'Shaw. North Star had niched itself a place in the Burger King parking lot. All sixteen of the club's cars were backed into position diagonally. Stagalee had the loudest music so he could serenade the lot. "Gangsta Gansgsta" by N.W.A. was the theme music for the gathering. Lapeace, who had ceased to lowride but still lent his support to the club, hadn't arrived yet. So the Northerners stood around and rapped, smoked pot, and filmed themselves with Ghost's camcorder. Lil' Slow Foe had suggested that they start filming their exploits on the 'Shaw, or wherever, 'cause if they were dumped on, jacked, or harassed by one time, they'd have some footage to use when it came time to exact revenge. Ghost and Lil Slow Foe were some smart young cats.

"Cuz," someone among the crowd said, "there go Lapeace at that light." Everyone turned toward the corner of Jefferson and Crenshaw. Sure enough there sat Lapeace's SS Monte Carlo, idling muscularly, waiting for the light to change. Lapeace sat cooling at the light, ten mm Glock in his lap, half a blunt hanging from his lips. He was twisted. He sat in the center lane, the Monte "C" on gloss. Next to him rolled up a green Grand National on some Lorenzo rims jamming "Piru Love." He looked over and locked eyes with Anyhow, whose face was fixed in an agitated scowl. They burned holes into each other. Since the sixth grade shoot-out, not one word had been spoken face to face to either. All their exchanges were rumors, innuendo, or, in most cases, lies fueled by back biters' jealousy of them both. Lapeace clicked off his safety as he stared. Anyhow never had his heat on safety. In his lap was an Israeli .44 Desert Eagle. The stares continued. The two muscle cars rumbled low under the music, rocking silently from the powerful explosions from under their hoods. When the light turned green neither car moved forward. Horns from cars behind them began to blow and this alerted Ghost to the problem.

"Stag," asked Ghost, one eye zooming in with the camcorder, the other squenching, "ain't that that slob nigga Anyhow's car next to Lapeace?"

"Hell yeah, cuz, that's him." Just then a caravan of lowriders came through the alley behind Burger King, serving the North Stars with rapid fire.

"Cuz . . ." was all that was heard and then the avalanche of gunfire. The Brims, with their Du-Low plaques exposed, were dumping with some heavy shit—tearing up every car in the parking lot. The North Stars ducked behind their vehicles as the Brims had their way. Ghost slid down next to his gray coupe, which was first, parked out toward Crenshaw, and kept filming the Grand National and the Monte Carlo. Bullets, however, kept ripping through steel and glass so Ghost went down on his belly, momentarily losing sight of Anyhow and Lapeace. Once he'd righted hisself he trained the camera back on the two. Both Lapeace and Anyhow raised their weapons at the same time and started firing. The muzzle flashes illuminated the dark interiors of both cars continuously and it looked as if they were welding inside. The 'Shaw was in rapid motion now, people running, screaming, jumping into their cars. Screeching tires and gunshots were everywhere. When Lapeace began to shoot he lowered his head, his strap angled sideways, blunt smoke in the air. Anyhow too had ducked when he started firing. Glass shattered and fell onto Ghost as he was filming—the Brims to the back were still shooting. The Grand National and the Monte Carlo began to roll forward slowly, still giving off the welding-like flashes.

Lapeace's first three shots went through Any's car; one struck the bumper kit of a gold coupe in the AM/PM parking lot, another hit a woman in the back, severing her spinal cord and paralyzing her instantly. The third shot hit a gas pump and the spark ignited an explosion. The explosion killed a number of people getting gas. Any's first four shots shattered the windows of the stores across the street, doing damage to nothing but property. The firing continued as they slowly rolled out into the intersection. The wailing of fire engines and other emergency vehicles could be heard in the distance. Two helicopters could be seen making their way across the night sky toward the havoc. In the intersection Anyhow's reckless firing ended the lives of two pedestrians waiting at the light. The firing continued. Wrecks were happening now as people panicked in their haste to leave the area and still the Brims were shooting. Lapeace's shots were now tearing holes in the body of Any's Grand National; two, three, four holes appeared magically in the money green exterior of the Buick. Any fired back with his last five shots: one blew out a chunk of Lapeace's Nardi steering wheel, another knocked a softball-sized hole in the driver's side door from inside out, and the others went who knows where. Lapeace kept dumpin', hand up head down. Out of shells, Any had to turn off, but he'd missed Jefferson, so he jumped the curb and began barreling down the sidewalk. He ran over two women, killing one instantly. Lapeace gave chase as best he could but the street was a mess. Any jumped back out onto the street on Adams and disappeared into the night. Lapeace, realizing that the area was being cordoned off, righted his car and slipped away. The Brims had torn up every North Star car in the parking lot but had hurt no Eight Trays. Every car had produced a shooter who'd emptied his weapon into the parked cars. Tires and windows were shot out completely and the bodies had gaping holes in them.

Across the street, in the AM/PM parking lot, chaos reigned supreme. The gas pump explosion was seen for miles around and now two helicopters illuminated the area and turned it into daytime. Fire trucks, ambulances, and hazmat vehicles dominated the intersection. Then came the media. Their first report had been "A shooting between feuding lowrider factions." Then, the next morning, it was "A clash between the Crips and the Bloods," and by the six o'clock news that evening it was "The carnage set in motion by the 6-Duce Brim gang and the Eight Tray Gangsters; at least one suspect is being sought for questioning." Lapeace watched every news broadcast from CNN to *Good Day L.A.* His car had not been identified. *Who was that suspect?* Lapeace wondered. Safi broke through his thoughts with a question.

"When you started shooting were you actually aiming, consciously aiming?"

"No, man," Lapeace answered, a bit agitated. "Like I said, when fool raised his strap, I raised mine. When I started dumpin', my head was down in the seat."

"Uh-huh," sounded Safi, writing rapidly in shorthand while Lapeace spoke.

"Do you know if your friend Ghost still has that tape, Lapeace?" asked Safi, putting down the gold-tipped *kalamu* from Saudi Arabia and leaning back in his chair.

"I got it. Took it and put it in a safe deposit box in Mississippi."

"Good, good. We'll need to retrieve it soon and view it. Perhaps we'll be able to use it in court for a—"

"Court? Wha'cha mean court?" Lapeace exploded, standing up wide-legged, hands clenching and unclenching.

"Calm down, brother. Control yourself," cautioned Safi sternly from behind the massive desk.

"Eh Safi, I was protecting my life, man. Dude was trying to *kill* me," Lapeace reasoned, easing back down into the soft leather chair.

"Yes, I realize that, but in the process of your defense and his assault eight innocent people were killed. Someone is going to have to be held accountable for those killings. Now we know

Alvin is cooperating with authorities. He, as you probably already know, is allegedly the Westside Night Bandit . . ."

"Yeah, I heard."

"Yes, well he is, from what I've been able to gather, using his knowledge of the Crenshaw killings to lessen the impact of the serial burglary charges."

"And?"

"And?" responded Safi as if to say *You don't know?* "Well, it's only a matter of time before your face and name are on every news channel in the country. We need to start building our defense now."

Lapeace ran one sweaty palm over his face in an attempt to wipe away the stress building on both sides of his temple. He really needed a blunt now.

"We still need to discuss this custody battle thing too."

"Man, fuck that bitch. I ain't even trippin' on that no mo'. Shit, Safi, the custody battle I'm most interested in is the one between me and the authorities, you know?"

"Yes, of course. Well, then, I'll move to postpone on the grounds that you are out of the country."

"That's straight, man. Eh, you got an address on her?"

"There is a P.O. box she uses in Ontario and you know she was staying with her cousin in Upland . . . the only address I do have is in Houston, Texas, where the boys are."

"Eight-three-oh-two?"

"Yes, I believe that's it."

"Awright, Safi, I'll get the tape. Any other suggestions, bro?" Lapeace asked, calmer now.

"Yeah, you shouldn't go home to your neighborhood or drive any of your vehicles until we've built up an adequate defense. Do you understand?"

"Yeah, I understand. You mean I should go underground?"

"Doctor's orders," answered Safi with a wink and a click of his tongue. "I'll be in touch."

"Yeah, you got my digits. Hit me on the hip," he said, standing and tapping the side where his pager was.

"Will do."

5

The notepad Mendoza began writing Anyhow's statement in was two pages from the end—back and front he'd written in quick, barely legible script—trying to keep up with Any's sometimes erratic narration. Their entire eight-hour shift had been spent beside his bed. The city council, pressured by the mayor's office, wanted this case solved. L.A. had suffered too many high-profile losses recently and needed a solid victory to restore faith in the city with its ability to police and prosecute criminals. There was the L.A. Four's victory, O. J. Simpson's acquittal, two hung Menendez juries, and Snoop Dogg's verdict of not guilty. So the district attorney's office was definitely out for blood on this one. They'd discussed the balance of things among themselves that would bring the most relief politically to the D.A.'s office—the prosecution of Alvin Harper as the Westside Night Bandit or using him as a participating state's witness in the "Crenshaw Massacre" case, as it had been named?

"Well," reasoned Garcetti, L.A. district attorney, "we certainly would gain the political, not to mention the ethical, backing of the West L.A. community by prosecuting the Night Bandit. Greater Los Angeles has been held in a grip of fear for over nine months by his invasions."

"Yes," countered Barker, a New Afrikan deputy district attorney, "but eight lives and thirteen injuries, seven of which are critical, occurred in the Cren mass. And we've got one of the shooters. Certainly lives take precedence over property."

"Possession," piped in the D.A.'s male secretary, "let me remind you, is nine-tenths of the law." Barker couldn't believe it, that they were going after a burglary conviction over a multiple-murder conviction—no doubt because the property was white and the bodies were black—the Amerikan way.

"What if we prosecute for both?" asked Barker. But the Amerikan prosecutors had begun to talk among themselves this time. It was Barker's call to the city council that changed the course of pursuit in the case. Anyhow would be offered immunity for the Night Bandit burglaries if he agreed to testify against the second gunman in the Crenshaw Massacre case. For it had been discovered by the ballistics experts that the ten mm had definitely done the most damage. Of course Any's statement reflected a biased slant, which painted him as being under attack by Lapeace—"A mad Crip who'd kill anyone." Mendoza wrote as a final note in his pad:

Suspect fully cooperative

Sweeney stared across the space of the hospital room and thought of historical bitter rivalries that had caused for so many an endless stream of struggle and strife. This feud, like those, had developed from personal conflicts and snowballed into polemics that could last for generation after generation.

"Why don't you like Lapeace Shakur, Alvin?" Sweeney had asked him earlier in the interview.

"Shit, I don't know man," Any had replied sulkily. "I just don't like that nigga." And that was that. Anyhow attached his own logic to those words and for him he'd pretty much explained himself about it. He'd now be moved from General Hospital and housed on the 8000 floor of Los Angeles County jail. It would serve as both a hospital ward and a protective custody module. Anyhow had entered a new phase in his young life—that of a police informant and a state's witness. He laid back on his bed after Sweeney and Mendoza had left and stewed in the decision he'd made. *Damn,* he thought, *I'm a rat. A snitch—no good. What will my homies think? My girl, will she stay with me? Good Lawd, what have I done?* A solitary tear rolled down his face as he reached over and took control of the Bic razor on the bedstand. Breaking its top, the blade fell onto his chest, shimmering in fluorescent glare. He moved robotlike, motivated by sheer disgust, with his right hand until it came to rest with the blade against his left wrist. With six rapid moves he cut deep into his dark skin. He grimaced and bit back a painful cry. The blood flowed quickly, warmly, plentiful. He laid back and waited.

At that same moment Lapeace was knocking on Shima's door. Hoping she'd answer before someone drove by and recognized him. On his third knock a female voice asked from behind the bars, "Who is it?"

"Lapeace," he answered, then added, "Is Tashima home?" A series of locks, bolts, and chains were undone before the lock on the bar door itself was opened and he was invited in. He stepped into the cool confines of the living room and was faced by a beautiful young woman wearing a Texas Rangers jersey and black biker shorts. Out from them gleamed thick muscular legs that were coated in baby oil. She wore no shoes, just white bobby socks. Her hair, like Shima's, was a massive tangle of braids. She was short and built like Linda Murray, the bodybuilder.

"What's up?" she chimed, extending her unpolished no-jewelried hand. "I'm Sanai, Shima's friend."

"Right on, good to meet you," said Lapeace, still captivated by her stunning beauty.

"Sit down, bro. I'll get Shi for you." And she sashayed off down the hallway. Lapeace took a seat on the leather love seat under the platinum CD of the Poetess's latest album and fiddled with his keys. When Shima came out she lit up the room with her brilliant smile and Clarion fragrance.

"Hey, Shima. How you doing?"

"I'm good, Lapeace, I'm good. And you? Did you speak with your attorney?" she asked him, leading him by the hand down the hall to her room.

"Yeah, we rapped and there's some things we need to talk about. I need you to—"

"Shi," interrupted Sanai, standing in the doorway wearing tennis shoes now, "I'm walking to the store. You need anything?"

"No, I'm cool, thanks."

"Walkin'?" asked Lapeace, questioning the logic in that.

"It's right up the street," Sanai answered pointing in the store's direction.

"Here, take my truck," he insisted, while fishing in his pocket for the keys. "And can you bring me back a small box of Phillies?" he added, handing her a ten-dollar bill. Sanai looked at Shima, who in turn gave her the nod of approval. She took the keys and the money and left the room. She came back after seeing the 'burb and said, "I am not driving that truck—no."

"Why not?"

"What's wrong with it, Sanai?" added Shima.

"It's got D's on it, girl. You know fools be trippin' over them rims."

"I'm insured, Sanai."

"Aw, girl, go on up to that store and stop trippin'," counseled Shima. Sanai thought a moment and then asked how to work the remote and left. She never knew what hit her.

At the corner of West Boulevard and Slauson, where she stopped in the right-hand turning lane behind a red Granada, a sista tapped on the passenger-side window and mouthed a question to her. She rolled down the window and at that moment the driver's-side door was opened and she was yanked out and shot once in the back of the head. It wasn't until the next day that Shima and Lapeace found out. The police left a message on his service that said his truck had been found and he should come down to the impound yard to retrieve what was left of it. Shima called Sanai's father and he told her that she'd been murdered by carjackers. Shima was stunned into a catatonic silence. "Hello?" Silence. "Hello, hello?" and finally Sanai's father hung up. Shima was out of it totally. Lapeace laid her down and retrieved a cold towel for her head. He hit Sekou on the hip and he called right back. He gave him the generals of the situation and within thirty minutes Sekou was there in a black Lincoln rent-a-car, with two AK-47s. They slipped out the back, got into the rent-a-car, and took Slauson to Crenshaw in silence. Then at Crenshaw they turned left and stopped at 60th Street.

"How we gonna serve 'em?" asked Sekou, signaling a left turn with his blinker.

"With the business." In other words, we catch all we kill. At 11th Avenue they pulled to an easy stop. Lapeace reached back and retrieved an AK, handing it to Sekou, and then the other. Checked the chamber and the clip, unlatched the safety, and got out of the car. The evening air was warm and cars were parked heavily on both sides of the street. Three things told him that it was the Rollin' Sixties that had killed Sanai and taken his truck: the area of the jack, the fact that she was killed 'cause they knew it was his truck, and the area it was found in. Now, they'd feel the pain. With his weapon down against his left side, he jogged nonchalantly across the street and began walking on the opposite side of a gathered crowd. Sekou stayed on his side and walked toward them with his weapon behind his back. When he had gotten within a house distance he raised his AK and opened it up. He shot down every standing body he saw. The fierce bark of the AK knocked loudly, adding to its strong recoiling kick, as Sekou dumped twenty-five times, dropping half as many bodies. He retained five rounds for his retreat. Silently, Lapeace watched from across the street crouched behind a gray '74 Pinto. Sekou got busy. When he disappeared back into the night, just as swiftly as he'd appeared, the wounded began to stir, moan, and wither. Those not hit came out of their camouflage to tend to their casualties. They were bending over their homies, walking in circles, crying, wailing, and swearing retribution when Lapeace sprinted from across the street and brought the noise again. After his thunder there was dead silence. And just as swiftly as he'd brought it, it ended and there was no more pain.

The funeral was a closed-casket event. The impact of the bullet had blown most of Sanai's face away. In place of her being seen, Angelus Funeral Home put together a video montage of still photographs taken throughout her life. Accompanying the photos being shown on the big screen was complementary music. "Stairway to Heaven" by the O'Jays; "Keep Your Head to the Sky" by Earth, Wind & Fire; "Angel" by Angela Winbush; "Zoom" by the Commodores; "Body and Soul" by Anita Baker; and "Your Smile" by Renee and Angela. The gathering was a solemn one, as family and friends huddled up tightly around Sanai's casket while the spiritual council offered up its prayers for her well-being. Lapeace stood erect with Shima leaning slightly against him. He was taking a big chance by attending Sanai's funeral. Word on the street was that detectives had been asking about him. And as of late, within the last three days, he kept receiving foreign numbers on his pager. He'd not called them back. There were unmarked cars, more than usual, combing his neighborhood (he'd been told), which added fuel to his suspicion. There'd been various agencies represented by several types of individual agents, police, inspectors, detectives, etc., etc., in the hood since they'd initiated the L.A. rebellion. When Football smashed Reginald Denny in the head with a rock and threw up the set—it seemed as if that was a call of the wild and every agency sent troops. The hood, at times, seemed to have more police in it than homies. This was compounded by the little homies' new fascination with bank robbery, which brought yet another collection of agents snooping. The spiritual council began to wind it down and Shima's lean became heavier. She felt personally responsible for Sanai's death. Lapeace tried to explain to her that it was more his fault than hers. And he even thought about telling her that there was more grieving than this right now on the street, but he realized that wouldn't help her none. He held her hand tightly.

"And so it is," chimed the Oba, representing Orisha, the spiritual path that Sanai and her family followed, "that our sista has passed her spirit on to another. One in whom it can carry on its meaning more fruitfully. We are thankful, however, that we were graced with its beauty in the person of sista Sanai. Let it be that she is amongst the remembered." Neither Lapeace nor Shima attended the house gathering after the funeral. They, instead, retreated to Shima's house, where Lapeace had been staying since Sanai's death. He still had not told her about his own troubles. Her white 300SC Lexus came to a smooth stop in the drive and she prepared to get out when Lapeace touched her arm.

"Babes, you can't afford to take this so personal. You are straining your nerves. Be easy, Shima, awright?" he said pleadingly, looking her deep in her brown eyes. Her eyes were crying but no tears came out. Her lips were quivering but no sound came out. She loved this man. She knew at that moment.

"Lapeace," she began, sniffing back a burst of tears, "she was the closest person to me in this world. She was all I had. Do you feel me? She was my soul mate, my alter ego, my . . ." She couldn't hold up and for the hundredth time she burst into tears. Lapeace leaned across the console dividing them and hugged her tightly while stroking her braided hair. She smelled pure and clean and he breathed her in like smoke. "Baby," sniffed Shima, breaking their embrace, "don't leave me, awright? I need someone in my life with me. Don't you go too."

"I'll not leave you, Shi. I won't go." His heart clutched tightly and he found it hard to swallow. How was he going to explain to her the mess he was in? That he was connected to the now infamous Crenshaw massacre? Soon, he knew, there'd be his photo and bio on *America's Most Wanted*. The local, regional, and world news would soon begin to pry into every aspect of his life. Shima wouldn't be able to handle that, not now and probably not ever. He was in knots knowing that, regardless of whatever he said or however he felt, he would have to leave her in one way or another. Inside the house Shima collected her messages from her machine and Lapeace sat cutting open a blunt. The cigar paper cut easily and opened like the skin of a sausage when touched with the razor. He emptied the tobacco in the kitchen trash and began applying adhesive saliva on his return. Once seated, surrounded in the living room by gold and platinum, he started packing the cigar skin with chronic, fresh and strong. It's aroma rose up and played with his sense of smell and for the thousandth time he wished someone would invent indo-chronic air fresheners. He rolled the blunt fat—thick as his thumb—and licked it sealed. He brought out his lighter and dried the saliva onto the paper. The blunt shrunk tightly around the chronic and Lapeace put it in his mouth and lit it up. *Time to get lifted.* The first inhale was always the most critical, for it set the pace for those to follow. The cough, the sometimes painful hacking, convulsive cough, was expected and welcomed—it opened up the zone for the powerful THC invasion. Lapeace blew out a light blue stream of smoke and went doubled over in spastic coughs that brought tears to his eyes. After several of these, resembling Muslim Rak'ahs, his lungs accepted the intrusion and he was beginning to feel the twist. He sat back into the comfortable leather sofa and closed his eyes. He relaxed as best he could. He'd taken off his Filas and his white tube socks looked to be glowing incandescently against the black carpet and dark furnishings. The silence was too ominous, he felt, and reached for the universal remote. He flicked on the tube and scanned the airwaves until he reached *The Box*. He sat through several videos. Skee-Lo, "I Wish"—wack. Mystikal, "Boot Camp Clicc" —phat. MC Lyte, "Keep on Keepin' On"—phat (and sexy as hell). Goodie Mob, "Soul Food"—phat. Geto Boys, "The World Is a Ghetto"—phat. Fat Joe—*click!* Off went *The Box* and on to BET. Donnie Simpson was sitting comfortably on the set's couch, looking blowed out as usual, talking to Faith Evans. *Damn, she's ugly,* he thought and turned the power off.

He aimed the remote toward the stereo but it wouldn't come to life. He took a deep drag on the blunt and hefted himself up to retrieve yet another remote atop the stereo cabinet. While at the stereo he selected a CD he wanted to hear and went back to his soft spot. He took another meaningful hit of the blunt and pushed play. "For My Lover" by Tracy Chapman came smoothly across the room, touched him, and sent him up and away. It reminded him of his ex-wife and he let the sultry sound take him there, for what he didn't know.

Damn, she dogged me out, he thought, in her presence having rode the indo and the music there. Things were cool for a while with he and her—or so he thought. She'd given him a place to live when Aunt Pearl had driven him from the house with her paranoid alcoholic antics. They'd had their first child, a boy. Lapeace had no job then but she did. When she'd be at work, Lapeace would be puttin' in work for his hood, his name, his propers. She seemed the perfect mate. Tall and elegant with long silky hair and a radiant smile. He smiled now to himself thinking of her beauty. But even then, she was exemplifying traits of poison. Being seen with other men in this car and that and eyeing his homies seductively. Once when he called her from across town, a male answered the phone and hung up on him. She said it was the plumber. While he was in Oakland visiting relatives, she'd had an affair with his first cousin, and when he found out about it she said he'd raped her. This caused strife and dissension in the family for a long time. His family, the little he had then, turned their back to her and tried to get Lapeace to leave her. But by then he was in love. They'd had young love, the kind seldom experienced in the midst of the urban turbulence they grew up in. They'd met in junior high school. Lapeace was a freshman and Tammy was a senior. She'd been one of the most popular girls in the school among her peers, but Lapeace was unaware of her. Her peers were not his—freshmen mingled with themselves, usually oblivious to most of what went on in the senior circles. The seniors looked down on the freshmen as immature, fresh-out-of-elementary schoolchildren. So, socially they seldom mingled. Lapeace, however, was an exceptional seventh-grader who came to Horace Mann Junior High with a tall bearing and a street reputation that demanded attention. Height-wise, he was as tall as any ninth-grader and almost as thick. He was accepted by them and preferred their company to his own peers. But because he was a thug, and maintained a strict code of allegiance to the M.O.B. ethic, Tammy never caught his eye.

It wasn't until late in the second semester that they actually met, though Tammy had long since known who he was. She'd watched him from afar, taking cats to the hoop, battling above the rim. Moving, she'd observed, like a graceful panther, with his smooth black coat glistening under the ultraviolet rays and beading sweat. His body was maturely developed from athletics with Pop Warner. His perfectly shaped chest heaved pistonlike when he halted at the top of the key. Then, bouncing the ball easily with a learned rhythm, he'd explode past his opponents, with two swift strides, and slam-dunk the ball with a ferocious roar. He'd hang on the rim, knees drawn up, stomach muscles bulging, wingspan tapering down to his thirty-inch waist, and taunt his opponents. Tammy would sit under the lunch area canopy and watch him run two or three games while she pretended to read or do homework. She'd carefully watch him gather up his T-shirt, bottled water, and Rawlings basketball and shake the others' hands with daps, climb the chain-link fence on Cimmaron Avenue, get into his lowrider, and drive off. She figured that if she didn't deliberately put herself in his path he'd never notice her. For it seemed to her that the popularity that garnished her meant zilch to him—if, that is, he'd ever heard of her in the first place. She knew he was a young thug, of that she was certain. Not only did his dress code reflect this but so did his associations. Tammy, nevertheless, was attracted only to roughneck types. All her previous boyfriends had been thugs in one way or another and all but one had been younger. She preferred it that way, for secretly, known, then, only to her closest girlfriend, she'd had seven abortions by the ninth grade. This produced in her a maternalism that bled over into her search for a mate and caused her to seek out young men she could mother. Because of her age and beauty the younger guys she dated usually stumbled over themselves vying for her attention. They'd go to outlandish lengths to impress her and she'd grow bored with them quickly and kick 'em to the curb. Her thing was really pursuit. She liked to do the chasing, and when she'd conquered her prey, mothered him, and gotten pregnant she'd disengage and move on.

Lapeace was the most intriguing and elusive of her preys. He was a self-possessed young man, confident and stubbornly independent. She was nonetheless sure of her ability to capture him in her web. She just needed the opportune moment. Lapeace had two girlfriends that he'd been able to have sex with. The first was Robin, who took his virginity on a box in his Aunt Pearl's garage. He'd never told her but feared she'd somehow known by the way he fumbled about. Which hardly equated with the way he spoke about it. His second sexual girlfriend had taught him gentleness, but it lasted too briefly. He was not hung up on sex. He could not be persuaded by it or misled into it. He'd grown up in the crack era and this produced, for him and his small clique, an attitude predicated on M.O.B. theory and practice. "Always," he'd been drilled, "it's money over bitches. Once you get the money, real women will be available, but in the thick of the grind you'll only attract bitches trying to get your riches." He'd grown up with this credo uppermost in his mind. So most women who'd tried to push up on him were viewed with suspicion and incredulity. It was in the wake of he and Sekou's big hit that Tammy first approached him. He'd been standing alongside the lockers that outlined the corridor of the main building, waiting for Sekou, when she materialized out of the crowd.

"Excuse me," she said with a direct approach. "Can I speak with you for a minute?" Lapeace looked down at his Hamilton watch and then up again into her brown eyes.

"Go. You've got fifty-five seconds," he said coldly.

"Come on, don't play," responded Tammy, flashing her ultrawhite teeth through sensuous red lips. "I need more than a minute really."

"Forty-five seconds."

"I know you ain't trippin' like that, are you?" she asked indignantly, overstanding that he was very serious.

"Look," responded Lapeace, scoping the crowd, moving to

and fro in clusters, for Sekou, "if you really had something to say, you'd have asked for more than a minute. That shows how little you think of me."

"It ain't that I think anything of you, it's just that—"

"Five, four, three, two—time's up, I gotta go." And he pushed up off the lockers, blended into the moving crowd, and disappeared. She couldn't believe his nerve, his coldness, his self-righteousness. And although she stood there, books held tightly against her chest, embarrassed, she was in her own way excited by his behavior. The chase was on.

She saw him again that day at lunch leaving the campus alone. "Hey," she called out, giving a girlish trot to catch up to him. "Can we talk now, or what?" Lapeace looked back over his shoulder and glimpsed her thick legs rising up and falling beneath her skirt as she trotted to catch up.

"Yeah, how much time you want?"

"Come on, don't trip on me, all right?"

"I ain't trippin'. I'm serious as cancer. Time is money. What you want anyway?" he asked, turning now to look at her. She stood next to him staring up in his eyes, using her most seductive look, trying to get an edge on his cool demeanor. Yet she saw in his gaze nothing she was familiar with. Nothing she could work with to ease his defenses.

"I only want to get to know you. Damn, baby, are you that raw?" she asked, deciding to use her straightforward, no-nonsense approach. That's what she saw in his eyes.

"First of all, I ain't a baby. And second of all, knowing me may not be good for your health." He'd started walking away again and she followed toward his car.

"Well, you should let me decide what's good for my health, don't you think?"

"Whatever," Lapeace answered, looking both ways before crossing St. Andrews toward his car. He didn't want any of his teachers and especially not security knowing he was driving to school. And yet he parked right out in front of the parking lot. He unlocked the door, pulled it open, stepped one foot up on the chassis, and rolled down the window. "So what's up? What's your name anyway?"

"I'm Tammy. And like I said, I was just trying to be friendly, that's all," she said in a pleading manner now. Her fingers rubbing the smooth lacquered body of his car.

"Uh-huh, well, I'm fin' to bank to Wings n Things, you wanna roll or what?"

"Yeah, I'll roll with you. What's your name?"

"Knock it off, you know my name. Don't you?" Lapeace watched her walk around the back of the car and refused to open the door until she responded.

"Yeah, okay, I do know your name, all right?" she admitted exasperatedly.

"Look, just come correct with me awright? Don't push up wrong, 'cause I'm not the one, you feel me?" Lapeace said over the roof of his car, looking directly in her eyes.

"I gotcha, Lapeace." He unlocked her door and she sat down in the Chevy, realizing for the first time how low it actually was. It felt as if she were sitting on the ground. Suddenly, without warning, the car jumped up with such force that she hit her head on the ceiling. "Ooh!" she screamed, startled by the sudden jerk, and then quickly tried to regain her cool. Lapeace paid her no mind. He pushed in "The Temptress Greatest Hits" and pulled off from the curb. He turned right on 68th Street and right again on Western Avenue. As they waited for the light on 69th and Western some students passed in front of them, eyeing the car closely. Lapeace pulled down his locs and eyed them back over the top. The car was in a normal-looking mode, whereas no one could tell that it was lifted. When the light turned green, Lapeace hit his three-wheel motion and pulled away slowly with the front left wheel a foot off the ground. Out of the sunroof he threw up his set. They cruised down Western Avenue until they hit 83rd, where Lapeace turned left and took Harvard to 84th and parked on the side of Wings n Things. After they'd eaten, each paying for their own, they rolled back down Western stopping once on 76th so Lapeace could get a bag of pot. He couldn't deny that she was an attractive woman. Tall, shapely, aggressive—much like he'd imagined his woman would be when he fell in love. Yet his distrust of the hood rat type was so strong that he'd kept his mind on his money and that was it. Now an unfamiliar feeling began to tug at his heartstrings. A feeling, he knew, that threatened the tradition of his ethics. But he couldn't resist the current, the pull, the gravity, the actual weight of this reality.

Soon, they were inseparable. Going everywhere together, hardly ever apart. She'd even begun to pull Lapeace away from his time with Sekou. A year passed, then two, and all was going good. Tammy had a job at a local market and Lapeace was making wise moves with his cash from the score. Tammy had said she was on birth control so Lapeace wore no condoms. Then, one day out of the blue, she called Lapeace, who was still living at Aunt Pearl's. "Lapeace!" she said excitedly over the phone. "Guess what?"

"What's that?"

"I'm pregnant!"

"You what?" asked Lapeace, half shouting, half screaming.

"Pregnant!" she shouted back without excitement and more with a challenged finality.

"I thought you was takin' birth control?"

"I was, but I stopped 'cause they were causing menstrual problems for me. What's wrong, Lapeace, ain't you happy about this?"

"Happy? Tammy, I'm fifteen years old . . ." She burst into tears and Lapeace could hear her sobbing convulsively through the phone. He knew her face was contorted into a mask of emotional protest. Mouth pulled to one side by her pain, cheeks drawn up, over which ran torrents of salty tears—but what about his feelings? What about how he felt? He was crying inside, not having learned yet how to cry outwardly, his innards in knots. *A child is such an awesome responsibility,* he thought. "Tammy?"

"What?" she responded through sniffs and muffled sighs.

"What we gonna do about this?"

"What you mean what we gonna do? What you gonna do? 'Cause I'm having my baby."

"You tricked me. You said you was on birth control. Now all of a sudden you pregnant. Talkin' 'bout menstrual cramps. That's bullshit." His anger was present but subtle.

"So what you sayin' Lapeace? You don't want this baby? Is that it?"

"What I'm sayin' is . . . you tricked me," he said, his voice beginning to elevate emotionally. "Now you want my advice and cooperation. But you didn't ask for it when your ass stopped taking them birth control pills, huh?" Tammy cried harder now. Heaving and coughing into the receiver and Lapeace wondered what her face was like then. The phone was dropped, then picked back up.

"Listen Lapeace, I only stopped taking them pills a month ago . . ."

"Only a month, huh?"

"Wait, let me finish. I was going to tell you, but it slipped my mind."

"I'll have to think about this. I'll talk to you later."

"Don't hang up, La—" Click. She slammed down the dead receiver and balled up into a fetal position and cried. Twenty-two blocks away, Lapeace paced the length of his room thinking about his future. He overstood one very real thing—he loved Tammy. And his love was pure, it was without blemish. It was (and she overstood this far better than he) blind. His blind love for her overwhelmed him. He surmised that since she'd had so many abortions before that this was it—she really and truly would do the right thing and lock on to him.

Their son, Sundiata, was born in Black August. Named by Aunt Pearl, he was a robust baby full of life and intelligence. He was the spitting image of Lapeace. *I'll never be without Lapeace now,* she reasoned, *not as long as I have his seed.* After Sun was born they took an apartment together on the west side of his neighborhood. The next year they'd had another child—another boy, who they'd named Tafuta, after Lapeace's father. Tammy had graduated the year before and Lapeace had long since escaped from the L.A. Unified School District. She was doing hair, working out of a shop Lapeace had leased for her. Plus she was renting out booths to other cosmetologists. So when Molly, Lapeace's personal accountant through family connections, informed him that there was an $85,000 discrepancy in his holdings, he couldn't believe it. He didn't approach Tammy with it but just quietly investigated her himself. He'd given her whatever she wanted, or thought she needed. He crossed his own lines of reality for her, for his new family, and she'd schemed him on everything. As his investments panned out and the revenue mounted, the deceit she'd begun to exemplify grew. And she'd lie through her teeth about the most trivial things. Lapeace began to despise her. She was foolish enough to think things were all good. Even as Lapeace plotted ways to teach her a lesson.

They'd moved into one of the bigger homes in the Eighties, over behind St. Andrews Park. Tammy, having gotten bourgeoisified, lived for the attainment of material possessions. She felt so less of herself as a result of all the wicked things she'd done behind Lapeace's back that she could only find appeasement in material things. They alone filled the gaping void in her twisted soul. First she'd tried filling it with men—sleeping around with most of Lapeace's homies and eventually his first cousin. If he'd had a brother she'd have slept with him too. When he found out about his cousin, she'd claimed rape. When he investigated further and found that condoms had been used, she confessed to the affair. His heart was twisted. Soon Molly informed him of diverted funds from her shop and it was then that Lapeace began to move on her. Tammy came home one afternoon—the boys hadn't been picked up from their Headstart classes yet—to find an empty house, stripped bare. He'd not even left the carpet. She stood in the foyer dumbfounded, stricken by the reality of material loss—the loss of the only things that made her miserable life worth living. She went into a rage. She called the bank to find Lapeace had closed the account. She rushed into her bare bedroom to find that her clothes were gone. Her jewelry gone. Everything—gone. She fell to her knees and wept with her hands over her face. She couldn't believe it. The phone rang and interrupted her sobbing.

"Is this Tammy?" asked an overly excited female.

"Yes, what is it?"

"Well, I don't know how to tell you this, but your boyfriend was just at your shop, the Hair Palace, and he gave away everything in there. Everything. Then he locked the door and put up an OUT OF BUSINESS sign in the window. Girl, he had bitches lined up for blocks gettin' your things. That nigga crazy. Hello?"

"Yeah, yeah. Thanks," she answered robotlike and hung up the phone. It rang again. "Hello?"

"Tammy, you better look out your window, girl. Niggas takin' your van," said Val from across the street. Tammy leaped to her feet and ran through an empty hall, out through the living room, just in time to see the back of her Aerostar van turn the corner on a flatbed truck. She bolted back into the house and grabbed up the phone. She called Open Ridge Headstart and was startled to find that Sundiata and Tafuta had been picked up early by their father. She slammed down the phone and paced the empty living room. She paged Lapeace and got no reply. Then, at 4:55 p.m. Lapeace called.

"Why you doing this Lapeace? And where are my fuckin' kids!" she screamed.

"Do you have a job?" he asked, ignoring her questions and sounding cool as ever.

"You ain't shit Lapeace . . ."

"Do you have a means of support?"

"You ain't gonna get away with this shit you mothafucka."

"Well, seeing as how you broke and ain't got no means of support, you can't possibly care for Sun and Taf. So I'll keep the boys until you get your shit together. Here, take this number." She scrambled for a pen, finding one in the junk drawer in the kitchen. And rushed back to the phone.

"What is it?"

"1-800-756-1637. You got that?"

"Yeah, but what number is this?"

"It's the welfare office you stupid beeyach!" and he hung up.

When she picked up the phone again to page him there was no dial tone. He'd had the phone turned off. Which is why he called at 4:55. She sunk to her knees clutching the dead receiver, crying loudly and jerking about. She couldn't believe the swiftness of Lapeace's moves. Within three hours, he'd closed in on her world and shut it down. Now she had to stew in her own makings.

6

Lapeace, still in his blunt-induced drift, noticed only slightly that the music had stopped. That around him was screaming silence, wrapped in dark leather and trimmed in gold and platinum. The blunt burned on between his fingers, but he found it hard to move it to his lips. He needed to, however, because he couldn't afford to allow depression to set in. Finally, using his tempered will, he eased up enough to rest his elbows on his knees. Whenever he thought of how happy he was with her at first it always turned to sour depression in the end. She had pretty much fucked up his mind and for the longest time thereafter he was very bitter toward women, yet he knew he had only himself to blame. For he had allowed her into his vibe and she did only what he was taught her nature required. He'd gotten taken. He slowly raised the blunt to his lips and got a hardy drag. The tip blazed red as he pulled the soothing smoke into his lungs. Held it for as long as they allowed and blew it out over the room. It was almost half gone. He looked at it for a long moment and for the umpteenth time marveled at the ingenuity of pot smokers to develop ever better ways to consume the plant. Who'd have imagined? Music, he reasoned, is what he needed to complete the groove. This time he chose something for the children. Before he got back to the comfort of the sofa, Gil Scott-Heron's "Save the Children" came at him.

Shima padded softly into the room and positioned herself next to Lapeace on the sofa. She gently took the blunt from his fingers and inhaled it slowly. She held it for a long moment and then exhaled an even plume of cannabis discharge and doubled over in a coughing spasm. Lapeace patted her back, but of course this did nothing. For nothing was caught in her throat. Rather it was an attempt by her lungs to resist the smoky invasion by using a cough defense. She coughed on until her lungs were satisfied that they'd expelled or neutralized the threat. By then, naturally, she was very high.

"What you know about Gil Scott, Lapeace?" Shima asked, lifting the blunt back to her glistening lips and inhaling.

"I was turned on to him by my Aunt Pearl. You know, she used to be into all that black movement stuff. So I was raised up on his music. Whenever I wanna wind down on some real shit, I throw on some Gil."

"Gil is definitely the man. 'Save the Children,' huh?"

"Yeah, that's one of my favorites. I remember whenever I'd hear it as a child, I'd feel safe and loved. Aunt Pearl would hug me and hold on to me and sing the chorus softly in my ear. I'd sway along with her and think about a bright future. Aunt Pearl didn't drink then. She'd smell almost like my attorney Safi's office. She'd be wearing all that Afrikan garb, you know, flowing robes, head wraps, sandals, and stuff?"

"Yeah," said Shima thoughtfully. Visualizing Aunt Pearl. "I know what you mean." She took another drag on the blunt.

"And she'd always be reading me things from this book or that. Quoting stuff and dropping names on me. But shit, all I remembered was the music. My Aunt Pearl never had no kids. Said the ancestors used her for something else besides bearing children. But she raised me, though, you know?" Lapeace was sitting on the edge of the sofa now, looking at Shima and gesturing his spiel with his hands.

"Babes, when you hear that song now do you think of your sons, about saving your children?" she asked, handing him the blunt. He looked hard at her, staring as if she'd breached a sacred burial ground of thoughts, though his glare was not threatening.

"I have so many thoughts when I hear that song. My first thoughts are of me. You know, wondering if I have a future, or was I destined to be . . ." He trailed off his discourse with clenched fists and his head down.

"What? What was you gonna say, Babes?" She took the blunt and put it in the ashtray and reached an arm around his wide shoulders.

"I don't know," continued Lapeace in a melancholy tone. "It's just that 'Save the Children' now seems such a small thing when so many of us adults are fucked up. I mean, damn, look at Aunt Pearl now. She's a wino, stumblin' around and shit. People smoked out, niggas killin' everybody, scandalous bitches chasing riches and on top of all of that, one time huntin' a mothafucka. This shit is wicked."

"I feel what you sayin', Lapeace. And sometimes I feel like things are hopeless for the black nation too. But we can't develop such a negative attitude toward our future. I feel that what Gil is saying is right and what you are saying is right. In order to save the children we've got to have some idea of what we are saving them from. Therefore, it follows, that what we are saving them from, we are already victims of. Do you follow me, Babes?" she asked, kneeling now in front of him, holding both his hands and squinting into his dark brown eyes.

"Yeah, I hear what you saying. Sounding like Aunt Pearl 'n shit. But that's just some theory. We need more than that . . ."

"Hold up a minute . . ." Shima said, standing erect, one hand on her hip, the other waving wildly with her index finger extended, ". . . don't be comparing me to your aunt. What I say is me, you got that?"

"Calm down, Shima, just calm down. I didn't mean it like that. I meant that it's been so much talkin' about the problem that it gets in the way of action. Shit needs to be done."

"I overstand that, but . . ."

"Wait a minute. Why you be sayin' overstand instead of understand? Which is another thing, y'all be using all these code words and shit. What's up with that?" he asked, honestly seeking an explanation.

"You know what Lapeace? Fuck you, all right. 'Cause you ain't tryin' to learn nothin'. You just wanna argue. I ain't got time for it," she said walking quickly toward her room, waving her arm dismissively.

"Come here, Shima," he called out after her. "I ain't tryin' to argue. I only asked a question." He watched her walk down the hall and disappear into her room. The door shut loudly behind her. Lapeace frowned and pushed back on the couch. A passing car backfired and he jumped slightly. When he walked and looked out of the window he was startled to see two black-and-white patrol cars parked in front of Shima's house. Both were empty. He felt a momentary panic by their presence. What now? Using the rotary adjuster he positioned the blinds so he could see out but no one could see in. Standing perfectly still, with the music off, he watched the street and the cars. *What the fuck are they doing here?* He eased over to the coffee table and retrieved what was left of the blunt, which wasn't much. He took one drag on the roach and put it back in the ashtray. At that moment two shadows moved across the blinds on the porch. Lapeace positioned himself in time to see the two officers collect themselves at the door and to see the blond one knock. He stood still and watched them look at one another. There came another knock. Lapeace stood firm. He hoped Shima wouldn't come back up the hall wanting to continue the argument. But to him it wasn't really an argument at all. The questioning she took as a challenge to her ways was but an honest pursuit by him to reach a synthesis in the dilemma she presented. There was yet another knock and this time Shima came out of her room and asked Lapeace who it was. She received no answer, yet when she entered the living room she saw Lapeace standing there looking out the window.

"What's up, didn't you hear someone knock?" she asked en route to the door.

"Shhh!" Lapeace hissed urgently, waving her back with a contorted face and exaggerated swings of his arms. Shima froze in her steps looking puzzled. Then she saw the two shadows cross the expanse of the window. She eased over to his side and peeped out as she saw him doing.

"What they want here?" Shima asked in a whisper, observing the officers walk to the next house and traverse up the walk.

"I ain't knowin' and really ain't tryin' to find out," he answered and moved toward the stereo.

"Why you didn't answer it, Babes?"

Bending down choosing a compact disc from the stored selection, Lapeace thought about explaining everything to her, but quickly decided against it.

"'Cause it smelled like pot up in here and you heard what happened to Snoop in Atlanta when the pigs smelled pot."

"Yeah, that's right," said Shima thoughtfully, stepping up to Lapeace and playfully pushing him on the head. "You got some brains in that ol' thick head of yours don't you?"

"Awright girl, quit playin'," chided Lapeace gleefully, relieved she was in a good mood. "Eh, Shima, what you know about this?" He pointed the remote at the stereo and out came "Strange Fruit" by Billie Holiday.

"Ooh, that's a phat ass song, ain't it? Sista-girl put it down! Hey."

"Yeah, but what you know about it?" asked Lapeace pressingly.

"She's talkin' 'bout lynchin' in the South." Then she thought again and added, "You know I gotta be up on it if it's my CD."

"Not really," he countered, "'cause a lot of folks slept on X-Clan. Got caught up in the beats and never under, I mean *over*stood the lyrical importance."

"Probably because X-Clan got too esoteric and the average hip-hop head couldn't fade it. But the production was definitely on it." "Strange Fruit" played on in the background as Lapeace busied himself with splitting the skin on another blunt. With experience he slit the belly of the densely packed cigar and emptied the contents on Ice Cube's face as it appeared on the cover of *The Source* magazine. Before going any further with the delicate procedure, Lapeace asked Shima if she had any honey. Promptly, she went to retrieve what she had. Intensely he watched her muscular mounds rise and fall with each step. Her ass was all over the room. Far too long he felt he'd been denied the opportunity to be intimate for any length of time with such a woman. From head to toe she was simply gorgeous. Tammy, he remembered, was never gifted with the ass of a sista. Really, as he thought more about it, her body was terribly unattractive, especially after the children. *Ugh.* In the face, she remained a stunning beauty but below the neck she was a wreck. And it had become, in the latter times in their relationship, a true test in anatomical will to get an erection for her. He grimaced just to think about it.

Shima aided in that thought's dissipation by entering the room. She wore gray terry-cloth shorts, no shoes or socks, and a midriff gray T-shirt that showed off her sexy belly button. Her walk was lively and modelesque, made all the more attractive by her bowlegs. She plopped down on the couch beside him and slid over the plastic honey bear. Lapeace wasted no time in applying the honey to the cigar paper packed with chronic. He rolled it expertly in his large hands allowing not one parcel of pot to fall out. Once complete, he laid it aside and moved to discard the cigar tobacco in the waste can in the kitchen. It was time, he felt, to tell her. Better now than never—which was really not realistic. She'd find out soon enough and more than likely from the wrong people. Those who always twisted shit, got facts blurred with fiction. Envious bustas, back-bitin' gangsta haters. Either them or the so-called news would exploit the fear and ignorance of the people and turn reality into a montage of white supremacist perception, as usual. He knew it was his responsibility and he'd never run from that. When he returned to the living room, having dumped the whole magazine in the trash, Shima had changed the music. Now playing was "Happy Feelings" by Maze featuring Frankie Beverly. Shima was simulating a slow dance, grinding her pelvis against an invisible partner, eyes closed, arms extended, hips swaying. He moved quietly to the sofa and sparked the honey blunt. The inhalation was sweet and smooth. The afterburn smelled of honey-roasted crescent rolls with a mint aroma. When she opened her eyes again he was passing her the bud.

"How long you been sittin' there watchin' me?" she asked and took a drag on the blunt.

"Long enough to get horny watching your sexy ass."

"That long, huh?"

"It only takes a second," said Lapeace, lustfully ogling her while rubbing his crotch area. He stopped abruptly and reminded himself of what he had to do. He sat up straight and cleared his throat. Shima passed him the blunt back and went to change the music. "Shima, leave it off for a minute, will you? I've got to run something to you."

"Oh, okay, Babes," answered Shima, and returned to his side on the couch. "What's up?"

Lapeace pulled hard on the blunt, making its cherry burn brightly for a long moment. He held the smoke in for a while, trained it up from his mouth to his nostrils, then exhaled heavily. "Did you hear about that big shooting on the 'Shaw last month?"

"Um," Shima thought, hand on her chin, legs drawn up under her tight little body. "I think so . . . Oh, hell yeah, wasn't that what they called the Crenshaw massacre?"

"Yeah. Well . . ."

"Oh, yeah. Now I remember. A lot of innocent folks got all shot up. Gas stations exploded and people got ran over and stuff. What about it?" asked Shima, hand resting on Lapeace's thigh.

"I was involved in that."

"We have a code blue alarm in one-twenty!" shouted the beefy male nurse over his shoulder as he ran down the cluttered corridor. In his wake, almost as if his wind alone had propelled them forward, the remaining staff followed his lead. He burst through the door with force. So much so that the heavy wooden door hit its rubber stop behind it and bounced back, almost knocking down the first following physician. Corbet, the beefy lead nurse, moved quickly to the bed whose alarm had been tripped but was astonished to find that he was not in distress at all. Perplexed, Corbet turned toward the other patient in the room, who was the dog-bite victim. He in turn raised a bandaged hand and directed everyone's attention toward the far corner of the room. There, under Anyhow's bed, was a thick, almost congealed pool of blood. His left arm lay extended off the bed, hand half clenched with blood flowing freely down, feeding the pool. His right arm was laid easily across his chest and his eyes were closed softly, as if he were peacefully asleep. The hospital staff flew into action under the commanding barks of the head doctor. Soon Anyhow was being attended to by half a dozen physicians. After an hour of intense work and critical care, Anyhow was listed in very critical condition with possible brain damage due to the massive amount of blood lost. Nurse Richter notified Sweeney immediately after she found the code blue to be for Anyhow. Mendoza and Sweeney were there within an hour of the call.

"How significant is the threat of brain damage?" asked Sweeney, leaning against Nurse Richter's station in a crumpled brown jacket and customary white shirt. His pink head was glistening from sweat brought on by the event, as well as from the bright four-foot fluorescent lights beaming down upon his naked dome.

"Well," began Nurse Richter, reaching under her counter to retrieve a Kleenex for Sweeney's sweating head, "we won't have any definite results on brain activity until a full CAT scan and EEG has been done. Which could take anywhere between two days to a week."

"We'll need to be kept abreast of his developments," Mendoza said, looking up from his notepad at Nurse Richter, who stared back evenly.

"Of course."

"You'll call me, should there be anything significant, then?" asked Sweeney, leaning over the counter in search of a wastepaper basket.

"Yes. As I did, I shall continue to do."

"Great."

Mendoza wrote:

8-27-96, approx. 6:30 p.m.
Suspect attempted suicide at Co. Gen.

Then he slapped the black leather notepad shut and pressed the DOWN button for the elevator. Instinctively his left hand went up to his mustache.

Sweeney stood silently brooding as the elevator descended from the thirteenth to the seventh floor, where a young New Afrikan deputy sheriff boarded. The descent continued. Each nodded his greetings but no words were spoken. Sweeney shifted heavily from one foot to the other as he contemplated the ramifications of Anyhow's actions. He tried to recall what he'd learned in the military about the brain and the various ways it could be damaged by blood loss. *Damn,* he critiqued himself, *need to brush up on my studies. Let's see,* he thought, focusing on the two-thousand-pound-capacity weight sign on the elevator wall. *There was the lobus occipitalis. The temporalis, the cortex . . . um . . . damn . . . the corpus callosum. So many connecting fibers . . . having lost the amount of blood that he had, causing a loss of oxygen to the brain, could result in a number of brain-altering maladies.* When he had been allowed to look in on him nothing by way of exterior observation seemed amiss. Though on the oscillator Nurse Richter pointed out the very low heart rate pronounced by the LED. He could only hope that Any pulled out with some degree of stability. Otherwise the case against Lapeace Shakur would be shot. Traveling back to the new prefab trailer station the 77th Division was using while its original location was being rebuilt and expanded, Sweeney spoke what he'd been thinking.

"You know," he began, eyeing the exposed girders of the 110 freeway, which had been under construction for years, "wouldn't it be something if the Mexican guy in the room with Harper slit his wrist?"

"Yeah, that would be something," replied Mendoza in an "oh yeah, sort of incredible" tone.

"No, I'm serious. I mean, shit, aren't the Mexican gangs and the black gangs at war?"

"Yep," Mendoza said while changing lanes. "So?"

"So? Don't you see what I'm saying? Look, all this guy had to—"

"The guy had a hole in his head, John. For Christ's sake, he was shot in the head! He has no motor skills."

"Oh. I didn't know that."

"Yeah, well I—you stupid fuck!" exclaimed Mendoza, slamming on the brakes briefly after being cut off by an older sedan. He quickly righted the Chevy and resumed the discourse. "No, I um . . . I took a peek at his chart while you were in the ICU with Nurse Ratched."

"Well, that kills that theory then."

"Yeah," chuckled Mendoza, "deader than shit." Then, with seriousness he said, "I can't see why you would think it was the Mexican guy anyway. What about the other patient, the black guy? Shit, they kill each other too. But you automatically assumed that the Mexican did it."

"I was using deductive reasoning. There was nothing racial about it, if that's what you're reaching for."

"Your thoughts speak for themselves, Mexican people cut."

"Oh, come off it, beaner!" Sweeney shouted and then burst into hysterical laughter.

"*¡Chinga tu madre, pinche yanqui!*" replied Mendoza as he wheeled the Chevy into the station's parking lot.

7

At his desk in the makeshift station, Sweeney sat reclining in his chair with his feet up. In his meaty hands was a blue notebook—the murder book, as it was called. He was studying the evidence to date, compiled in chronological order in the binder. These collective pieces were of great importance to his case, but alone, without the assistance of an informant, they could not win a conviction. The murder book's binding was covered with a strip of masking tape that ran from top to bottom, drawing one's attention easily to it. There, written vertically in black marker, was:

Lapeace Shakur—Cren Mass: 1996.

Sweeney knew Lapeace well—or, actually, knew of his exploits well. Only once had he been in contact with him. A "slickster" is how he thought of him. Educated, smooth, loyal, and, without a doubt, a killer. Although he'd never been convicted of murder, his reputation spoke for itself. And somewhere along the line he'd gotten a lump sum of cash, Sweeney knew. Yet his name had never been associated with drugs. Not only that but up until this case his name was not even on the neighborhood wire. Sweeney turned the page and was confronted with a slew of photographs, which depicted every victim framed in the finality of death. Photographs taken by crime-scene specialists showed grotesque holes and gashes torn into the bodies of innocent bystanders. Page after page froze the lifeless from an angle different from the one preceding it. He turned each page slowly, carefully. From the explosion site body parts were circled in chalk and photographed. An arm here, a leg there, pieces of skull with the hair and scalp still attached were pictured in glossy colors for pages on end. Sweeney had never gotten used to the murder book photos or now, as it were, video shots of the scene. It was a macabre ritual. He closed the book with a sigh and began to sift through scraps of notepaper scattered over the plastic blotter. Finding the number he wanted scrawled sloppily on the back of a Chief Auto Parts business card, Sweeney picked up the phone. On the third ring the line was answered by an adult male.

"May I please speak to Robert?"

"This Robert."

"Little Huckabuck?" Sweeney questioned with suspicion, hearing the monotones of exchange in the background.

"Yeah, this him."

"Listen, Huck, this is Sweeney. I need your help on something. Now I know you've been doing all you can on the Stoney case, but we would really be grateful if you could poke around and see what you can find on Lapeace."

"Lapeace?" Lil Huck asked, and before Sweeney could answer he added, "Man, I'm a tell you, Lapeace ain't doin' nothin' that I know of. He don't slang or nothin'."

"Well this ain't got nothing to do with dope. We need to know about his involvement in the big Crenshaw shooting earlier this month. Poke around, see what you can find. It'll do you some good."

"Aight, man. I'll get on it. Is that it?"

"Yeah," answered Sweeney, drumming his pencil on the blotter top. "Oh, hey, how the feds treating you?"

"Shit, man, them fools still owe me money and niggas startin' to ask questions about me. It's gettin' kinda hot."

"Well, you be safe and keep your nose clean."

"Aight then."

Sweeney replaced the receiver in its cradle and again picked up the blue book.

Once Lil Huck had returned the receiver to its place, he rejoined his homies in the den. There were five there, lounging, getting high, and playing Sega. The room was replete with indo smoke and the acrid scent of the chemical compound PCP. C-Fish held the small iodine bottle filled with the sluggish urine-colored liquid still while he dipped in the marijuana joint. Once it was totally saturated he pulled it gently from the bottle and laid it on top of a strip of tinfoil. No one paid him much attention, for they were all into the Sega game. When the joint had dried sufficiently, C-Fish sparked it up. It caught with a blaze of fire, which he had to blow out. "Damn, cuz, this shit da bomb," said C-Fish.

He got no response. He began to smoke the joint. After two big drags he handed it to Baby C-Dog, who refused it.

"You know I don't smoke that shit, nigga."

"Here, cuz," exhorted C-Fish pushing the chemical joint toward Stagalee. "This shit is monkey piss loc."

"We'll see." Stag took the fat stick of pot, laced with twenty-two different chemicals, and pulled on it hard. The harsh invasion of indo smoke was all but subdued under the wetness of the PCP and no recoiling cough spasm occurred. Yet the effect of the indo's strength was felt strongly as the PCP took Stag down into a dark mental abyss and seemingly rolled him around on a bed of pointy nails that tingled every nerve fiber in his body. Then came the flow of saliva and the need to spit—but by then he was embalmed and couldn't move. His Sega control lay alone on the floor and he stared out into the virtual reality created by the drug. The joint was taken from his hand and pulled on by Lil Spike, who after three hits was comatose in a vertical position, legs wide apart, forehead beaded with sweat. No one else wanted any of it. It was, as C-Fish said, da bomb. C-Dog and Lil Huck played on with the Sega and let the others enjoy their trip. It was true, Lil Huck's name had begun to leave a sour taste in some homies' mouths, for word had come out of the county jail and the Federal Metropolitan Correctional Center that his name was linked unfavorably to some cases involving bank robberies and murder. Those who still hung around him were there only at the behest of Sidewinder, who had instructed a team of little homies to cover him until a definite word came down regarding his fate. There was a knock at the door and Lil Huck went to answer it. C-Dog was left alone with the zombies. He looked pathetically from one to the other. Pitying each in his own way, wishing for the millionth time that his loved ones would stop using PCP. Their motor skills were shot, unresponsive to any directive sent from the brain. They stood and sat as motionless as statues. Burning up.

"What up loc?" Sam Dog said cordially as he bounced up into the den.

"Aight, homie," responded C-Dog with an extended hand. Sam Dog clasped his hand over Lil C-Dog's and went through the ritual shake.

"Ain't no need in greetin' these other niggas, they wet!" said Sam.

"Yeah, they been in that monkey piss," said C-Dog before he bent to pick up Lil Huck's Sega control. "Here cuz, play this nigga's game 'cause he's takin' too long."

"Uh-unh," protested Lil Huck entering the room. "Gimme my shit. I can play my own game."

"Well, commo' then nigga, damn. Trying to run from this ass whuppin'."

"Yeah right. Sam, sit your black ass somewhere."

"Where? These niggas all over this muthafucka."

"F-F-Fuck y-y-you, c-cuz," Stag managed to say and then just as quickly slumped back into his trance.

"Yeah, yeah. Save it Stag, you drippin' wet. But hey, I ain't mad at you. Just keep yo' ass off the street like that. We can't afford to let nobody kill you."

"Eh, Sam," said Lil Huck while frantically pressing control buttons on his control pad. "What up wit Lapeace? I ain't seen cuz around in a while?"

"I seen Lapeace the other day in a phat-ass Lexus with some bitch."

"Cuz he be doing his thang in the North. Havin' his chips, helpin' homies out," answered C-Dog while working his controls just as quickly.

"The homies from the North got they lolos shot up by some rims on the 'Shaw last month," added Sam Dog watching Lil Spike tic as if he were afflicted with Tourette's.

"Oh yeah?" replied Lil Huck. "I didn't hear 'bout that. What happened?"

"Shit, off brands from the Du-Low Car Club caught 'em slippin' and dumped. Toe up all the homies' shit. Lapeace was there. Him and that nigga Anyhow was goin' at it. Ghost say them niggas was really tryin' to kill each other."

"No shit?" Lil Huck had put down his joystick and sat looking at Sam Dog.

"I don't know, but Ghost say he got that shit on tape. A couple homies from the North say they seen it."

"Who got the tape now?" asked Lil Huck.

"I don't know. Eh, cuz, what you got to eat in this raggedy-ass muthafucka?" asked Sam, catching C-Dog's eye and the sign to change the subject.

"I ain't got shit fo' yo ass. Take yo' ballin' ass to the sto' and get somethin', if you that hungry."

"Fuck you. I'm outta here. Eh C-Dog, let's bounce, cuz."

"Naw, I'm a hang here till the homies come down. I'll hit you off later though. And watch yo' self." Sam exited the residence and C-Dog and Huck went back to their game. Lil Huck needed to get to a phone. Needed to tell Sweeney that a tape existed.

"Wait a minute Lapeace. What you mean you was involved? Involved how?" asked Shima, looking directly into his brown eyes.

Lapeace eased back onto the couch, trying to escape her glare, but found that it was still quite intense. Then he stood up and began to pace in short strides in front of her.

"I was up there flossin', you know, movin' the Super Sport, when this nigga name Anyhow—who I been beefin' wit fo' like life—rolled up on me and started dumpin'. Shit, so I start dumpin' back, you know. And—"

"I don't even wanna know no more, Lapeace," Shima interrupted, voice cracking, eyes filling up with water, her hands moving nervously.

"Oh, you just gonna shut me down like that? You ain't gonna listen to my side or nuttin', huh?"

"I can't handle this right now, Lapeace—y'all black men are breakin' my fuckin' heart with this stupid-ass shit! Ahhh!" she cried and threw herself back onto the couch and kicked her feet like a child in a tantrum. With one mighty thrust, she kicked over the glass coffee table, its top flipping over twice before it came to a rest over by the stereo. Lapeace moved around the flipped table and sat down easily next to her.

"Shima," he whispered in a soft husky tone, "I need your strength right now. You've got to see, Shima, that I didn't start all this crazy shit. I just grew up in it and naturally became a part of it. I'm not bangin', Shima, you can see that, can't you? I was, at one time, but this wasn't no bangin' thing. Me and dude been at each other since we was nine years old. Aw, Shima, I ain't into killin' no black people. I'm pro-black. Come on now, can you feel what I'm saying Babes?"

"Lapeace . . . you . . . knew . . . you'd never be able to stay with me as you promised no more than three damn hours ago . . . why you lie to me, to my heart?" Her voice was cold as ice, her stare forward and unrelenting.

"I do plan to stay with you, Shima. We can leave this country. I've got chips and I got—"

"Be serious, Lapeace," persisted Shima. "I am CEO of my own company. I can't just take flight with you. Think about what you sayin', man."

"Oh, now I'm just 'man,' huh?" asked Lapeace sarcastically as he got up and moved toward the hallway. "You are a trip, Shima. You're only concerned with yourself. But don't even trip, I'm a get outta your way and let you do your thing." He moved on down the hall toward her room. Shima closed her eyes and wept softly to herself. Damn, she loved that man. She had become addicted to his darkness, his style, speech, smell, and way of treatment. It had been only a short time that she'd known him personally, but in that time he'd shown her nothing but righteousness and respect. And she'd heard of him long before they'd met—their circle wasn't that big. She overstood, perhaps better than he, that he was but a victim of circumstance. That his activity in the wicked realm of banging was but a response to a reality that was there long before he was born. *But why,* she mused, *do all the good brothas have to respond to that shit?* She knew that the backbone in the New Afrikan Nation was its women, that while sexism was hella prevalent in the nation, New Afrikan women still exerted the underlying power in the final equation. He was right in that regard, he needed her strength. She'd have to call on her sista friends for auxiliary strength. When Lapeace came back up the hallway and entered the living room, he had his bags with him. When he looked over at Shima, he no longer saw a tantrum-throwing child but an upright New Afrikan Woman waiting to aid her man. Her strength was radiant throughout the room. He stood still, bags in both hands. Drinking and soaking in her power. It was certainly reviving.

Shima stood up and opened her arms to Lapeace. He dropped his luggage and rushed to her embrace. They held each other tight. Eyes shut over each shoulder the vibe was electrical and sure.

"Babes, we gonna deal with this shit together, aight?" Shima said, leaning back away from him and looking up into his moist eyes.

"Aight, Shima, I feel you . . . all over me."

"Good, 'cause that's a permanent feeling. Now, let's start workin' on your defense. You gotta—"

"I got an attorney already."

"Oh? What's his name?"

"Safi Wazir, in West L.A."

"A brotha?"

"Yeah, he's a Muslim."

"Good. Still, I want my attorney Chokwe Lumumba to look at this case too."

"Aight."

"And," continued Shima, retrieving a notepad from atop a speaker, "I am callin' in my girls to roll back the Amerikan press, 'cause you know it's gonna be negative."

"Yo' girls? What's that mean?"

"Well, let's see," said Shima, looking down at the list she'd been compiling. "We got Poetess doing the Agenda on the *Beat.* We got Sheena who's the editor in chief of *Rap Pages.* Monifa writes for the *Malcolm X Grassroots Movement Newspaper* and has a radio spot in New York. Dream and Asha are out there too. Mujah and the New Afrikan Women for Self-Determination are in Oakland. Muasia's in Delaware. Thandisizwe is editor of *By Any Means Necessary* in Georgia. Latifah is at Ruthless. I'm at Rap Life. Marsha is at the *Sentinel.* Kay is at Power 97 in Philly . . ."

"Aight, aight. I get the message. Damn, y'all got that communication thang on lock, huh?"

"I thought you knew? Don't you know that it was women who brought Kwame Nkrumah to power?"

"No, I didn't know that."

"Yep. And it was women who took his ass outta power. See, while y'all runnin' round slangin' all that testosterone—being men—women communicatin' with each other. Now, go on and finish tellin' me what happened, Babes."

"Wait, not all y'all communicatin'. Don't front. Don't even try it."

"Naw, I ain't sayin' it's like that. But I am sayin' that we ain't got a lot of the hang-ups that y'all got."

"Hang-ups?"

"Yeah, hang-ups."

"Shit, the only hang-up I got is a nigga tryin' to peel my damn cap. And then that nigga got the hang-up—he can hang up his damn life! Ha, ha, ha!"

"Not funny, Lapeace. What I'm talkin' 'bout is, you know . . ." There came a loud knock at the door which cut her monologue. They looked at each other without moving. The knock erupted again. Shima got up and moved toward the door. She peeped through the peephole and fixed her eye on the visitor. "It's your boy Sekou, Babes."

"Oh, I forgot, when I was packin' I called him for a ride. Let him in."

"Damn, you was really gonna leave, huh?" asked Shima while undoing the blots and locks.

"I was outta here," replied Lapeace playfully with a jerk of his thumb like an umpire.

"Hey, Sekou, what up?" Shima said, greeting him warmly as he entered.

"That damn door—y'all got mo' locks on that muthafucka than Pelican Bay!"

"The times we live in," said Shima, rebolting the door with its many locks and chains.

"Shit," responded Sekou, stepping over to Lapeace for a shake. "It's only what you make it to be."

"Sekou?"

"Yeah, Shima."

"Why you always quotin' Tupac? Everything he say, you say."

"That's my nigga. Plus, everything he say he gets straight from the street. Most times we been sayin' it fo' years."

"I'm just checkin'."

"Check on, baby, check on. I ain't mad at you." He grinned at the realization of another Tupac quote. But he didn't really do it on purpose; he was just a slang-speaking thug. He and Lapeace sat and began to talk while Shima righted the coffee table then walked down the hall. "Hey," said Sekou, looking about the room, "you ready to bounce or what?"

"Naw," replied Lapeace, standing and moving toward the sound system. "I'm a chill here. We pretty much straightened it out. You know how shit be in the heat of the moment."

"You in love ain't cha Peace?"

"I don't know yet. Why you say that?"

"'Cause, nigga, you quotin' R and B titles and shit. Fuck R and B—this rap fo' life!" exclaimed Sekou loudly, fixing his hand into an "R."

"Oh yeah? Well what about this?" He pressed the PLAY button and out came "Freakin' You" by Jodeci.

"Aw, man, that's really hip-hop, though. Plus, I just can't fade that candy-ass R and B that cater to pop audiences. You know what I mean?"

"Yeah, but it's R and B."

"Killa," shot back Sekou. "You wiggin'. Eh, you got any chronic? You got some Alizé?"

"We got Hennessy."

"What you think about the upcoming fight with Tyson and Golden?"

"I ain't into that shit, really. Why I wanna pay to see a fight when niggas fightin' daily in the streets. Now, what you wanna do, fight or get bent?"

"What you think—get bent. Guess what?"

"What's that?"

"One of the homies, Ghost I believe, filmed that shit with you and Anyhow. Got it on tape."

"Yeah I'm already up on it. I hurried up, scooped that shit!" Lapeace exclaimed.

"Good, 'cause Lil Huck been askin' 'bout the damn thang."

"How he hear 'bout the tape? Who ran they fuckin' mouth?"

"C-Dog say Sam Dog did."

"Aw, fuck," complained Lapeace, disgusted.

"Exactly. We gotta shut Sam up and kill all thoughts 'bout that tape, man. You need to tear that shit up. Burn it or somethin'."

"Yeah, I plan to."

"Dig this, let's move to the hood now. This way we can put down some damage control. What you think?"

"Yeah," answered Lapeace, rubbing his chin thoughtfully, oblivious to the music now. "Let's do that." He picked up his bags and walked them down the hall to Shima's room. She was sitting on the edge of the bed, one leg drawn up onto the comforter as she painted her toenails. He explained what he needed to do without telling her about the tape. She didn't need to know every detail about his involvement. And it wasn't like he lied to her. He just didn't tell her *everything* he knew. This was a tactic he'd learned from Tammy. She'd always do him like that. Tell him only half or three-quarters of the truth while conveniently omitting the rest. She wouldn't lie; she'd just be evasive. Shima overstood his point in what he'd said and bid him farewell with a passionate kiss that sent him reeling.

In Sekou's Explorer, engulfed in a cloud of indo smoke, they traveled east on Slauson Avenue. Sekou's truck was black with gray interior. From without it looked to be a stocked Ford Explorer but inside it was a virtual office. Sekou had a fax installed, fitted just below the A/C unit. The glove compartment had been removed. Now a five-inch television was set into position with such precision that it looked as if it were a standard option that came with the truck. Two cellular phones adorned the console. One he used strictly for business purposes between he and his accountant, broker, and real estate agent. He gave this number to no one else. Nor would he call anyone other than them on it. The other was his in-truck social line. Two Sega control pads were attached by Velcro strips on the dash next to the TV screen and the windows were so tinted that even on the sunniest days the inside looked like dusk. The music, of course, was top-of-the-line Kenwood. His amps, a thousand watts each for his rear speakers, were so huge that they came equipped with fans for cooling. After breaking several windows in his truck with his sounds, he'd finally gotten all his glass except the windshield replaced with quarter-inch Plexiglas.

Sekou was of medium build, light-complexioned, and resembled, in an almost remarkable way, Cuba Gooding Jr. In the summertime he turned a vibrant bronze and the tips of his hair changed to golden embers. When not in braids (usually cornrows) he wore it in a 'fro, combed out evenly and full. Neither he nor Lapeace wore hats. Hats, they overstood, were targets. Targets as sure as blue and red flags. Sekou's dress style was baggy hip-hop gear. Walker Wear, Phat Farm, and Kani. He'd never taken on a nickname. Never found it expedient. Besides, most folks figured that "Sekou" itself was some sort of nickname. And only but a few of his homies knew its correct spelling. He'd seen on several occasions where in the course of a sprawling role call spray-painted on a wall, his name would be spelled "Say Coo." That didn't much matter to him, as long as they pronounced it correctly. The soothing thing to him, however, was that most people he knew had changed their names to sound hard: "Killer," "Mad Dog," "Evil," "Devil," "Snake," etc. Sekou meant "fighter" and he'd been given that at birth by his mother. So he always considered himself a natural. A born fighter.

The hood gobbled him up not long after it had eaten Lapeace. Sekou and his family had relocated to South Central from the East Bay. He was an only child in a single-parent household. He'd met Lapeace over his back fence one July morning. Lapeace had been rumbling through some boxes in Aunt Pearl's garage and came across a case of Beefeater gin unopened. He figured that Aunt Pearl must have forgotten it, 'cause the dust upon it was so thick that blowing on it only moved the top layer. Lapeace tore back the cardboard cover and viewed the sparkling clear bottles secreted in their individual spaces. He'd never drank anything but beer and even then it was not much. Only what his older homies had given him. Looking down at the twelve bottles of Beefeater gin gave him a curious feeling. One that beckoned him to experiment. He lifted out one of the bottles and gazed upon its label, looking at the funny-dressed white man, before closing back the top. He took a single bottle and went out behind the garage, where he nestled himself in between some boxes and the ivy-covered chain-link fence and began to drink the gin. It burned from the time his young lips touched the bottle. His lips, tongue, throat, and stomach were aflame from the liquid, but he guzzled it still. Sekou was out in his backyard emptying the trash when he noticed the indentation in the fence. The ivy-laden fence sagged miserably under the weight of Lapeace's drunken body. With a quarter of the gin gone, drunk in huge gulps, Lapeace was rubber under its control. Sekou could hear guzzling sounds through the ivy, but due to its density he could not see anyone. He put down the garbage pail and crept closer toward the sound and the sag. "Gulp, gulp, gulp, ahh!" It sounded to Sekou like the person was enjoying whatever was being drunk. He bent and peered through a small opening in the leaves. The person, he could now see, was a young man.

"Hey, wha'cha doin' man?" asked Sekou through the fence.

"Who dat?" asked Lapeace in an obvious drunken slur. The sag shifted as he attempted to come off the fence. But his body and mind were not one; alcohol was running interference.

"Sekou. What's that you got?"

"Say who?" asked Lapeace, perplexed by the complicated name.

"Never mind," said Sekou, not worried if he'd get the name. He wanted to get an answer to the question. He asked about the drink. "What's that you drinkin'?"

"It say Beefeater. Some gin or some'em."

"Can I get some?" asked Sekou through the little opening in the leaves. His hands were on both of his knees.

"Climb on over . . . wait a minute." Lapeace held on to one of the boxes on his left and hefted himself up to his feet. He turned and looked at the thick ivy. "Nigga where you from?"

"From?" asked Sekou quizzically. Not overstanding how Lapeace meant it.

"Yeah, who you with. What set you claim?" Lapeace asked, talking into the ivy.

"I'm from Oakland. We just moved down here. I ain't in no gang."

"Aight, then. Come on over," Lapeace said and stumbled back a pace or two. Sekou scaled the fence and landed on the other side awkwardly. Lapeace handed the bottle to him and he tipped it to his lips. Sekou took a big gulp and felt the powerful liquid burn all the way down to his belly.

"Ahhh," he said, handing the bottle back to Lapeace. "Whew! That's some mean shit!"

"Yeah, this gangsta shit," said Lapeace and took a long swig. They sat there behind Aunt Pearl's garage, between the boxes and the fence, and talked and drank. Postured, posed, profiled, and drank. When Aunt Pearl, worried as to where Lapeace might be, wandered into the yard, she found both Sekou and Lapeace laid out asleep. The bottle of Beefeater on its side, empty.

"Who you gonna hit up first?" Sekou asked, wheeling the Ford Explorer around the corner on Slauson Avenue and Western heading south.

"Let's go straight to the south side and try to catch Sam. Then we'll double back and holler at Ghost. Didn't you say that he was showing the video?"

"Yeah, that's what C-Dog said."

"I wonder if he made a copy of the damn thing? That would be foul, huh?"

"Yeah, but it ain't like it was copyrighted or nothin'. It ain't on Ghost."

"Naw, I know that," answered Lapeace, reading the writing on a graffiti-packed MTA bus. "But he could at least have some discretion about showing it. He knows what happened up there. And if one time got wind of that tape, they gonna raid the whole hood looking for it."

"Yeah, you right about that. Shima still taken Sanai's death hard?"

"Not as much as she did at first, but still kinda buggin'. Eh, check these muthafuckas out," Lapeace said, indicating the adjacent car, an AMC Pacer packed with Mexicans playing loud mariachi music. The driver was sporting a big ten-gallon hat and had a mouthful of silver teeth.

"What's that question Mr. Marshall asked 'bout the hood?" asked Sekou.

"Oh, when did the neighborhood become just the hood?"

"Yeah. Well, there it is," Sekou said, pointing at the Pacer. "When we stopped knowing our neighbors."

"No shit. And you know what else?"

"What?"

"If homies don't start clearing these hat dancers out, our hood's gonna fuck around and become their *varrio*. And that's real!"

"You ain't lyin' 'bout that." They came to a smooth stop outside of Sam's house on 79th Street and sat momentarily while Sekou retrieved his weapon from its spot. Then they exited the truck out into the warm evening air. At the door they were met by Sam's sister Pat, whom they once called "Big Butt Pat," but she'd not been called that in years. Pat had been smoking crack for three years straight and her emaciated body was pitiful. Her face was sunken in so much that her jaws were almost touching. The remaining teeth she had were yellow and green with rot and decay. They were concealed by dark purple lips so dry and chapped that whenever she spoke they bled from little splits.

"Y'all lookin' fo' Sam?" she asked coming out of the filthy screen door onto the porch.

"Yeah," answered Lapeace. "How you doin' Pat?"

"Bad," she answered quickly. "I'm tryin' to get some money to get my hair did." And when they looked at her hair they knew she was lying. For she had hair only on the top. The sides had long since broken off.

"Oh, yeah," said Sekou, looking at her head, "I can see you need it done. You also need your head replaced."

"Ah, fuck you bastard. Hold on, let me go get Sam, fo' I have to whup Sekou ass out here."

"Yeah, you go do that, 'cause you ain't whuppin' shit here."

"Whatever." And she disappeared into the house. When Sam came to the door he was shirtless. The first noticeable thing about Sam with his shirt off was the huge block EIGHT TRAY tattooed across his chest. It was shadowed in against his light complexion, evenly and dark green. He had on a pair of gray cutoff khakis, which hung off his ass revealing blue cotton boxers, white tube socks, and corduroy house shoes. His hair was covered by a Jheri curl bag, which almost concealed his boyish face. His eyes were bright and intelligent.

"What up, cuz?" Sam asked in a greeting tone.

"Ain't nothin', just bailin' through the hood, thought we'd come check you out," said Sekou.

"Eh, you wanna move wit us?"

"Where y'all goin'?"

"On the North, we'll bring you back," replied Lapeace.

"Yeah, I'll move wit y'all. Hold up, let me get my shirt on."

Lapeace and Sekou waited until Sam had come back with his shirt before the trio stepped off the porch and headed out to the truck. On the sidewalk they all paused as a brown Cutlass came to a menacing stop in front of them and the driver's-side window was lowered.

"Where y'all from?" asked the passenger across the driver's stare.

"Where *you* from?" asked Sekou, easing his hand toward his weapon. Feeling his adrenaline level rise immediately.

"Hoova Criminal," answered the passenger with a *now what?* type of tone.

"Fuck Hoova!" Sam shouted and was immediately answered with a burst of gunfire from within the car. The trio split. Sam rolled leftward and came up firing with a nine millimeter. Sekou dove behind his truck, came up on one knee, and started dumping into the body of the Cutlass. Lapeace followed Sekou behind the truck. Another short burst of what sounded like a Mini-14 was let off from the car before it sped off full of holes.

"Come on," shouted Sekou, running around to get in the truck without looking back, "let's get them niggas."

"Hold up," said Lapeace, seeing what Sekou hadn't. "Sam is hit. He's down."

"Damn!" Sam lay on his side, statuesque in his stillness, weapon still clutched in his hand—dead. Blood pooled around his body in an oval on the sidewalk and ran off into the grass thickly. His eyes were open still but the bright intelligence was gone. Lapeace was down on one knee staring at Sam's lifeless body when Sam's mother came running out.

"Oh, no," his mother said screaming and holding both sides of her face. "Not my baby! No, not my Samuel! Nooo . . ." She fell to her knees next to his lifeless body, pushing Lapeace roughly aside. She was busying herself with picking the debris from Sam's hair and brushing off the accumulated dust and dirt when Pat tried to loose the weapon from his clenched fist. And in the most chilling tone imaginable, Sam's mother looked up at Pat and said through clenched teeth, "You leave that goddamn gun in his hand. He will be buried with it." Pat eased away from mother and son, clearly knowing that the time to protest was not now. "And you two," she turned directing her glare at Sekou and Lapeace, "I think you've done enough. You may as well leave us alone! And unless you are going to get buried with that one, you'd best put it away."

Sekou put his weapon in his right pocket, wearing it like a cowboy. He looked over at Lapeace who had a menacing look on his face and thought a few years back and a dozen homies before, when he would have been all over the ground crying, pacing, and swearing. But he had seen too much death, caused too much death, and had known firsthand the acute pinch of suffering emotional trauma to take each death personal anymore. Lapeace knew what war was about. They stood their ground for a minute or two and listened to Sam's mother hum the melody to "Mama's Little Baby Loves Shortnin' Bread" and then they left.

"What you wanna do, Lapeace?" asked Sekou as they drove east on 79th toward Normandie Avenue.

"You know what I wanna do, Sekou," answered Lapeace, staring out of the window with a fixed scowl on his face, his brow furrowed tightly.

"Damn, the homies trippin' with this Hoova-Gangsta war. Man!" added Lapeace trying desperately to overstand how their toughest ally had become their latest nemesis. "I'm gonna tell you now, Sekou. I ain't bustin' on no Hoovas. Fuck that, we should leave that shit to the baby locs. Matter of fact, let's go over to the Bacc West and alert them lil niggas now. Damn, man, Sam was dumpin', too wasn't he?" asked Lapeace looking over at Sekou.

"Yeah, after fool 'nem dumped, Sam got off 'bout fo', five shots. That's fucked up."

"Yeah."

"I feel you on not wanting to bust on no Hoovas, but damn . . . them niggas killed Sam. Shit, they killed Baby Evil too. They shot—"

"Aight, aight Sekou, I hear you shit. I know what they've done. It ain't like the hood ain't dropped none of them."

"Yeah, but . . . I don't know man. It's just hard seeing the lil homies go through this shit—young, losing their clique members just like us in the early eighties."

"That wasn't us, our clique. We was too young then. Shit, that was Monster and Crazy De 'nem."

"Yeah, you right. I'm a tell you though, them Hoovas can't win against us. You know why? 'Cause they ain't no real combat hood. They ain't really killed no Nine-0s, One Elevens, or Bloccs. The Hoovas is too big, got too many chapters to win against us. Our hood been in mortal combat with the Sixties for what, seventeen years now? And as much as I hate them niggas, I gotta give 'em props for being killas."

Lapeace looked over curiously at Sekou because he'd not said one word as he was talking. Usually he'd butt in. "What's up, Sekou?"

"Eh, Peace," sounded Sekou staring straight ahead, "let's go kill some Hoovas."

"Man . . . ain't you heard nuttin' I said?" Lapeace said in exasperation.

"Yeah, I heard everything you said. But did you trip on Sam's moms? Huh?"

"Yeah, she was trippin'."

"She went crazy right there, Lapeace. Mrs. Jones ain't gonna never be right. She gon' be like Twinky moms—just gon'."

"Fuck it . . ."

"But you know what I'm sayin' homie?"

"I feel you, Sekou."

"But did you feel Sam's moms? Man, she was like out there. She was like 'My baby . . .'"

"Sekou—"

"'. . . noooo, not my Samuel . . .'" said Sekou, mimicking her voice.

"*Sekou* . . ." Lapeace tried to stop him.

". . . I mean, she was like . . ."

"Hey! Aight, man, aight. Let's go get some Hoovas, fuck!" Lapeace exclaimed and slapped the dashboard hard. The little Sony television came on and they looked at each other and laughed. It was a tension-breaking, long-overdue laugh. One that kept them from crying. They made one stop on the Bacc West, then began their foray into Hoova hood.

"You know how I wanna go out Lapeace?"

"Naw, how's that?" answered Lapeace through applications of saliva to the blunt paper now heavily packed with chronic.

"Aight, dig this . . . Damn, look at her ass, shit!" They sat idle at a red light on 79th and Vermont Avenue watching a stacked woman sway her lower half into a liquor store.

"Just drive. We on a mission 'member," Lapeace quipped.

"Okay, I ain't gonna live to be old, I know that. So when I get killed . . ."

"'Bury you smilin', wit g's in your pocket, have a party at your funeral, let every rapper rock it, let the . . .' some ol' Tupac shit, right?"

"Hell naw, this some real shit. Check it, hold up, is that them niggas there?" They both eyed the throng of youth intently.

"Naw them fools is kids. Keep drivin', I know where they be. Go on 81st."

"Okay, now listen. I wanna be cremated. Right? And then have my ashes stuffed into shotgun shells, and then I wanna be shot into some muthafucka's chest."

"You are just outta your damn mind, ain't you? You sick, Sekou."

"But tell the truth, don't that shit sound phat? Come on, give me my props. And you know, I don't care which enemy I end up in, just as long as niggas don't miss. Can you see to that, Lapeace?"

"I might go before you. Then what?" Lapeace was putting fire to the blunt.

"I'll shoot you into a muthafucka . . ."

"Naw, shit naw. Just bury me like everyone else. There they go! How many you count?" Lapeace choked off his cough and fanned away the smoke.

"One, two, three . . ."

"Just circle the block and park. We gonna lure they stupid asses." Once they circled the lively block, which was bustling with people traversing to and fro, they stopped the truck in the middle of the block on 82nd Street, walked as if they were going into an apartment complex, and scaled the rear fence. Sekou stayed put in the back of the long drive serving the olive green duplex apartments. Lapeace strolled out front onto 81st Street. Once out on the sidewalk, he waited until he'd found a Hoovalette passing and asked her if this was Hoova hood? She replied yeah that it was and then inquired as to his set affiliation. To which Lapeace replied none of her Snoover-ass business. She couldn't run away quick enough to tell her homies. Within a short breath, a clump of Hoovas began to walk briskly toward Lapeace, who feigned fright and began his descent into the driveway from which he'd come. As they picked up speed so too did Lapeace until his silhouette was one with the darkness at the end of the drive. He jumped up and onto the parking fence and then paused momentarily. Just long enough to lure them closer. And closer they came. Threats and all. "*Now!*" he shouted and Sekou stood up with his weapon steady, trained on the charging throng. A shift of light crossed the shaded passway through a naked window and highlighted a square of cinder block. As soon as the first pursuer entered the light, Sekou squeezed off two rounds. Both shots hit him center mass and propelled him into the others, who had no time to react. The nine's flash created a strobe-light show of surprise and pain. With each round, illuminated by the muzzle flash, the Hoovas were caught in different stages of decline. Once the strobe light stopped and the barking nine was quiet, Sekou joined Lapeace on the other side of the fence and they walked nonchalantly to the truck.

"Shiiiit," said Sekou proudly as they exited Hoova hood, "this gangsta fo' life!"

Lapeace added, "Not fo' protection!" They slapped a high five.

"'Nuttin' but a gangsta party. It ain't nuttin' but a muthafuckin gangsta party . . .'" Sekou sang. Lapeace sparked up the blunt as they traveled west on 83rd Street. At Normandie they turned right until they'd made their way to Ghost's house. As usual a pack of young homies was standing out in front. Some were slanging, others were drinking beer and talking loud, clowning. The vomit green dwelling was adjacent to an alley off Florence Avenue facing east. The porch was packed with males and females who propped themselves up on the stucco banner and listened to music through the opened door. In the darkness, cherries on the tips of blunts, joints, and cigarettes burned brightly, looking from a distance like infrared beams. Ghost had long since repaired his gray coupe and it sat on the street. Sekou brought the Explorer to a stop across from it. Lapeace retrieved the blunt from Sekou and he pushed in a fresh clip for the nine. "Aight, now, what we here to do?" asked Sekou, looking from the gathering to Lapeace, nine in his lap.

"Pull Ghost up 'bout showing that damn tape. See if he's got a copy and get to it."

"Okay, then. Let's do this and then get off the street. 'Cause shit might heat up." And with that they left the truck and stepped quickly across the street. Once in the yard the pack of youth shifted and gravitated toward Sekou and Lapeace. They explained about Sam Dog, but the lil homies had already heard and in fact had sent three cars into the Hoova's hood right before Lapeace and Sekou drove up.

"We surprised y'all didn't see 'em," said Shady Macc. And, of course, they hadn't. Lapeace asked where Ghost was and was told he was in the house. They pushed on through the crowd and went into the house. Ghost sat on a long playpen couch hugged up with his girl. When he saw Lapeace and Sekou, he broke into a wide smile, gapped teeth shining brightly through the dimness.

"What up, cuz?" greeted Ghost jovially.

"You," shot back Lapeace, crossing his arms over his chest.

"With your handsome ass," added Sekou. Easing down on the arm of the couch, offering the blunt to Ghost.

"There you go," answered Ghost in a self-deprecating tone.

"We need to holler at you, loc."

"Right." And Ghost disengaged himself from his woman's grip and motioned the homies to follow him. They walked down a short hallway and into the back room. Ghost closed the door behind them and sat on an old bed that sagged in the middle.

"Ghost, who-all you show that tape to?" Lapeace asked.

"Uh," Ghost began, brooding over the question as he inhaled the pot, "shit, 'bout five or six of the homies. But that was fo' you scooped it up."

"Did Lil Huck see it?" asked Sekou.

"Fuck naw! I wouldn't show that rat-ass nigga shit."

"Before I scooped it up, did you dub it?"

"No, homie," said Ghost as he handed the small blunt to Sekou, "I didn't."

"Cool."

"Well, you know, that fool Anyhow workin' with Bob Hope tryin' to get some other shit off him."

"Naw?"

"Yep, nigga straight snitchin'. But he ain't knowing nuttin' 'bout the tape is he?" asked Ghost.

"Naw, but Sam Dog, rest in peace, slipped and mentioned the tape to Lil Huck . . ."

"Which means before long, Bob Hope gonna know 'bout it and then gonna start tearin' up the hood."

"So we needed to know if you dubbed it or not."

"Naw, cuz, on the hood, I didn't," swore Ghost.

"Good, good. And eh, tell the homies you showed it to, to keep that shit on the D.L., aight?" Lapeace said looking Ghost straight in his dark eyes.

"I got 'cha cuz."

"Oh, and you might wanna clear the spot out 'cause we knocked on the Hoovas befo' we came here," added Sekou over his shoulder as the trio made their way up the dark hallway. In the front yard they clasped as many hands as possible in passing before reaching Sekou's truck.

"Where to?" asked Sekou starting up the truck and stashing the heat.

"Take me back to Shima's."

8

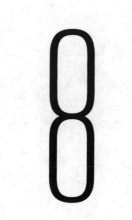

When Sekou's Explorer entered Shima's drive, she was already out on the porch. Her dark skin blended perfectly with the night. As did the black attire she wore. Black sweatpants made of thick terry cloth over which she had on a matching sweatshirt. Her braids were pulled back into a bun and fastened with a tie. Her tennies were black Nike Air. She was pacing to and fro along the length of the porch. Disappearing now and then behind one of the two wooden pillars that supported the structure. Her arms were folded snugly across her breasts. Lapeace had phoned from the vehicle to announce their arrival.

"Damn," said Sekou as he manipulated the stick into neutral, "like that?"

"Like what?"

"I mean, one call and you got baby on the porch waiting for you?"

"Well, you know," said Lapeace, exaggerating his body movements and blowing on his fingernails, "what can I say? I'm a boss playa."

"Killa. Now you best get your ass out there to her 'cause she stopped moving and is just standing there tapping her foot."

"Aight, love one, I'm out then. But watch yourself. Hit me off tomorrow, huh?"

"Yeah, I got 'cha."

"So, who you got on the fight tomorrow?"

"Um," Sekou said, as if really contemplating the opponents, "I might roll with Golden."

"Man, fuck you. Tyson's gonna smash old boy with the swiftness. But if you serious, we can put a slight wager on it? Say, this truck for my bike?"

"You wiggin'."

"Let me know it then."

"You know, we should bail out there to the fight. It's in Vegas, ain't it?"

"Yep, but I ain't trying to be around all that. I'll watch it on cable."

"Aight, then, Loco Love, I'm outta this area."

"I'll hit you tomorrow," Lapeace said and closed the Explorer's door. Sekou gave one sound of his horn and was gone. Lapeace stepped up onto the porch and into the awaiting embrace of Shima's warmth. In the house, seated comfortably on the sofa, Shima began to tell Lapeace of the connections she'd made regarding the counterpublicity sure to erupt around the Crenshaw shooting. Lapeace sat lazily and listened to the endless list of names associated with this organization and that, one newspaper and another. Shima carried on excitedly. Once she exhausted herself they moved to the kitchen where she began to dish out portions of the hearty meal she'd prepared. Stuffed bell peppers, angel hair pasta, hot-water cornbread, and for desert she'd made peach cobbler. Lapeace gathered the glasses for the beverages from the cupboard. The kitchen was a cozy affair. Replaced tile of chessboard black and white covered the floor. The wide Admiral refrigerator was packed thick with magnets of miniature replicas of appliances, fruit, and people, etc. Shima had been introduced to them by Sanai and became obsessed with them and their attainment. Above the table spun a Tiffany ceiling fan with four flowered light fixtures appended to its belly. The necessary amenities for contemporary kitchen use were strategically placed around the counters. These included a microwave, blender, food processor, and toaster. The window above the sink was covered by yellow curtains trimmed in white lace. The double sink was spotless, as was the rest of the kitchen. Lapeace retrieved the Sunny Delight from the fridge and poured their glasses full. Shima brought out the napkins and they sat down to eat. Moving with a start, Shima quickly excused herself and went to the service area. When she returned, Kody was in tow. She was so enormous, even at her young age, that she seemed to fill up the room.

"I'd almost forgotten about my baby," said Shima standing at the cupboard, looking for an appropriate bowl. Kody sat attentive on her haunches licking her chops.

"She sure bounced back from that Parvo, didn't she?" asked Lapeace, looking down at the big rottweiler's shiny black coat.

"Yeah, thank God. I didn't know what to do. They said it was like AIDS for dogs and that rottweilers were especially prone to getting it." She reached under the sink and to the left to retrieve a big bag of Milkchuck dog food, mixing this with a big bag of Kennel Train. She bounced about on her feet as Kody grew impatient and began to whimper.

"Yeah, that's heavy. Maybe we should let Kody meet Ramona. They'd probably get along, huh?"

"I'd hope so since we got it goin' on. So really they got no choice." Shima put the bowl down and Kody began immediately to chomp away. After washing her hands, Shima sat down to eat. "You know," she said in between forkfuls of bell peppers, "I got front-row seats to the Tyson fight. Do you wanna go?"

"You know, Sekou just asked me the same thing. Truthfully, it ain't my scene, but if you really want me to roll, I'll go with you."

"Well, I didn't pay for the tickets, they were sent by Simon as a gift. We try to stay in touch. So really it's not like I've made a specific engagement. I got cable, we can watch it right here."

"Yeah, that's cool," answered Lapeace, moving to clear the table. After the meal Lapeace washed the dishes while Shima dried. He swept the floor and Shima mopped it. Then they made their way to the living room where they selected a movie on video to watch. They watched *The Spook Who Sat by the Door*. Lapeace rolled the blunt and Shima retrieved and poured the Alizé.

Brims, dressed out in full gear, stood in the shadows of the massive concrete gym at Harvard Park. There were ten to twelve of them huddled closely together around an awkwardly built man who had, by his commanding voice, their full attention. Night had long since descended upon the City of Angels, which seemed, in this area, a signal for demons to surface. The tennis courts were deserted and their gates locked with muscular chains. So too was the rest of the modest little park that had always been the Brims' domain. The gym was a relatively new feature of the park, but it too was locked after nightfall. The Brims weren't concerned with locked gates or doors. Their job was to patrol the park, be visible—represent their reality. And that, of course, they did. Roving over the empty park until the wee hours of the morning like ghosts, as it were, through an abandoned cemetery, accosting trespassers and spooking nonbelievers. Harvard Park had a pool, the only pool in the area except for Jesse Owens. But that park was occupied by Crips. Great success in recruiting potentials happened as a direct consequence of the pools. For in the summer's sweltering heat, all the neighborhood children flocked to the pools. Then the Brims would put on gala festivals of pageantry—a miniature Nuremberg. Flags, loud music, posture, and poses. All to impress the youth into an alliance with them. Those standing now in the huddled conclave listened with rapt attention as the uncomfortably built man spoke with quick flicks of his tongue and sharp hand gestures.

"I was there in the room with him. I know who he is and I know what he said. Listen," said the man, pausing momentarily to scan the youthful faces looking upon him. "When one time came up in there, it was that fat bald-headed white boy who used to work around here. Swanson, Swade . . ."

"Sweeney," interjected one of the Bloods.

". . . Yeah, yeah, that's him," continued the man. "He was poking his finger into brotha man's bullet hole and stuff, telling him to talk about the shootin'. Man, listen, fool, the white boy. And he had a Mexican pig with him—went mad on brotha man torturing him. It was wild."

"But what happened, doe?" asked a Blood who'd grown tired of the generals and wanted the particulars.

"What happened? Man, brotha man told everything he knew and then some."

"Nigga you lyin'. Anyhow ain't no rat!" shouted the impatient Blood. The small gathering shifted wildly and unpredictably as mumbles were exchanged in the dark. The man in the center could see only silhouettes against the backdrop of a streetlight across the way. And even then hats, caps, and beanies disguised anything substantial. He grew frightened.

"I ain't lyin', man. And then, right after the police left, just like in *The Godfather,* brotha man cut his wrist!" The man was looking desperately from one unfriendly face to another in search of some solace, comprehension, and overstanding in the reality that he was but a conveyor of the news. He was old enough to know the ravishes caused by an informant. Now in his capacity as a bringer of what he believed to be good news, the Brims were turning hostile and getting agitated. Within the gathering of youth, with their strong sturdy-built bodies, he'd be hard-pressed trying to break through and, even if he did, he couldn't run as fast as them. Especially since he'd been mauled by the K-9 unit. And besides, he lived in their neighborhood.

"Hey, brothas, I ain't gonna come out here and lie to y'all. Come on, man. I'm only trying to help y'all out. This is crazy. Hey, hey, all right," said the man, trying a different approach. "I remember when this area was all Black Panthers. Man, it was a good time for black people. That nut J. Edgar Hoover had them feds runnin' all through here. Informants was everywhere, but we got 'em out and fast . . ."

"*Pow!*" The man saw only a quick movement and then felt the surging pain shoot up all over his face. "*Crack!*" And then he felt himself losing consciousness as his head and face were drenched with warm blood. Luckily for him he was unconscious when he hit the ground because there began the traditional L.A. stomp. His teeth were kicked out with chunks of gum still attached. His nose was kicked to one side and lay almost flat against his right cheek. After the Brims had satisfied their thirst for blood, leaving their victim in a fetal position mortally still with his head swollen beyond the size of a basketball, they lifted up and left the area walking east. At Normandie Avenue and 61st, they crossed to a brown stucco dwelling. In through the front and out the back where they each in turn rinsed off their steel-toed boots. Blood and small pieces of skin washed off into the thick crabgrass easily. One held the hose for another. Back inside the small house, which was a Blood commune paid for by collective proceeds from drug deals, they sat stoically around the huge oak dining table that monopolized the front room. Ben Dog went to the kitchen and brought back three forty-ounce bottles of Olde English. The 4-0 on the label was ripped off per gang rules—the Brims were mortal enemies with the Rollin' 40s.

"Blood," began Stack, leaning back in the chair on two legs, "I can't believe that shit about Any. Damn."

"Yeah," said Ben Dog after a thick guzzle of the charcoal-flavored liquor, "that's real. That nigga ain't no rat. Shit, as much shit as we done did with Blood, naw. I 'member when Kurt Dog and Big Bruno put boy on the hood. Blood ain't no rat, I'm tellin' you."

"How do we explain the extent of what dude knew about him?" asked Bingo, an OG Brim who'd recently been released from Pelican Bay State Prison after serving eight years for killing a Crip. He was, no doubt, the most educated of the bunch.

"Aw, Blood, that wasn't no extent. Anybody could have knew that. All you gotta do is call the hospital, they'll give up the drawings," said Crazy Be.

"Well," countered Bingo, in his slow, thoughtful manner, "in any event we'll need to follow this up. Me, personally, I feel that dude had some weight behind his words. And what's frightening is, if dude made it up, why? Or if he did just call up the hospital how could he have known about the one time's name and that he cut his wrist?"

"Yeah," chimed Blister, from a corner seat. "We didn't even know 'bout that. Plus, did y'all see blood's face and hands? Fool had dog bite marks all over his ass. So he could've been in the hospital with Any."

"Was old boy a smoker?" asked Bingo.

"Naw, he just came out of nowhere and started talking to me about the homie. He ain't no smoker that I know."

"Ben, call Any's house and ask his moms how he's doing."

"Bingo, now you know how that nigga mama is. Shit, I'd get a better talk outta Hillary Clinton 'bout Chelsea's big booty-ass than her. I ain't callin her. Besides, it's damn near tramp in the mo'nin'," Ben completed his thoughts and took a swig of the beer.

"We gotta get some hard copy info on blood's health, physical and otherwise. This ain't no way to be. Sittin' here in limbo and shit. And I'm a tell y'all niggas now, if any of dis shit real, 'bout Any and that fat cracka Sweeney, on da Blood Nation, they both gotta die."

"Be down den Blood-B-Dog fo' life! And when we get to hell, we gonna be straight. Why?"

"Because Satan is a Blood!" answered RedFace forcefully.

"Nigga, how can I tell?" asked Bingo.

"Because we pray to the big homie for strength and guidance."

"And?"

"And because we send him nasty souls to feed on daily."

"And?"

"And because as Bloods our flames burn bright in honor of our lord and redeemer, the ultimate flame, Lucifer—the red light bearer, king of the dark side."

"Well den, let us pray to our redeemer for our bloody souls," added Bingo.

The three empty beer bottles were placed on the floor and out came a black ruglike cloth over the wooden table. In its center was a circle with a pentagram in it. A fat red candle was placed in its center and lit. The Brims then donned black robes with hoods and held hands around the table. Bingo led the prayer.

"O baphomet, illuminated king of our lives, anointed bearer of our bloody existence, we offer to you our meager lives in hope of you finding a useful task for their existence. Our bodies, but first our hearts and minds, belong to you for purposes not yet known to us. Please, O baphomet, do with us what you will. All praise be to you O baphomet, we are your humble servants."

"*Damu!*" shouted Bingo.

"Insogani!" answered the collective.

"Damu!"

"Insogani!"

The following day Lil Huck sat comfortable in the big leather recliner chair fully extended in proverbial lazy boy fashion. In his lap was a big Tupperware bowl half emptied of salted and thickly buttered popcorn. He was watching *All My Children*. The den was empty except for him. His wife and her parents were at work. He'd had his own apartment for a couple of months but had no steady income other than his wife Stella's. Which wasn't enough to keep them housed. There was a flood of money at first coming from the crack he was selling. But when word got out that he was a possible snitch, his homies killed the supply. He resented them for this. However, he wasn't wise as to why they'd stemmed the flow. All he knew was that he was being shook. Whenever Mary was paged, so he could re-up, she'd never return his calls. When by chance he'd see her rolling, she'd say she was in traffic and keep going. No one else would give him work either. His closed future was the best-kept secret in the hood. Of course in his own mind his cooperation with the authorities was justified by his love for his family. He'd been shot in the hand by some of his own homies as they were summarily executing yet another homie accused of being a snitch. Irony is as irony does—it turned out that the executed one was acquitted posthumously of being an informant. Yet when Lil Huck went to the hospital for his hand injury and the authorities were called to report on the gunshot wound, and questioned him about the murder, he spilled his guts. People went to jail and then to prison for extraordinary lengths of time. And still others found themselves jailed in lieu of a confidential informant, inexorably heading to an upstate prison. His days were numbered and the designated hitters had long since been set upon him. They were, in fact, his closest companions—he played dominoes with death daily.

The telephone rang and broke his concentration on Palmer's scheming, yet even as he reached absentmindedly for the phone he kept his attention on the television.

"Hello?"

"Robert?" asked the caller who sounded familiar in a non-threatening way.

"Yeah, Sweeney?

"Uh-huh. What's up buddy?"

"Nothin', just watchin' my soaps. Eatin' some stale-ass popcorn."

"Hey, man," joked Sweeney, "those two in combination will make you senile. You'd better regulate your intake."

"Who you telling shit, if I could stop I would, but this shit is tha bomb."

"Yeah, the bomb, *kapoom*—your fucking heart!"

"Never that."

"Hey, listen, I called to see if you'd gathered any info on Lapeace. Shit, the guy seems to be squeaky clean, but his name is all over this damn Crenshaw shit."

"Uh-huh. Well, I did some snooping just like you asked me to. And you are right, he is squeaky clean. But you know what—and you ain't gonna believe this—there is a videotape of the whole thing!"

"You gotta be shitting me?" asked Sweeney excitedly, not believing his good fortune.

"Naw, people done already seen it. And you remember . . ."

"Hold on, you mean to tell me that Lapeace is showing people the tape?"

"Nooo," crooned Lil Huck. "Ghost was showing it to people right after it happened."

"Ghost?" Sweeney asked more to himself than to Lil Huck. "Ghost, Ghost, Ghost," Sweeney was saying to himself trying to remember the given name. "Kevin . . ."

"Madison," Lil Huck said finishing the name. "And you know what else?"

"What's that?" asked Sweeney, checking the tape on the recorder he always attached to the phone whenever speaking to Lil Huck.

"'Member when Samuel Jones . . ."

"Sam Dog."

". . . Right. Well, he got killed the other day and Lapeace and Sekou—Sekou Higgins was with him."

"No, I didn't know that."

"Yeah, now, what I believe is that they was comin' to kill Sam they self, but the Hoovas came up instead and did it for them. Not really *for* them, but you know?"

"Yeah, yeah. But why would they want Sam Dog dead?"

"'Cause Sam was going around runnin' his mouf 'bout the tape. Braggin' on the homies and shit."

"Uh-huh. Listen, Robert. Can you tell me more about that tape?"

"Naw, all I know is what I told you. A tape exist of the shooting that shows Lapeace clearly."

"And that Ghost—Kevin Madison—has it, right?"

"Last I heard, yeah."

"Hey, how can I help you? You've been a tremendous help to us."

"Well, you could do what you did for me that one time, 'member?"

"Yeah," said Sweeney and reached over to turn off the recorder. "Uh-huh, I know what you mean Robert."

"This time, since I helped you out so much, you could make the package bigger. Say, a whole kilo?"

"That's a bit much to be moving, but I'll tell you what. I'll give you half of that. You know I've got others to take care of, right?"

"Yeah, I know that. Awright man. When can you get it to me? I'm doin' hella bad. Muthafuckas over here ain't given up no work."

"Um, I can come to our designated spot at say four o'clock. How's that?"

"Today?"

"Yep. Unless tomorrow is better?"

"Naw, that's straight."

"Good, good. Okay, now go through this with me will ya?"

"Awright."

Sweeney leaned his hulking body over the desk and switched back on the recorder. He cleared his throat and said, "Robert, are you there?"

"Yeah, I'm here."

"I asked what it was I could do for you?"

"Just keep those streets clean as you been doing and I'll be fine."

"Okay, buddy, you've got it. Good-bye."

"Bye."

Sweeney hung up the phone and slapped the desktop loudly, causing several detectives to look up startled from their work. "There is a God," he said boisterously, "and he has a hard-on for cops!" He stood and pulled his pants up farther around his sagging belly, wiped his head clean of sweat, and went to the captain's office to relay the info he'd gotten from Lil Huck. The captain was a gruff man, with an agitated scowl permanently affixed to his face. He appeared always to be either in pain or in the declining stages of a migraine headache. These looks, however, betrayed his jovial personality. Yet he used his looks to ward off unnecessary conversations with those below him. He and Sweeney now sat listening to the tape of Lil Huck. Mendoza walked in during the last portion of it.

"Okay, here is how you proceed with this. Get warrants to

search the Madison residence, including the garage and his vehicle . . ."

"Excuse me, sir," interjected Sweeney respectfully. "Shakur lives in an apartment and, um, his vehicle was taken in a murder-robbery some weeks ago."

"Hmmm, I see. Well, the apartment will do. Perhaps we should attach some sort of surveillance to him?"

"No one claims to have seen him, sir. And from what the landlady of the apartment complex says, he's not been home for some time."

"Is he wise to our investigation?" asked the captain.

"It's possible, sir."

"Well, then use extreme caution. We'll use a surveillance unit to pick him up in hopes of our warrant causing him to try and move the tape. And we'll just use his activities with others to glean more of who's who."

"Okay then, I'll get these warrants signed and we'll move first thing in the morning."

"Fine, fine," said the captain, both hands on his small waistline. "Incidentally, this guy wouldn't be related to that gangster rapper boy Askari would he?"

"I don't think so, sir," answered Sweeney.

"Same tribe, probably, sir," added Mendoza with a humorless chuckle.

"Yeah, right," the captain said. He closed the door behind the exiting detectives.

When Sweeney returned to his desk his line was ringing. He answered it to find Nurse Richter sounding rather impatient and a bit peeved. She said someone had been calling asking about the health of Alvin Harper. First saying they were family, then calling again to say they were with law enforcement.

When neither yielded the information sought, due to a lack of proper identification, she'd hung up and called him. Harper, she'd also called to convey, suffered a massive stroke as a result of the amount of blood lost during his suicide attempt. He could no longer speak and was paralyzed on the whole of his right side. He was not in control of his bodily functions and would more than likely be a vegetable for the remainder of his life. Sweeney's luck had never been greater. He no longer needed Anyhow as a witness. His statement, perhaps a last dying testament, coupled with the tape would be more than enough to seal Lapeace's fate and close the books on the Crenshaw massacre case. He thanked Nurse Richter for her diligence and returned the phone to its cradle. Life was great.

9

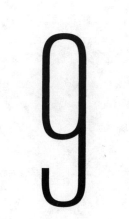

Sekou rolled out of his bed, as he did every morning, and did fifty ten-count burpies straight. Then he sat down in his favorite corner chair and prepared his morning blunt while watching the morning news. The usual shit was happening, some irate commuter was shooting folks on the freeways; the presidential mudslinging was getting dirtier. But the big news was the Tyson-Golden fight scheduled for tonight. He'd decided that he was going to drive over to Vegas and watch the fight. He'd probably swing by 662 and chill for a while, spend the night, and double back to L.A. Sunday afternoon. He needed to get the truck washed, waxed, and detailed too. He picked up the phone and dialed a number that was answered by a female.

"Can I speak to Maniac?"

"Hold on . . . Maniac? Here he is."

"Hello?" asked Maniac.

"What up, Ridah?"

"Oh, what's up Sekou. I thought you was Peanut. Been waiting for cuz to hit me back 'bout some work."

"Eh, you wanna bail up to Vegas with me to see the fight?"

"Cuz, my chips ain't right. Shit, I'm waiting on this nigga Peanut," Maniac said disappointedly.

"Don't sweat no chips, it's on me. You got someone to handle your biz?"

"Yeah, baby here. Shit, hell yeah homie, I'm with the bail."

"Aight then, check it. I'm gonna get the hoop detailed and then I'll come through, huh?"

"I'll be posted up waitin' loc."

"Aight den."

"Aight, cuz."

"I'm out." Sekou put the phone down and went to take a shower. Having completed his hygienic care he sparked up the blunt and chose his gear. The summer had not yet gone so it would be a hot day. Vegas would be even hotter. For his day wear, he slipped on a white cotton Stafford T-shirt and a pair of sea blue three-quarter-length menace shorts, white baby tube socks, and Grant Hill Filas. Watch, one pinky ring, three gold loop earrings, and a linx chain. Hit himself three times with the Obsession and chose his gear for the fight. Having completed this, he banked out to the truck. On Florence Avenue he flirted with a sista in a green coupe on Dayton's. Her man's car, no doubt. *She'd better return it or find herself walking,* he thought, *or worse.* He pulled to a stop on Manchester and McKinley in front of Big Jack's Detail Shop and blew his horn three times. Big Jack came lumbering out dressed in old blue khakis, a dingy light blue denim shirt, and worn combat boots. His mass was evident even under the loose shirt. Jack was an original East Side Crip and formerly Tookie's roommate. Now he owned his own detail shop and a few other things. Sekou and Lapeace had been knowing Big Jack for years and always came to see him and patronized his business. Jack instructed Sekou to bring the truck up into the lot where Squeeky, Jack's assistant, took control of the detailing. Jack and Sekou went into the shop's air-conditioned office.

In the briefing room for detectives, which had come to be known as the "war room," Sweeney stood behind a utilitarian wooden table, atop which were heavily armored flak jackets, helmets, P-24 batons, a battering rig, and a Plexiglas shield. On the chalkboard behind him were crudely drawn layouts of both Ghost's and Lapeace's residences. He'd briefed his men on the possible dangers of both raids and the significance of finding the tape. Out in front of him, situated in a cul-de-sac-like semicircle, were eight other homicide detectives listening closely to what he was saying.

"And so gentlemen, it will be in our interest," added Sweeney, head glistening with a high gloss, "to take into custody every VHS, BETA, and adaptable tape we find. I needn't continuously tell you the seriousness of these guys we are serving these warrants on."

"Are these actual arrest warrants or evidentiary warrants?" asked Detective Rupert.

"We are in search of evidence which could possibly nail these bastards to the wall. Again, a CI brought to my attention that there exists a videotape of the Cren mass. Madison has been showing the tape and Shakur is the shooter. And men, these are Eight Tray gangsters, I needn't tell you of their pedigree. Any questions?"

"Yeah, um, who should we anticipate encountering at these residences?" asked Rupert.

"At the Shakur residence, no one. Though our surveillance units have seen an elderly woman there as of late. She is believed to be an aunt, Shakur's guardian."

"And the other?"

"Well, we could encounter anyone from Mad Bone to Monster Kody there. It is a hanging spot for them. So use caution, please. Okay, with me to the Shakur residence is Mendoza, Rupert, Schnell, and Stuart. Baker, Lance, Lucero, and Decker will hit the Madison residence. We'll be on tac two gentlemen. Let's do it."

They each picked up their vest and baton, and Sweeney, as the lead of his team, grabbed one battering rig and a shield. Decker grabbed the other as lead of his. Then they filed out into the parking lot. The morning air was fresh and the sun was heating up the city.

"Hey," asked Lucero, the youngest detective of the nine, "are these guys out of jail? I mean, could we really encounter Monster Kody and Mad Bone?"

"Hell no," answered Lance. "Both of them are under someone's jail. I'm sure. Sweeney meant that as a watch-your-ass type of thing."

They mounted up and rolled out of the parking lot bumper to bumper, all unmarked cars. Sweeney relayed to dispatch for additional black-and-white coverage to meet them at the respective residences. Estimated time of arrival, ten minutes.

* * *

For some reason Lapeace felt the need to talk to Aunt Pearl. He'd not called his apartment in three weeks, and he thought that the phone might be tapped. So he had Shima retrieve his messages from a pay phone as she traversed from work nightly. He'd gotten his motorcycle out of the shop and had it stored in Shima's garage and handled some other business transactions through his accountant, but for the most part he stayed close to Shima's house. He'd even taken to having Sekou park his truck all the way in the back when he came over to avoid any possible surveillance with he, Sekou, and Shima. This morning, however, he wanted to hear his aunt's voice and tell her he loved her. He also wanted to see how Ramona had been holding up. He missed her too. He picked up the phone and dialed his number. The phone was answered on the third ring by his answering machine. The music of Randy Crawford singing "Rio de Janeiro Blues" played as Lapeace instructed the caller to leave a name and number. He sounded sort of foreign to himself. He was no longer the same man he was when he'd made that recording, but still he had no idea what he was becoming or who. He could, however, feel Shima working on him, healing him from some injured past of broken hearts and twisted dreams.

"Aunt Pearl, pick up the phone. It's me, Lapi."

Silence.

"Aunt Pearl, if you're there pick up."

Silence.

He knew that if she didn't pick up soon, the machine would cut him off and he'd have to call back. He hoped she wasn't in a drunken stupor this early.

"Aunt Pearl if—"

"Hello?"

"Aunt Pearl, it's me Lapi. How ya doing?"

"I'm fine, baby. How are you?" answered Aunt Pearl crisply.

"I'm good."

"That's great. It's about time you called. I was beginning to worry for you," said Aunt Pearl, her voice sharp and clear. No sign of an alcohol slur or drag.

"Well, I've been outta town a couple of days," Lapeace lied. "But I'm straight, though. I miss you Aunt Pearl. I hope to see you soon."

"When? Is everything all right with you? Why don't you come home Lapi?"

"I am soon. Just gotta tie up some loose ends. Hey, how is Ramona?"

"She os round here crazy as a bedbug in boiling water. She misses you Lapi—we both do. Now you make it here as soon as you can, you hear?" she demanded with a sternness Lapeace hadn't heard for years. A sternness that made him think of his youth.

"Yes ma'am. I just have to pull some things together."

"You said that. Now I'd wish you'd stop pussyfooting around and come on *home*." Ramona had begun to bark wildly, twisting and growling at the front door.

"It won't be—" his answer was cut short by Aunt Pearl, who'd begun to shout.

"Lapi," shouted Aunt Pearl, straining to be heard over Ramona's hysteria, "call me back after I've taken this dog out for a walk. I can't hear you over her barks."

"Okay, Aunt Pearl. I love you."

"Me too. Bye now, baby."

"Bye."

* * *

When Ghost reached for the phone, which seemed to be ringing in surround sound, he caught a glimpse of the digital clock displaying red numbers illuminated brightly against the darkness of the bedroom. Seven-forty-five, a.m. *Who's calling at this hour?* he wondered through a foggy consciousness reaching for the antagonizing phone. Next to him lay his lady friend Sandra in a deep sleep. Lank strands of her ultra-blue hair streaked her soft face. Both were in the nude. The sun had begun to intrude slightly through openings in the miniblinds on the window above the queen-size bed. It played pinpoint light bright upon spreads, waves, and ruffles.

"Hello," gruffled Ghost into the receiver. He'd propped himself up onto his right elbow. Instinctively his eyes scanned the night table for cigarettes. Finding them he reached out, but then stopped abruptly. He strained hard with his ear to hear into the phone. His senses were on alert. He'd gotten no reply to his answer and yet there was an eerie silence that belied a twist.

"Hello," he said once more and then the connection was broken. In one fluid motion he swung back the covers, hung up the phone, and opened the drawer on the nightstand and retrieved the nickel-plated ten mm Glock. He ran up the hallway naked toward the living room in semidarkness and stumbled forward over the sleeping bodies of Lil Opie and his girlfriend Kimba. Lil Opie, startled by the sudden abrasion and the swift movement, reached to his left and gabbed up his weapon, a Taurus PT nine mm. He sat up ready to shoot.

"Cuz, it's me Ghost."

"Damn, nigga," said Lil Opie straining for adjustment in the semidarkness. "What you doing?"

"I think one time fin' to hit us," exclaimed Ghost, leaning over the couch and peering through the blinds toward the street, his eyes taking in every car he could see, looking for unfamiliar models. Trees, bushes, and fences he stared at until he was certain there were no people behind them. "Get these niggas up and get 'em ready."

Ghost trotted back down the hall paying little attention to his own nakedness. Then in the room he began to rustle Sandra from her sleep. Meanwhile, Lil Opie awakened Kimba, who sat up rubbing her eyes clear of sleep, her firm young breasts exposed to the morning chill. She rubbed her eyes into focus and noticed Lil Opie with his gun in hand waking up the others. She scooped up her sweatshirt, stood, and wiggled into her Levi's and then took control of her own gun. Up now were Lil Stagalee, his companion Tray Girl, Baby Diamond and his girl Zion, Lil Hit Man and the home girl, Lil Sista Monster. Weapons were in the hands of all. And stern thoughts of combat and resistance were in their minds.

Ghost pulled on his khakis, sweatshirt, and Converse All Stars while Sandra busied herself with her gear. Other than quick trips to the bathroom, the house stayed eerily quiet. Everyone was posted at designated windows watching and waiting.

"Say y'all," asked Lil Stag around the room. "What we gon' do, just wait for Bob Hope to run up in here on us? Or are we gon' bail up out this bitch?"

"The call," answered Diamond, "is on Lil Ghost. It's cuz's house. So if he don't want us to hold it down, we bail. If he say post up, well, then we shoot it out with Bob Hope."

"To me, it don't matter," whispered Zion while peeking through the olive green drapes, her gun on her lap. "'Cause whichever way it falls we gon' still have to deal with Bob Hope one day."

"And that's on the gang," confirmed Lil Sista Monster.

These bangers had grown fed up with police tactics of intimidation, false arrests, no-knock raids, and summary executions that always seemed to accompany their public "protect and serve" image. They had made a pact to stand and fight when confronted without an escape route. It's not that they wanted to die—or necessarily wanted to kill. Most felt their meager existence was but a living death anyway. A sinister pre-hell sort of purgatory. And so to die on the trigger was just a consummation of a slow-motion death already lived. And while they were not trapped without a means to escape they were a determined young band of urban guerrillas.

"Los Angeles Police Department. We have a warrant—open up!"

The command was answered by silence as each officer looked tentatively at the other. They stood huddled at the door, adrenaline coursing heavily through their bodies, piquing excitement and fear.

"It's the police department, open up, we have a search warrant."

Still, despite the knocks and the assertive commands, there was only silence: the closed and locked door. A collective shift in stance was done: a steel-toed boot was put forcibly into the door, which shook only slightly. On the second attempt to jar the door a handheld battering rig was swung by Officer Stuart at the doorjamb, which gave way easily. The officers entered the dwelling as if sucked through a vacuum tube. Guns leveled and aimed in anticipation of an occupant. Through each room they burst only to find emptiness and silence.

"Clear," barked Mendoza with finality as he stood holstering his service weapon. The others, in turn, followed suit.

Mendoza radioed to Sweeney that they'd found an empty apartment at the Shakur residence only to be told that they too had found only an empty house on Halldale. They commenced to search both premises only to find a lot of nothing.

10

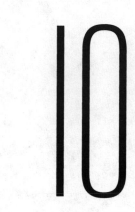

Ghost and the others had decided not to defend the spot. Nothing of significance had been left behind. A call was made to Sekou, explaining the situation. He felt there was going to be a raid and thus, moving on instincts, honed in the grimy streets where the slightest movements caused the greatest calamities, Sekou evacuated the homies and situated them in a safe house not far from his own residence. He in turn was able to watch the house in safety. And sure enough they came in force, but met no resistance, found no usable evidence. He knew it had to be in search of the tape of Lapeace and Anyhow on Crenshaw.

Sekou confirmed as much. He instructed Ghost to lay low and keep in touch. He in fact asked Ghost if he wanted to go to the Tyson fight in Vegas, but he declined. They exchanged regards and hung up. Sekou rang Lapeace at Tashima's.

"Hey Shima," spoke Sekou, "how're you this mornin'?"

"Fine, just fine. You know, trying to keep up with your boy as he bounces off the walls over here."

"Yeah, I can imagine. Let me holla at the ol' man, huh?"

"Yeah, sure, you take care, huh?" said Shima as she padded down the hall to where Lapeace was sitting reading through an issue of *Rap Pages* magazine in her room.

"Here you go, love. It's Sekou."

Lapeace was handed the cordless.

"What's crackin'?"

"Hey, homie. Look here, Bob Hope had a concert at See Throughs rest not long ago—this morning."

"Yeah?" queried Lapeace and tuned to the codes spoken.

"Yeah, I was thinking that there may be another concert not too far from there. And that maybe you should try to call Ticketmaster or any available ticket outlet to see if there are any more available."

"Hmmm. I think you're right. Well, I talked to A.P. not long ago and there was no noise. But hold on, I'll reconnect on the tray-way."

Lapeace dialed the number to Mrs. Delaney across the street from his complex and was told that, yes, a whole mess load of armored police were in, around, and all through his complex. But that Aunt Pearl was not there. He calmed her worries, bid her well, and broke the line.

"Well, there it is, huh?"

"Yep," Sekou quipped. "What's the game plan now, cuz?"

"Shit, I guess I'll be going up to that fight with you now."

"That's what I'm talking 'bout, homie! Get on then! The homie Maniac is movin' with us. So it's all good. What about Shima?"

"Naw, I don't want her up there in all that."

"Cool, I'm a go get dressed and I'll be movin' your way in a few. Should I pick Maniac up first?"

"No," cautioned Lapeace. "We'll have his girl drop him off at S-Macc from Trouble's pad and we'll scoop him there."

"Oh, aight then."

Aunt Pearl spied the comings and goings of the platoon of officers as they made sojourns through the complex and up and down the steps leading to Lapeace's apartment. She, along with Ramona, stood idle in the recess of a neighbor's yard watching with anxiety and a sense of foreboding as armload after armload of property was taken into custody.

So this was why, Aunt Pearl thought to herself, *Lapi hadn't been home. Well,* she reasoned, *my Lapi right, my Lapi wrong; right or wrong, my Lapi. And I'll be damned if I let them encase my man-child in tomb and kill him like they did his father.*

Aunt Pearl waited up the drive in stealth until all signs of the intruders were gone. She made her way, led by Ramona, along the street on the opposite side. Up the drive to the porch she went and calmly rang the bell. It was answered at once by Mrs. Delaney.

"Oh, Pearl," she stammered with a sense of peril, "I'm sorry to see things going as they are."

"I know, I know," soothed Aunt Pearl, pulling nervously on Ramona. She felt Mrs. Delaney's sincerity and knew she was genuinely concerned.

"Come on in here, Pearl. Bring Mrs. Ramona along as well. Lapeace called not long ago. Come, we'll talk over a cup of decaf."

Aunt Pearl led Ramona into the house and was directed to a love seat in the living room. Ramona, like Aunt Pearl, sat regally quiet as Mrs. Delaney made haste with the decaf.

Mrs. Delaney was an old trusted friend of the family and a community activist in her own right. She'd been responsible for the founding of the Black Scouts Youth Brigade, which cultivated survival skills and cultural awareness among neighborhood youth who would otherwise have been susceptible to criminal or gang activity. She was a stalwart standard-bearer who practiced public clandestiny, which was simply: what I do ain't no secret, it's just nobody's business but my own. She'd lived in the same community, in the same house for thirty-seven years.

"Thank you, Belva," Aunt Pearl said as she took the cup and saucer and blew lightly on the steaming coffee.

"Oh, don't mention it. Can I get you anything else while I'm up?"

"No, this'll be fine."

"Well," began Mrs. Delaney, sitting now across from Aunt Pearl and the ever vigilant Ramona, "he called this morning, early. Asked simply was there any abnormal activity on the block, or at his house particularly."

"Hmmm," sighed Aunt Pearl as she sipped and slurped the hot black coffee.

"I told him, yes, in fact there was. This was about seven or six-fifty or so."

"They'd been there since then?"

"Oh Pearl, you wouldn't believe just how close they'd come to pulling up before you and Ramona left."

"You saw us?" Aunt Pearl asked incredulously.

"Pearl, now you know I see everything. Well, no sooner had you turned the corner there on Harvard did they come crawling up in various cars, vans, and trucks and what have you. Lapeace called soon after, I told him what the weather was like and that you had not been caught in any storm."

"Well, thank goodness for that. I don't know what he'd have done without knowing what was going on."

"Ain't that the truth," commented Mrs. Delaney before taking a sip of her coffee. "Now Pearl, what is all this about . . . Why are the authorities on Lapeace?"

"I wish I knew. But I plan to find out and then fight like hell for his freedom."

"I know that's right. And you know you can count on me," add Mrs. Delaney firmly.

Detectives Sweeney and Mendoza sat with looks of dismay and trepidation on their faces. Captain Killingsworth was pacing menacingly to and fro behind his desk. Both raids had proven to be busts. Not so much as a bullet, let alone a VHS tape of the Crenshaw shoot-out was found. Mostly taken from the Shakur residence were tapes containing Pop Warner football games, a few photos said to be of gang members, Lapeace's computer, some articles of clothing, and seven books supposedly of a subversive nature. Less than that was taken from the Madison residence. The captain was fuming. Not only had there been no usable or damnable evidence seized but now the suspect would be wise to their investigation.

"What have you to say for yourselves, gentlemen?" Killingsworth stood, hands on either side of his narrow waist.

"Sir," began Sweeney, "my CI, as you heard on the tape,

led us in this direction. Which is not to say that just because we didn't find a tape today doesn't necessarily mean it doesn't exist."

"No, no, you're right. It's not that that has me pissed, but how were we eluded by both parties?"

"Well, captain," spoke Mendoza, "these bangers are wise to some of our tactics. Being that today is Wednesday, they could have very well felt that we were gong to hit 'em."

"Yes, well—" began Killingsworth but was cut off by Sweeney.

"Besides, we had no choice, really. We got the info and we moved on it accordingly."

"Yeah . . ." the captain spoke noncommittally.

"It's all we could have done, really."

"Well, you two get back out there and beat the bushes. I want something soon on this shit. We're losing the initiative here. We need something solid on this. The assistant chief is breathing down my neck. So bring me something."

"We'll do our best, sir," Sweeney said, lumbering to his feet.

"No," whispered the captain, turning his back away from the exiting two, "you'll do *better* than your best. You'll do your very best, now won't you?"

"Yes sir, we will," said Sweeney solemnly.

"Thank you."

Sweeney followed Mendoza to their work cubicle. His mind was racing a million times a minute. He needed to forge a solid lead to the tape. He needed to get that tape. Or, at worst, find someone who at least had seen the tape. The tape was the key to the case since no one was talking and Anyhow was now useless. He sat with a plump in his work chair and leaned back with his feet up on the desk. His brow was knitted into a thinking scowl.

Certainly, he reasoned, Robert hadn't sent him on a blind mission. No, that thought he dismissed almost immediately. For Robert had proven most reliable in the past. *Fuck!* He thought as he scooted his chair up to the desk and began shuffling through a stack of papers he'd compiled from the Cren mass, which had yet to be filed into the murder book. There had to be something here. The papers were filled with notes, inadvertent statements, names, phone numbers, and addresses of various people he and Mendoza had talked to over the past two months. Most names on the sheets were of gang members from a variety of sets. Who said bangers weren't informants? Most of what he knew on every gang killing or shooting was gotten from the combatants themselves. Mendoza had gone to get coffee and had now returned.

"Hey," Sweeney suggested. "Ever do a call back on this guy Bennie . . . last name Weems?"

"No," Mendoza answered, setting down the coffee, "but he's in L.A. County on a few burgs if you think he's worth the trip."

"We don't got squat else at this point. So what's say we make that trip?"

"Sure partner, why not," Mendoza answered while tugging on his mustache. He knew the phases they had to go through to piece together the puzzle of a murder investigation. All the little, seemingly stray and disconnected pieces came together to form a coherent whole—or rather a full picture leading first to the killer, then to a conviction. All leads had to be followed up on. And no lead was too small.

The Los Angeles County jail, or Men's Central jail, is a behemoth structure of windowless concrete that stands defiantly on the outskirts of downtown L.A. It's a lonely and sad-looking building that holds no paint. Its original gray concrete had recently been attached by an enclosed bridge to a nother-painted jail consisting of two towers. The Twin Towers jail is a modern septagon made detention center that stands seven stories above the ground. They are beige and light brown. L.A. County jail, including all its facilities, is notorious for having eighteen thousand prisoners housed at once, at any given time: vicious waves of racial violence sweep regularly over the captive population as the New Afrikans frequently do battle with the Mexicans, each cutting, stabbing, and beating the other into submission until the next clash where the loser avenges his humiliation.

Sweeney and Mendoza turned onto Bauchet Street, which housed both the Men's Central jail and the Twin Towers. They motored their Crown Victoria up the street to the back of the jail where they showed their law enforcement credentials to a service technician who guarded the gate leading to the PERSONNEL ONLY parking lot. They traveled up two stories and brought the Crown Vic to a crawling stop. At the front bar entrance to the main corridor they again had to show their credentials to a deputy behind a one-way mirrored booth. They explained who they'd come to see; the sheriff's deputy sent for the prisoner to be brought down to a designated interview room.

The prisoner, Bennie Weems, also known as Freedom, was a supposedly stand-up guy who had owned a few businesses out in L.A. before succumbing to his cocaine addiction, which evaporated the whole of his business adventures and got him caught up in a series of commercial burglaries that ultimately landed him in the L.A. County jail facing a fifteen-year term. He'd already escaped once, running from an ass whipping he was sure to get in wayside from a group of prisoners who'd caught him breaking into lockers. His family persuaded him to turn himself in and now he was kept in the 1750, Men's Central jail, Module of High Power. He paraded himself as his own attorney but was in fact an undercover informant. He'd given reliable information on several occasions and had always held out on the juiciest tidbits of information, culled from conversations with real high-powered criminals, in hopes of getting some of the strain off himself.

"Weems," spoke a deputy's metallic voice over the intercom speaker, "you have an attorney visit." This prompted Bennie to get dressed into his high-power orange jumpsuit and splash some water onto his grizzled face. He dried off his mug and pulled his dreadlocks into an offending bun. Deputy Fernandez came onto the tier with a set of waist chains and proceeded to bind and cuff Bennie until he was secure. Fernandez signaled to the control booth to open the designated cell and the prisoner came out onto the narrow tier and ambled up toward the exit, giving and receiving greetings from most as he passed.

Once he and deputy Fernandez were out of earshot of the other prisoners he was told that he didn't really have an attorney visit, but a pass to 6000 control. This, Bennie knew, was more than likely a visit from some law enforcement agency seeking information. And he'd picked up a few good things off the tier. He was more than willing to bargain the info for his freedom. Walking slightly in front of his escort, Bennie ambulated his six-foot-five frame along the corridor until he'd reached the solid door he knew all too well. There he was led into the room, greeted by Mendoza and Sweeney, and chained to the chair.

"Hey, Bennie," Sweeney greeted, with his stubby hand extended and a fake, shallow smile, "how's it going?"

"Things aight," Bennie countered.

"You remember my partner, Mendoza, huh?"

"Yeah, sure I remember him." Bennie struggled to find a comfortable footing in the little chair and in the conversation, where in negotiations for his info he often felt like he was in a poker game with professionals.

Sweeney and Mendoza laid out their leather-bound notepads and scooted their chairs up to the table.

"Well, we are here in hopes of you being able to help us on a serious matter we are investigating," spoke Sweeney while scribbling Freedom's name atop the notepad.

"Well, you know my stilo. I help you, you help me. I am soon coming up on my sentencing date and, well, you know . . ."

"Yeah, we know," Mendoza said sarcastically. "You want us to bargain . . . or should I say haggle, with you, huh?"

"I mean—"

"No, we know what you mean," interrupted Sweeney in defense of Bennie's fragile pride. "We'll keep all options open as we go through the motions of what's useful and what's not. Is that all right with you?"

"Absolutely," Bennie confirmed.

"Good then, let's see what we got. Um, do you know anything about that big shoot-out a couple of months ago on Crenshaw where a whole lot of innocent bystanders were killed?"

Bennie frowned and looked toward the floor. "Yeah, I have a few lines on that. A friend of mine was killed at the gas station. She was burned to death."

"Really?" questioned Mendoza. "What was her name?"

"Kimberly Byrd."

Mendoza immediately flipped through his notepad to the list of victims and deceased. He thumbed his way down the list and stopped at number five. He shot a furtive look toward Sweeney and said, "Yeah, she's here."

"How were you acquainted with her, Bennie?" Sweeney ventured.

"She used to boost clothes for me. We had a cipher of boosters and she was a pro. I'd known her a few years."

"Intimate?" asked Sweeney.

"Naw, just business."

"Okay," soothed Sweeney, while he and Mendoza both wrote down their thoughts. "What have you got?"

At that moment Sekou, Lapeace, and Maniac were crossing the state line into Nevada at Whiskey Pete's. Lapeace was sitting low in the passenger seat reclined to a ninety-degree angle. He was thinking about his life. Wide-open spaces made that possible a lot. He'd often go out to Santa Monica Beach alone and either walk or sit on the sand and think. He'd look out over the Pacific, into that vast sea of water, and let his thoughts go. Some of his best ideas on stocks, interior design, lifestyle, and friendship were initiated or developed in wide-open spaces.

Now as Sekou's SUV floated over the state line and the sound system banged out "Shorty Wanna Be a Thug" by 2Pac, Lapeace peered out over the vast expanse of sand and desert and contemplated his future. It had been difficult as of late to smile. His usually jovial persona had grown pensive with the weight of the coming doom. The pad had been raided. Obviously the word was out that a tape existed. *Shit,* he thought, *gotta put a lid on this before it spills all the way out.* He reached for Sekou's mobile phone, signaled for him to turn down the music, and dialed his attorney, Safi. He'd have to tell him about the raid. Plus, he'd need to know what kind of warrant had been served. He was concerned in the extreme about his status. Was he at that moment a fugitive or not? Crossing the state line could, if he were, be cause to insert the FBI into the situation for interstate flight to avoid prosecution. Lapeace was put straight through to Safi by Erma.

"Assalaam Alaikum, Lapeace," spoke Safi over the phone.

"Walakum assalaam, Safi. Listen, I won't say too much over this horn, but your client's residence was raided this morning and he needs to know the status."

"Hmmm," pondered Safi, "I see. And my client, is he in Allah's hands?"

"Firmly."

"Good. Keep him thus until which time the matter can be investigated. Is that clear?"

"No doubt."

"Good, may peace be upon you, brother."

"And you too. Later."

Lapeace cradled the mobile and stared out the SUV's tinted windows across the desert.

"Lapeace, man, I didn't know you was Muslim . . ."

"I ain't," answered Lapeace. "I'm a gangsta."

"Well," began Maniac, putting down his Sega control that he'd been playing from the backseat, "why you say them words that they say?"

"That's just a greeting. It means *peace be with you.*"

"Yeah? So, you ain't gotta be no Muslim to say it?"

"Naw, not really. My attorney is a Muslim cat. So when he greets me in peace I greet him back the same. It's like a custom, dig?"

"Yeah," piped in Sekou while maneuvering the Explorer around a slow-moving Camry. "Like when we say 'Gangsta's Movin'—that's a custom, right Lapeace?"

"Not exactly. See 'Gangsta's Movin' is our slogan. It's our way of promotin' our set. A custom would be like as Crips, we say 'cuz,' see?" instructed Lapeace, ever the alpha.

"Yeah, yeah," agreed Sekou, "that's it. You're right, Lapeace."

Maniac sat back in thought and contemplated the exchange. It wasn't every day that he was exposed to conversations like this. He always enjoyed being around both Sekou and Lapeace. And they'd always been generous to him. He sat now with two thousand dollars in his pocket. One from Sekou and another from Lapeace. And he wasn't expected to pay it back unless, of course, he won big at gambling. Then out of gratitude and respect he'd be obligated to return the money. He wouldn't have made two thousand dollars sitting at home selling dope, for sure. He'd perhaps have made $800 and that's only if the spot was poppin'. He'd have taken $500 of that and reupped with a zone, putting the $300 away as profit and coupling it with the first $300 to get two zones and thus working toward a seven-hundred-dollar profit to be reinvested and flipped. All this against the backdrop of constant drama and danger. And still he had to pay bills, eat, dress, and rep the turf. Notwithstanding having to dodge one time, jackers, and a legion of haters.

So this brief reprieve of a Vegas trip, to watch the Tyson fight, no less, was certainly a welcomed opportunity. Maniac was a young homie who had lived in the hood since elementary school. He'd come up through the rigorous ranks of the set with guns blazing. Ever the trooper, he'd come into the favor of the upper echelons of his set by a daring daylight duel with a rival opponent that left the enemy assailant down and out—weapon in hand. Those who witnessed the exchange said Maniac had terminated his nemesis with extreme prejudice without so much as a blink of his eye. He was, without question, a bona fide gunfighter.

Standing a solid five feet, eleven inches, Maniac was menacingly muscular. He'd done his obligatory stint in youth authority where he weight-trained like a mad Russian. His complexion was light brown, as were his eyes. His hair was long and cornrolled. He was a skilled fighter and would regularly demonstrate his ability when it was determined that someone needed to be disciplined. Both Lapeace and Sekou thought highly of him. They moved along the interstate at a steady clip. Soon to be in Sin City.

II

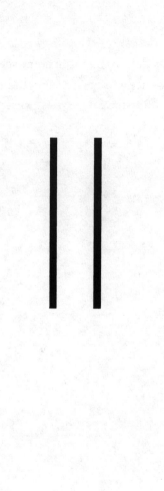

Tashima hung up the phone and pushed back in her recliner satisfied with her latest acquisition. Her A & R had brought her a demo disc of a new hip-hop group known as Fear None. West Coast battle rappers with a gangsta edge. She'd listened with trained ears to four songs on the CD. The lyrics were good, metaphorically insightful, and their production wasn't that bad. It was not up to Dr. Dre standards, of course, but it wasn't that bad. By signing Fear None to RapLife Music, they'd be in a financial position to work with a broader array of producers. So on that point their songs could only sound better.

Fear None was the fourth group she'd signed since June. Her roster held five active, on-the-radio groups. She had a steady presence on Billboard's top ten in hip-hop. Three of the five acts had gone platinum plus and the other two were beyond certified gold. They'd broken the East, South, and the Midwest markets with stunning success. She had been named as one of the ten CEO's to watch in the next five years by *Entertainment Weekly* magazine. Tashima was a keen and competitive businesswoman. She was bold and always outspoken.

The two weeks that had passed since Sanai's funeral and Lapeace's revelation of his involvement in the Crenshaw shooting had definitely taken their toll. She felt drained and strained against the weight. She reclined to the max of the chair's ability and massaged her temples. *Ignorance,* she thought for the briefest moment, *is indeed bliss.* Had she not been told about Lapeace's predicament she would be better off, she reasoned. But then, she knew, had she not been told and found out by another source she'd have blown a gasket and never trusted Lapeace again. And even now, now that she'd fallen in love with this man, what was she doing? Although she'd *always* been attracted to the roughneck thuglike man, she wasn't attracted to the criminal type. But was Lapeace actually a criminal? He'd explained his position in life: in his neighborhood he'd once been an active banger but had grown up and mostly—for the most part—out of that.

He didn't hang out, sell, or use drugs. Never even had a nickname. He was a doting father, a once-married *young* black man. But still and against all that he was responsible for the deaths of at least eight people. And soon the whole country will know this. *Dang,* she mused, *I'm stuck between love and a murder charge.* But I'd rather go blind than to see him walk away from me.

Tashima was interrupted in thought by a soft knock on the half-closed office door. It was Cora Roach, Tashima's personal secretary. A capable woman and all around troubleshooter,

Cor had been hired by Tashima immediately after they'd met at a Soul Train Music Awards after party where Tashima had gotten into a row with a particularly obnoxious employee of Violator Management who had insisted that RapLife owed Violator some credit for the success of Makanation, which had won three Soul Train Music Awards that evening.

Cora Roach had stepped in and shouted down the Violator employee and all but killed him with natural thugee. It was a sight to behold. And unlike Shima, who knew next to nothing about Cora Roach, the recipient of her rage was well versed in her aggression and backed off immediately. He skulked away with his head hung low. From that day forward, Cora Roach had been Tashima's personal secretary and bulldog.

"Yeah, Cora, come on in."

"Oh, sorry if I interrupted you napping, girl."

"Naw," Shima said swiveling around in the chair and leaning up into a regular sitting position. "I was just brainstorming. What's up?"

"I have these category A and B forms that need your signature and a sample clearance signature on some loops that Makanation is using. You aight?"

"Yeah . . . well, um, look Cora, let me ask you a few questions."

"Sure, Shima, shoot," Cora invited in her sisterly, soothing way.

"You ever been in love?" asked Shima, staring Cora straight into the eyes.

"Love? Well, I thought I was once. You know, I felt all mushy and warm toward him. I tingled at his touch and lusted after his scent. I thought always of him in some abstract kind of fairytale way. Yeah, I think it was love. But I came home early one day, girl, and found this nigga in a pair of my panties posing in the mirror."

"Oh, shit!" Shima said, holding her manicured hand over her mouth to surpress a laugh.

"Oh shit is right! And it wasn't even the fact about my underwear—goodness knows he looked better in them than I ever could—but he was sneaking doing it. This brought down all kinds of thoughts, doubts, and questions. I just thought I knew him! You know? I felt betrayed since I thought we were a true team. Me and him against the world. But after I learned about his little fetish I felt it was him against me and the world, you know?"

"Yeah . . ." Shima said absently, having drifted off to another train of thought.

"You ain't even listening to me, Shima," Cora pointed out with an edge of pain in her voice.

"No, no I am listening, Cora. It's just that the discloser of secrets or being honest is *not* one of the problems I'm facing. Actually it's the opposite. Nothing as freaky as cross-dressing, mind you. But still scary. I know I love this man and I am a committed person. But damn, we are headed for some rough waters. And, well, I'm just not used to being in such choppy waters. I mean, this music business ain't no walk in the park . . ."

"Who you telling?" Cora interjected.

". . . but still it's not life or death, freedom or jail."

"Hold up, girl. What are you talkin' 'bout? You in some kind of trouble? 'Cause if so, I know some headbangers who are with whatever in a major way . . ." Cora was now standing with her hands on Shima's glass desktop. She was leaning over into Shima's face.

"No, I don't need no headbangers, Cora. Lawd knows I have

enough of them around me now. No, it's just I've been seeing this guy . . ."

"Black?" questioned Cora.

"No, fool, *green*. Come on now."

"Just checking."

"And, well, I'm in love with this man. He's who I've been looking for. A perfect fit. But he's coming with some baggage. Not really issues but baggage. You know what I means?"

"What's the difference between issues and baggage? Shoot, I thought they were one in the same."

"Nope," quipped Shima, leaning back into her recliner. "Issues are like long-term, almost psychological defects, which cause a relationship to be always strained."

"Like what?"

"Well, um, like for instance if he has an underlying hate for women, like if he resents his mother. Or was always beat up by his older sister or . . ."

"If he wants to wear my drawers?"

"Well, um, yes I guess that's an issue."

"And baggage?"

"Baggage," began Shima, "is some burden that's carried around like a suitcase or something. It's not as deep as an issue, to me. It's some circumstance imposed from without, I mean onto an individual. An issue is *inside* an individual and becomes a part of their character, I think."

"Go on," encouraged Cora, "you're making sense."

"To me, my man hasn't got issues. He's as mentally healthy as any black male could be growing up in the inner cities of Amerika. I mean this with all that this entails. So it's not issues. My man is saddled with a situation I describe as baggage."

"How so? And do you mind if I sit down?"

"No, of course not girl. Sit down."

Shima told Cora the whole situation. After swearing her to silence, Cora listened intently, showing her friend concern, feeling the hurt in her voice, hearing the stress caused by even having to convey the circumstances surrounding Lapeace. Shima left nothing out—she needed to exorcise her thoughts; these new demons had begun to tear her soul asunder. She was grateful for an unbiased ear and a comforting shoulder.

"So what do you think?" questioned Shima in an exhausted manner.

"I'll tell you this much: it makes my panty issue seem like nothing!" Cora spoke in a joking manner, which made Shima chuckle a little before admonishing her to "Be serious, girl."

"I mean . . . it wasn't his fault, really. The other guy was trying to kill him. What was he to do? Is he wrong for being alive? For defending himself? I don't think so," Cora added quickly, answering her own questions.

"I feel the same and just needed to sound this off of somebody. I appreciate you, Cora. Thanks."

"Don't mention it. Though you could show it, say, with a few zeroes on my paycheck."

"Yeah, right. Girl, give me those papers to sign and get on out of my face with that foolishness," chided Shima in banter with Cora.

"Oh, aight then," Cora said and left the room.

12

Bingo sat alone in the spot cleaning an arsenal of handguns. He'd field-stripped each and laid them out on a dark green oilcloth. He was meticulous in his application of gun oil as he handled every weapon with genuine care. In the background, *Parliament's Greatest Hits* beat at a respectable level. And the cleaning, reassembly, locking, and loading went on until every weapon, twelve in total, was ready to go. This was Bingo's therapy. It was while he field-stripped and cleaned his weapons that he felt most relaxed and did his best thinking.

The hood was hot. On fire. Every few minutes patrol cars could be seen crawling at a snail's pace through the residential area of the Brims. Bingo had warned his homies to lay low. Stay clear of the LAPD's dragnet. Though he knew all too well that he was spitting in the wind. For all too often bangers who were not bound by any organized contractual agreement to a designated leader would do as they very well pleased. This was both a burden and a relief. The burden, of course, allowed for deep penetration of sets by law enforcement who'd often catch numerous members in various acts of lawbreaking and turn them during interviews where the average banger was ill-equipped mentally to handle the barrage of questions and interrogation. This brought raids, arrests, convictions, and, inevitably, prison sentences.

The relief, conversely, was that because there was no organized central structure of L.A. street gangs none could be theoretically saddled with R.I.C.O. (Racketeer Influenced and Corrupt Organization) status under federal crime laws.

The contradiction served its purpose in an ironic way. Bingo hated the ignorance but enjoyed the freedom it brought with it. After having served eight straight years on an eleven-year manslaughter conviction in which he shot a rampaging Crip inside the Slauson swap meet, Bingo came home to a set in shambles. The Brims were the premier black street gang in Los Angeles after the demise of the Black Panther Party. It was the emergence of the Black Panther Party in L.A. that had superceded the older black street gangs. These gangs, like the Slausons, Gladiators, Businessmen, and the Farmers, had come together, in 1965, under the color of a truce, to do battle with the LAPD and National Guard during the Watts riot.

By 1968, when the Black Panther Party came to L.A., the older gangs were incorporated into either the party or their rival, the United Slaves. The Brims came out of the smoldering wreckage of the Panthers and United Slaves. Wayward youth without leadership pounded the pavement in frustration and confusion. In L.A. these young folks wore stingy brim hats and thus became known as the Brims. The Brims evolved into Bloods, the Bloods became enemies of the new street gang, the Crips, and voilà—decades of mortal combat.

Bingo locked and loaded the last burner and began to move them all to a steel footlocker he kept secured by a heavy-duty padlock. No one had the key but him and Bruno, another trusted member and longtime friend. Two burners, both SIG-Sauer P228 nine millimeters, he left out before locking the chest. He dragged the footlocker to the back bedroom and put it into the closet. He showered and chose his gear: brown Armani pinstripe suit, white silk shirt, brown Bostonian shoes, and of course a brown stingy brim. He hustled along as he knew his ride would be there shortly. No sooner had he collected his watch and hit himself with a cloud of Aramis cologne did a horn sound and draw his attention toward the front of the house.

Bingo drew back the heavy curtains and spied the stretch limo idling in front of the spot. Made one full swoop of the house, making sure the windows and back door were locked before scooping up the two-inch-thick stack of hundred-dollar bills from the coffee table. He made his way out to the waiting limo and was let in by the Amerikan chauffeur. Inside he was greeted by his fellow Bloods, Blister and Blain. They, too, were dressed to the nines in brown suits. Bingo exchanged greetings and daps with his people and the limo pulled off from the curb and floated into the stream of traffic.

"B, did you bring my hammer?" Blain asked as he made a drink for himself. Blister busied himself with the remote for the CD player.

"Yeah, here you go, dawg." Bingo came out with one of the SIGs and handed it to Blain. "I just cleaned it and everything so you good to go."

"Asante," said Blain, using the equivalence of "thank you" in Ki-Swahili. Like Bingo, Blain was a veteran of California prisons.

"Sikitu," Bingo acknowledged as Blain pulled back the slide and popped out the clip. He checked the breach, pushed back in the clip, and put the burner on safety. He laid it on the black-carpeted floor.

"What about Blood?" Blain was indicating Blister, who was still preoccupied with the remote. "He gifted too?"

"Naw, just you and me, homie."

"Aight then." Blain finally took the remote from Blister and programmed the CD player. Blister noticed the SIG on the floor through the ceiling mirror as he sat back into the comfortable leather seat.

"Oh, you heated, huh, Blain?" Blister asked genuinely curious.

"Hell yeah. Ain't no telling who gon' be up in Vegas at the fight. Shit, I'd rather be judged by twelve than carried by six. You feel me?"

"Hell yeah. And I appreciate y'all allowing me to bail too."

"Ain't no thang, Blood. I love your life, homie."

"Yeah," smiled Blister in appreciation of the adoration. "Homie, I'm feeling you."

Blain looked over at Bingo, who was otherwise occupied by his own thoughts while gazing out of the window. His train of thought was broken by the thump of music flooding the limo. They rode in silence while Sly and the Family Stone sung "It's a Family Affair."

Both kids are/ good to Mom. Blood's/ Thicker than the mud,/it's a family affair. It's a family affair.

The big, ten-passenger limo floated along the 60 freeway east on its way to Vegas. Its occupants busied themselves with the art of splitting, breaking down, and folding up blunts. They drank and smoked and drank and smoked all along the four-hour ride to Sin City. Everybody had money on Iron Mike.

When Sekou brought his shiny black Ford Explorer to a stop on the strip where it was crossed by Tropicana, he felt exhausted. He was a bit overwhelmed by the amount of people packed on both sides of the street and cars were bumper to bumper along the fabulously lit strip. Lapeace shook himself out of his slumber and pulled his reclined seat to an upright position. He rolled his tongue inside and around his mouth and pulled down the overhead visor to scope his face. Maniac was still laid out along the backseat asleep. Closing the visor, Lapeace looked over at Sekou and, seeing his gaze, followed his vision out into the throng of people traversing the strip.

"Gang of folks, huh, homie?" Lapeace said as Sekou blinked and pulled out into the intersection and across Tropicana. The Explorer was crawling at a snail's pace, bumper to bumper.

"Man," exclaimed Sekou with a huff of frustration, "too many mothafuckas if you ask me. Shit, I wasn't even trippin' about it being this many folks. We should have drove up yesterday."

"Yeah, I hear you."

"Or flew up to this bitch. Man, I hate all this. Lapeace, get Maniac ass up. Let him suffer with us."

Lapeace reached back and roused Maniac out of his slumber. He stretched and yawned his way to a sitting position.

"Cuz, is we up in this bitch or what?"

"Damn nigga, can't you tell?" quizzed Sekou with irritation.

"Yac, you ain't never been here?" Lapeace asked turning almost around in his seat.

"Nope. Was gonna move out here with Big C Wack a few months ago but I got a violation and was on lock. I heard we got some troops out here, though."

"Yep," Sekou confirmed while maneuvering the SUV into the valet parking drive of the Luxor Hotel. "We got homies out here, but unless we see 'em at the fight we probably won't see 'em at all."

"How come, loc?" asked Maniac, holding on to the back of Sekou's and Lapeace's seats, looking from one to the other like a child.

"'Cause, nigga, we ain't up here to get caught up. Them the homies, but it ain't gangsta to drop in on cats unannounced. We'll bounce back this way in due time. We up here to see Tyson smash this nigga Golden, gamble a little, and let Lapeace get some space. So it's like more business then pleasure."

"Cool, I'm just glad to be up out the hood for a minute. So, whatever."

"That's right."

They coasted to a stop and were approached by valets and hotel bellhops. Before getting out Sekou popped the back latch and it slowly raised. The three lumbered out of the truck and into the sweltering Las Vegas heat. Sekou retrieved his suitcase and let the bellhop roll it along as they entered the luxuriously air-conditioned lobby of the Luxor Hotel. Luckily the three had dressed down for the occasion because the lobby appeared to be peopled by nothing but youth in hip-hop gear, gold chains, medallions, and hundred-dollar tennis shoes. They were boppin' around in a school of giggles and horseplaying. Some sat on love seats and grand couches that made up the decorative layout of the gold and glass lobby. As the three swept the crowd visually, none appeared to be bangers so they kept their pace toward the front desk.

Sekou gave his name to the receptionist. She checked in the computer for the reservation and checked it against his identification.

"Your room key, sir," said the Amerikan woman with a bright smile, "please have a nice stay at the Luxor."

"We will, thank you," Sekou responded and was directed by the bellhop to a bank of elevators. They were lodged in suite 2027. The suite was a large two-bedroom affair. One entire wall, facing out, was a tinted window that afforded them a vast view of the strip facing east. After setting in and blowing two blunts, they ventured out to find a department store where Lapeace and Maniac could find them some fresh gear to wear. Sekou alone had brought a bag with a fresh change of clothes. He was meticulously fashion-conscious. Which is not to say that Lapeace wasn't, but Sekou tended to be a bit more concerned than most.

The fight between Mike Tyson and Golden was a big-ticket showdown that drew thousands to the gleaming desert that never slept. Unbeknownst to any, there would be over thirty street gangs from Los Angeles represented by numerous members, some numbering as many as twenty-seven soldiers, others no more than four. It would be an adrenaline-packed powder keg of danger. Most combatants drove to the sports event and brought their weapons. And there'd be no shortage of them.

John Sweeney pulled into his driveway and turned off the engine on his white 1993 Ford Bronco. It was called an "O.J.

Special" by his fellow officers. No matter that it was the same year and same color as the one owned and driven by O. J. Simpson during his low-speed chase along L.A. freeways last year. No matter; it served him well and he was content with it.

He climbed down out of the cab and pulled his tote bag along the front seat. Inside his house he checked his mail—junk and bills. He showered quickly and laid out naked across his bed. He stared up into the ceiling and thought for the millionth time how he could get the goods on Lapeace Shakur. The case had begun to disrupt his peace. He was becoming obsessed with it, especially now that the searches had uncovered nothing. *Shit,* he cursed in his mind, *gotta get some fuckin' headway on this.* He rolled over to his nightstand and pulled open the drawer. There he retrieved a pack of Camel nonfilters and pulled one from the pack. He studied it for a long moment before taking it into his mouth and lighting it. He inhaled the strong Turkish and domestic blended tobacco and closed his eyes and relaxed.

His head beat hard until it hurt. A headache overtook his thoughts until he could concentrate no more. He sat up on the end of the bed, put out the butt of his cigarette, and began to dress. He had to pursue his ideas and needed to work this out. If his informant said there was a tape of the Cren mass then he very well believed it. He'd need only to prove it now. This may call for some extralegal methods of investigation, but that hardly wrinkled any feathers of his. He'd learned to employ such methods from his pals out at the rampart division. A wild bunch of cowboys, to be sure. They *always* got what was required when needed.

Sweeney put his nine-millimeter Beretta service weapon onto his hip by clip and belt loop. He then strapped a black leather holster to his right ankle. In it was a .380 Smith & Wesson automatic. It was an unregistered, untraceable "throwaway"—that is, a gun that could be used in a confrontation and thrown away or planted on a perp. This was standard operating procedure for most officers who'd worked in the CRASH units that did their tours of duty in the zones. Sweeney felt it necessary to call on his ol' friend Frank Beton, who worked out of the Rampart CRASH unit. Frank had basically taught Sweeney every dirty trick in the book. He felt now that after he employed his upcoming pony trick he'd seek Frank's counsel. First, however, he'd have to call and make an appointment.

"Hey, Frank," Sweeney spoke, easing out of his front door, holding his head against his shoulder while cradling the phone.

"Yeah, this is Frank. What's happening?" said Frank, on guard.

"Listen, this is John, John Sweeney. From the Seventy-seventh."

"Oh, hell yeah, what's doing, partner?" Frank spoke, unguarded now.

"Well, I got an issue I'd like to run by you if I can get near you this evening."

"Well, um," Frank said, hesitantly in contemplation, "you see . . . oh, what the hell. Come out to the house. Me and some of my unit guys are gonna watch the Tyson fight. If you don't mind any of that?"

"No, no, that'll be good. I'm going to make a stop now and then I'll boogie on out, huh?"

"Sure thing, buddy. See you then."

"Good." Sweeney broke the connect and backed on out of his driveway. But instead of driving north to Simi Valley where Frank Beton lived, he drove south to the 10 freeway and drove it to the Harbor 110 south—heading the way he'd go to work.

The way, that is, to South Central. The windows on the Bronco were limousine tents and were virtually impossible to see through. Around his back license plate were the alphabets KMA and the numbers 639. Unbeknownst to pedestrians and civilians this code identified the driver or registered owner as a law enforcement–related employee. The vehicle would be seldom, if ever, pulled over.

The sun was just beginning its descent from the sky and into the Pacific Ocean. From daylight hours to dusk there were about two hours left. He hoped to get in and out before the sun extinguished itself.

He slowed the Bronco to a stop on the run-down corner of Gage and Hoover. The area was, of course, a gang-infested, depressed, and dilapidated community of vice and graft. On the northwest corner sat a minuscule caricature of a park, though it was barely big enough for a swing set and a bite-size merry-go-round. Across from it was a gas station of a foreign name that was cluttered with crack heads eager to do whatever for some change. Some had squeegees and others had crudely made signs. They harassed every driver that came into the lot. Across Hoover Street from the gas station sat a liquor store. Gang members in full dress stood post in its lot hawking their drugs as if they had a license. On the opposite corner stood two obvious prostitutes in tight hoochie mama spandex and obnoxious colors. Wigs resembling unkempt poodles were haphazardly piled upon their heads. And they stood stilted upon platform shoes too humongous to be practical. Their shapely hips were thrown out seductively for passersby to glimpse for shopping. One worked a wad of gum as furiously as a major league pitcher in a World Series game. The other looked sullen and evil. No children played in the park. A homeless bag lady sat on one of the swings.

The light changed and Sweeney pushed the Bronco around the curve on Gage leading to Vermont. Once across Vermont he punched in a series of numbers on his cell phone.

"Yeah," said the recipient. "What's crackin'?"

"Robert," spoke Sweeney, coming to a California stop at Normandie and taking it south. "I'm in your area and I really need to see you. 'No' is not an option."

"Aight," Lil Huck said. "I'm around. Where?"

"Our usual place. But make it snappy. I'm almost there already and I'm in my personal vehicle."

"Aight, I'm coming now."

At 4:55 p.m., the continental limo eased on to the Las Vegas strip with Bingo, Blain, and Blister loaded inside. It crawled through traffic at a shooters' pace while its occupants blazed their last blunt of the ride. Bingo called ahead to the hotel to confirm their reservations as Blain tucked his burner in his waistband and combed his thick mustache with a palm comb. Blister took in the crowds with a predator's beam. There was a reason that Bingo didn't want Blister heated. Blister was an infamous jacker. He'd rob anything, anybody, anywhere, though his m.o. wasn't strong arm. It was *armed* robbery. Thus with him it was simply a matter of keeping him unarmed. Not that he wasn't a fighter or that he didn't have heart. No, it was just that Blister was a gunfighter. His allegiance was to arms. He preferred them because he had to say little to get someone's attention. He'd draw and take what he wanted.

Because of this, however, certain homies of his would keep him gunless when they had bigger fish to fry. And while this sporting event wasn't a mission per se, it presented too many options for a serial jacker like Blister to be armed, especially since they were out of state. Being OT—out of town—gave people, though especially bangers and criminals, a false sense of freedom by not being known to the native inhabitants or the local constituency and they tended to believe they could commit any outlandish act and get away. But in Las Vegas—especially on or around the strip—cameras could very well spell an assailant's demise. No chances could be taken under conditions as these. Burners would be used as a last resort, not a first.

They'd rented the limo service for twenty-four hours at an enormous rate, which included lodging for the driver as well. No sweat, because both Blain and Bingo were paper'd up. They'd grown ghetto rich by hangin' crack. To rent a limo for a twenty-four-hour period was as easy as batting an eye.

Lapeace, Sekou, and Maniac exited the elevator at the twelfth floor. They were immediately confronted by three men, one of whom was Askari, the world famous hip-hop artist.

"What that Mob Piru like?" asked the darkest of the trio. His hands were thrown out to his sides in a relaxed cross. His tone was probing but also menacing. The other fell back against the wall and posed in a strike-first position. Askari, in a gold Versace suit, black silk shirt, big gold medallion, and black shoes, smiled sinisterly. His eyes were almost closed from the bomb weed he'd been smoking.

"It don't Piru like *nothin'* here. This gangsta Crip," Maniac responded with venom.

The little Piru and Maniac began to advance on each other. Askari and Lapeace stepped up simultaneously between them, Lapeace's hand on Maniac's shoulder, Askari's on Lil Flame's chest.

"Hold up, players," said Askari, looking at Sekou and Maniac. "We don't need all that."

"Naw, really we don't," responded Lapeace. "It is what it is."

"Yeah," Askari said through a toothy smile. "We recognize you, potna."

"Eh Askari, what, you a Piru now, or what?" Sekou asked.

"I'm Death Row M-O-B," Askari focused on Sekou and answered in his husky tone heard always in his records. "It is what it is, know what I'm sayin'?"

"Yeah, well, whatever. Look, I'm Lapeace Shakur. We gangstas. We ain't up here to rumble with you cats. We come to see Tyson smash ol' boy. But if y'all bring it, we will respond like gangstas."

"Yeah whatever," said Lil Flame. "This P-funk nigga, all day."

"Wait, hold up. You are Lapeace who?" asked Askari incredulously.

"Shakur," said Lapeace facing Askari but towering over him. "I'm a Shakur man, just like you."

"Who's your folks?" quizzed Askari, one eyebrow raised higher than the other.

"My folks?"

"Yeah, your folks—your bloodline. How you become a Shakur?"

All the others had now fanned out to watch the exchange between Askari and Lapeace. A most fascinating confrontation to be sure.

"My mother, rest in peace, was Asali Shakur of the L.A. Black Panther Party. She died when I was born. My father, rest in peace, was Tafuta Shakur, of the Amistad Collective of the Black Liberation Army. He was a prisoner of war and died while a prisoner. I'm a Shakur by birth."

"Yeah," Askari said, looking now at Lapeace with a renewed interest. "I've heard of your folks through my moms who was—"

"A New York Panther and a part of the Panther Twenty-one case in 1969," Lapeace said, interrupting Askari and finishing his mother's legacy.

"Yep . . . so you know that, huh?"

"Of course. And your stepdad is doctor Mutulu Shakur, who is a prisoner of war and a comrade of my father's. Am I right?"

"Right again, player," said Askari. "I'm feeling you. So y'all going to the fight, huh?"

"Yeah, that's what we up here for," said Sekou.

"Well, after the fight, which shouldn't last too long, why don't y'all swing by six-six-two and party with us? It's gonna be a gang of bitches over there," offered Askari, pressing the elevator button.

"We might just do that," answered Lapeace.

"Aight then, *Shakur*," Askari said to Lapeace and issued his troops onto the elevator. They boarded orderly.

Sekou and Maniac turned to leave and Lapeace was still standing there watching as the elevator doors began to close.

"Okay, then, *Shakur*," Lapeace said excitedly acknowledging he and Askari's tribal connections.

Sekou seemed to be perturbed by the confrontation. He stalked off to the room in a huff ahead of Maniac and Lapeace.

Maniac and Lapeace entered after Sekou who, by their entrance, was pacing in front of the glass wall-window with one arm folded across his chest and his other hand pulling thoughtfully on his chin. Eyebrows connected, humming an indistinguishable tune under his breath.

Lapeace went to the bathroom. Maniac sat on a lounge chair and grabbed the remote.

"Hold on before you turn that on homie. I wanna get at you and Peace for a second."

"Oh, aight then." Maniac put down the remote and eased back into his seat. He crossed his legs and laid his head back on the soft upholstery of the headrest.

Lapeace exited the bathroom and walked into the silent vacuumed atmosphere projected by Sekou's tension. He looked quickly from Maniac to Sekou.

"Hey Peace," Sekou asked, "my question is this: what just happened out there? I mean, was we banged on by some Pirus and Askari?"

"Cuz," spoke up Maniac in defense of himself, "hell naw, we wasn't *banged on*. If anything we banged on them. And that nigga Askari . . . man, it's so obvious now where he at. I mean, they banged they shit and we banged ours. We could have did whatever. And Askari ain't said he was a Piru. He said he was Death Row, M-O-B. Sekou, you know as well as I do that they claim that shit means money over bitches. Them other niggas was RU's. But, shit, them niggas didn't want none of this."

"Was we heated?" asked Sekou, looking over at Lapeace with a hard stare and a frown. Maniac, too, looked up at Lapeace for an answer.

Lapeace looked from one to the other as if to say *Are you crazy?* and raised up his white T-shirt revealing the fat butt of the semiautomatic nine millimeter.

"What, you thought, Kou? Huh, a nigga wasn't burnin'? Miss me, homie. You of all cats should know my steez, Kou." Lapeace put his shirt down and walked over to the bureau and pulled out a seat. He eased down into it and put his elbows on his knees and eyed Sekou.

"Well, that's a relief to know. At least we had iron with us. 'Cause I seen ol' bog in the back, behind that midget nigga with the mouth, he had a burner in his waist. I was on his ass, though. Soon as it would have jumped off I'd have smashed that fool. That's on the gang," exclaimed Sekou with animated exaggeration. He paced now in rapid motion in front of the window.

"That's gangsta," confirmed Maniac, joining now in the revelry.

"Man, I couldn't even believe that nigga Askari. *Death Row M-O-B*. Fuck Death Row! I mean, damn, this ain't New York or even Oakland. L.A. is the Crip and Blood capital of the world. Niggas can't come out here and swing it like us. This red and blue shit a nigga gotta grow up in, can't come out here and choose a side. That's how foreign niggas get smoked, cuz. This on the land, nigga, if we had run across them three niggas anywhere else other than this janky-ass desert hotel, I'd have blazed on 'em," Sekou announced, getting fired up now.

"On me!" chimed in Maniac. He, too, stood now and began to Crip-walk around the room. Hands held up the turf, head held high, rhythm on time to a beat in his memory no one else could hear. Maniac did the war dance to a time resplendent with soul. He was one of the best C-walkers in his turf.

"You know what?" sighed Lapeace, tired of the chest thumping—though really he had no doubts about either's seriousness. "That would have been something to see. Since neither one of y'all was burnin'. I had the only heater."

"Oh, oh," jived Sekou now in a boisterous imitation of Askari. "*All right then Shakur.*"

And then Maniac joined him as Lapeace's voice "*Okay then Shakur.*" And then they both doubled over in laughter. Then Sekou added in a mock Martin Luther King Jr. voice. "I have a dream that one day little Red Shakurs and Little Blue Shakurs will join hands and sing 'We Shall Come Over, We Shall Come Over.' "

Maniac was on the floor, now bawling with hysterical laughter. His knees were drawn up to his chest in convulsive coughs of comical laughter. Sekou was leaned up against the wall laughing with his head down. Lapeace sat calmly looking from one to the other pathetically, not in the least enjoying the little charades being played. He got up from his chair, took the burner from his waist, and laid it upon the bureau top. Its heavy metal to wood sound ended the laughter in a hurry. Both Sekou and Maniac were now quiet and attentive. Lapeace took his long-strided walk toward his room.

"You niggas is twisted and sick. I ain't fuckin' with y'all."

"Aw, come on, Peace," responded Sekou in an attempt to sooth Lapeace's inflamed pride, "I was just bullshittin', man. Damn. Oh, now you workin' with feelins', huh?"

"Ain't got time to play with you, Sekou. It's time we got dressed for the fight." At that Lapeace closed the door to his room and began to shed his clothes.

"He'll be all right," Sekou said to Maniac, looking at the closed door. "He's just a little touchy right now. But that shit was funny, huh?"

"Hell yeah," Maniac said, standing up to mimic Sekou. "You killed that shit. 'Little Red Shakurs' . . . On me, you kilt that, loc."

"Right, right," Sekou said accepting the compliment graciously as he turned to go into his room to get dressed. Maniac took his cue and went over to his new clothing and began to pull out his gear for the evening.

13

Sweeney took Vermont south to Manchester, passing through some of the most volatile terrain South Central had to offer. At Manchester he broke right and headed west. At Harvard Boulevard, after waiting forever for the light to change, he banked left and then left again on 87th Street. There he floated to an easy stop. Not three minutes later Robert's van came to a halting stop behind the white Bronco. Robert ambled over to the passenger side and climbed up into the truck.

"Hello, Robert."

"Hey, Sweeney. Look, we gotta make this quick 'cause the fight fin' to be on, you know? So what's up?" Robert asked across the expanse of the leather seats.

"You know, we hit Shakur's and Ghost's this morning, huh?"

"Yeah, I heard 'bout it, so?"

"So," said Sweeney incredulously, "welp, you see, buddy—we came up on *zilch, nothing*."

"No?" Robert said.

"No. Now, we are back at square one. No evidence, *no* corroboration, *no* fucking Lapeace."

"He wasn't there, I guess?"

"Hell no he wasn't there. We got nothing, Robert. What do you make of that, huh?"

"I can't call it. But if—" spoke Robert but was cut off.

"No, you see, this is not how it works, Robert." Sweeney was showing anger now and his bald head began to glisten.

"I mean—" Robert began again to finish his point but was cut off again.

"This is *not,* I repeat *not,* how it works. I gave you what you wanted. I came through for you. Got you your 'work.' And you said what you had for me was surefire. But we know now that this wasn't surefire, was it Robert?" Sweeney's eyes were beginning to bulge. His voice was elevated.

"Man, Sweeney, I gave you what I was told. Sam ain't had no reason to lie. It's what he said. Said he seen it, man. You know I ain't into lying to you. You been straight with me, Sweeney." Robert was starting to plead now. He felt a bit unnerved at Sweeney's suggestion that he'd given him bunk information. The cab of the Bronco began to feel smaller and definitely warmer. He felt distressed and a little desperate. He scanned his memory for something useful. Anything juicy enough to keep Sweeney's mania in check. He squirmed uncomfortably in his seat and focused on a tan van a few parked cars up the street.

"So what's up, Robert? I need something. I need another link to finding this tape. You've made me look like a damn fool in front of my boss, man."

"I'm thinking . . . ," said Robert defensively. Though his brain was working overtime looking for links to Lapeace, his thoughts came to rest upon one individual. He'd been one of Lapeace's crew members and a leading figure in the North Star Car Club and thus probably more than likely there the night the shoot-out went down.

"Aight, look," said Robert in relief and resignation at having found for Sweeney a possible connecting fiber, "check out Greg Dawson. He goes by the name—"

"Lazy," Sweeney said before Robert could. He knew the name well. He investigated him before when as a CRASH officer he'd conducted a traffic stop on a blue-and-gray '68 Chevy Impala and found Greg "Lazy" Dawson in possession of a semiautomatic MAC-10, .45 caliber. He'd taken Lazy to the 77th, but no sooner had the booking process been completed than Dawson was bailed out. Fighting the gun possession from the streets he was able to draw the case out over a whole year and resolve it with a sentence of five weekends in the county jail and a one-year probation. To Sweeney's knowledge he was no longer on paper.

"Yeah," Robert said, looking over at Sweeney in surprise, "you know him, huh?"

"Yeah, I know him. Lives on Seventieth, huh?"

"Right. Between Halldale and Denker," added Robert, feeling a bit better for himself and Sweeney.

"You think he'll have a line on this thing?" Sweeney asked Robert while all along trying to work out an advantage point in his mind that could be used against Lazy in order to make him talk.

"Yeah, well he's in Lapeace's crew and he's in the North Star Car Club. He was more than likely there that night. Hold up," said Robert, thinking hard now. "He *was* there 'cause one of the homegirls told me his car was shot up. And *all* the North Stars cars were shot up by the Brims that night. So, yeah, he was there, I'm sure."

"Okay, look then," consulted Sweeney, raising his right leg to the seat, drawing the small semi out of its holster. "I'll need you to take this weapon and tape it under the front left fender—the wheel well—of his everyday car. What kind is he driving now?" Sweeney had placed the gun between himself and Robert on the seat. He'd carefully wiped it of any of his prints.

"He pushes a green Acura. It's a newer model. He leaves it on the street so it'll be easy to do."

"Good. I'll have a patrol unit pull him over tomorrow and alert me. I'll take him into custody on the weapons charges and grill his ass. But Robert, listen, I'll need you to keep your ears to the pavement on this. Help me out buddy."

"Naw, I got you, Sweeney. Don't trip."

"All right, buddy. You go on and do that taping job for me. And wear gloves, will you? *No prints,*" Sweeney demanded with a wink, a wipe of his sweating head, and a click of his tongue.

"Got it. Don't worry, I got this. Now, I gotta go handle this and watch the fight."

"Okay, be safe buddy," said Sweeney, starting up the truck and putting it into drive. Robert closed his door and the truck pulled off and turned left on Normandie Avenue and disappeared into the night.

* * *

Tiny Monster stood leaning against his pearl white 300 SC Lexus. He was talking with Baby C-Dog out in front of Lazy's house. A few more homies were across the street on the sidewalk laughing and bullshitting. Lazy came out from behind the chain-link fence and walked over to where Tiny Monster and Baby C-Dog were standing. They were locked in a debate when Lil Huck turned the corner. The conversations stopped as everyone got on guard. Tight discretion was the watchword around Lil Huck as everybody was only waiting for the word. Lil Huck got out of his van and instead of coming up to Tiny Monster, C-Dog, and Lazy he threw up a salute and went over to where the other homies were standing. He greeted them all in turn and lukewarm salutations were returned.

"Cuz," spoke Tiny Monster, "that nigga is foul! Why he keep comin' round here? He know niggas ain't feelin' him."

"You know the business on fool, TM. It's just a matter of time," Baby C-Dog said, digging into the top pocket of his work shirt to retrieve his pager and check the time.

"Whatever, cuz," responded Tiny Monster and added, "Niggas need to serve him and keep it movin'."

"On me," said Lazy. He looked at Tiny Monster and said, "You ready to bounce?"

"Yep, we out of here Baby Dog. I'll holler tomorrow. We gon watch the brawl on the big screen." Tiny Monster and Lazy then climbed into the Lexus.

"Aight gangstas," C-Dog said in farewell, "reach at me tomorrow."

"Fo' sho—three minutes," came the double salute from inside the fresh Lexus and they skirted out. Baby C-Dog saluted the others from across the street, got into his car, and left as well. Lil Huck acted as if he, too, was leaving by getting into his van and pulling off down the street.

He parked far up the block across Denker and watched the throng of homies, hoping they'd leave, too. But they stayed posted. He waited for twenty minutes in silence and contemplation for them to find another loitering spot, but nothing doing. He watched them posing, laughing, doubling over, and bullshitting. He could tell who was leading the war story and who was the group clown, but they still wouldn't move. He couldn't very well plant the weapon while they stood as sentries across the street. He knew that was no good.

No, he'd have to risk it on a late-night creep. 'Cause, to him, this shit wasn't as important as watching the Tyson fight. So later, he reasoned, starting up the van, he'd come back and do what he'd been ordered to do. No sweat, he thought, he'd get it done.

Tashima sat cross-legged on the sofa watching the prefight hoopla as she went over a few details of a recording contract she was going to offer an alternative rock group that had caught her ear by way of a close girlfriend.

She contemplated her current circumstances and coupled them with the conversation she'd had with Cora Roach earlier. She was certainly in love with Lapeace and was going to support him with her all. She needed him and was sure he needed her. She put down the sheet of papers and rubbed her fingers along Kody's healthy black coat. Kody in return slowly batted her eyes in a lazy, sleepy way. She was curled up on the sofa next to Shima totally relaxed. It was the ringing of the phone that broke both Kody's and Tashima's trains of blissful thought.

It was Aunt Pearl calling to tell Tashima about the early-morning raid. Tashima, aghast at the news, offered to come and retrieve Aunt Pearl from Mrs. Delaney's house, where she'd been all day. As she readied herself for the drive across town the phone rang.

"Hello?" answered Tashima while lacing her Reebok tennies.

"May I speak to the sexiest lady in Los Angeles?" spoke Lapeace with his husky baritone.

"Yeees," preened and purred Tashima into the phone while not trying to hide the pleasure in her voice, "this is she. At your service your highness."

"How are you this evening Babes?"

"I'm good. Just on my way out to scoop up Aunt Pearl. She been at a neighbor's all day. You know why I take it?"

"Yeah I was laced by the same neighbor you are going to get A.P. from. They also had a get-together at another spot in the land. I didn't know where or how A.P. was so I called the neighbor and was told she missed the bus. So, what, she called you?"

"Yeah, Babes. Not ten minutes ago. So I'm going to scoop her and let her kick it over here with me."

"That's cool. I appreciate it, Shima." Lapeace was watching out of the window of the limo at the masses of people traversing up and down the strip. Sekou and Maniac were huddled along the jump seats whispering.

"You cool with this, then?"

"Oh, yeah, I'm straight with it and, again, thank you."

"Mister man," said Shima in a mock voice, "you know you got it like that. And you know A.P. gots it like that." Tashima was smiling.

"Cool in the gang, then. I just called to tell you I love you and that I'm missing you out here."

"Well, that's a big ol' boomerang on the love. But we are going to have to do something 'bout these . . . these folks. I mean, are they trying to put the warrior on ice?" She learned quickly to use other words in a roundabout way.

"I called Safi but have yet to hear back. I'm telling War to take it as they are. Has there been anything on the news?"

"No. But then again I've been on the prefight stuff. But I'll notify you if anything comes on tonight. Call me after the fight, aight?"

"Yeah, fo' sho. I love you, Shima."

"Me, too. Talk to you tonight, huh?"

"Yeah."

They broke the connect as the limo pulled into the valet parking square at the MGM Grand. Sekou, Maniac, and Lapeace exited the limo and were ushered into the hotel lobby by their driver. The trio moved like royalty through the crowds, heads held high, eyes on alert. Gangstas movin.'

People dressed elegantly in tuxedoes and elaborate gowns were standing around chatting noisily with others dressed out in hip-hop's finest gear. Gold chains and white gold bracelets screamed their existence against dark skin and darker cloth. Diamonds of various sizes, cuts, and karats were on display in generous amounts. People gleamed and glammed and sparkled and blinged from earlobes to toe rings, from pinky rings to teeth. Lapeace spotted Askari with his entourage.

Of Pirus standing near the main floor entrance, Lil Flame was spotted too. Lapeace, Sekou, and Maniac kept it moving as their path was cut by their muscle-bound driver. It had been Lapeace's idea to go right to their seats as opposed to idling around in the midst of unnecessary confrontation. The idea was to come up here to get away from the zone and relax, not to bring the zone here and continue the business as usual. *Shit,* Lapeace mused, *if that was the case I could just heat up that whole section over there and slump all them fools.*

He changed his course of thinking when they made it to their seats. Lapeace scanned the seating section and felt comfortable in their positioning. He tipped the limo driver a hundred and sat down.

Bingo, Blister, and Blain's limo floated to an easy stop in the valet's square and they bailed out of the back like bloodhounds in search of prison-break suspects. Bingo in his brown Armani, red silk scarf on display just so in his top pocket, stood head and shoulders above both Blain and Blister. His gaze was beaming with a fixed scowl, which tended to discourage most. Standing at the rear of the limo he adjusted his tie and cocked his brim at a forty-five-degree angle—right-sidedly, of course. Seeing this, Blain did likewise, while Blister shuffled out a few feet and ogled the massive fight-goers' jewelry like a starving man at a buffet.

"Dawg," barked Bingo at Blister, "control yourself."

"Naw, naw," responded Blister, not looking over at Bingo but still feasting his eyes on those standing and moving into the hotel lobby. " I got this, Blood, don't even trip."

Bingo stepped quickly over to Blister and all but blocked his view of the fabulously dressed people. No doubt there to floss but also to watch and cheer Tyson on.

"Blood," Bingo began, staring down into Blister's sparkling, lust-filled eyes. "I ain't fin to end up in no Vegas prison for some dumb shit done by you. So control yourself, homie."

"B, what you woofin' 'bout, homie? I'm straight. Aight?" Blister had disengaged his sights and was now looking up into

Bingo's hazel green eyes. He held no fear of Bingo nor of Blain. But as his big homies he respected them to the fullest.

"Aight, homie," Bingo sighed. "Let's bail upon this bitch."

At that their driver led a path through the crowd and into the posh lobby of the MGM Grand. Once inside Blain immediately recognized Lil Tray from Compton's MOB Piru and Lil Flame. He guided Bingo's attention over to the band of Pirus. Blain gave Bingo a look of *why not?* At once they cut a b-line toward the right entrance and over to the Pirus.

"What's up Lil Tray, Lil Flame," greeted Blain jovially and shook hands with both young Pirus. He then saw Askari, Simon, and Lip Dog. "Oh, what up Askari, Simon, Lip Dog, how y'all be?"

"We straight."

"Cool."

"P-funkin'."

A chorus of responses, handshakes, and hugs came all around. Death Row and the Pirus were there in force. Fancying themselves a mafia-style organization, they sported an assortment of gold, platinum, and diamonds. Versace, Hilfiger, Kani, and Fubu. Red, black, white, and burgundy clothing in various stages of cut and floss hung impressively from the bangers as they stood about in conversations. Curious onlookers passed and gawked at the gathering as Simon and Askari preened and posed for pictures and autographs. Even passing Crips not locked into immediate war with Compton's Piru mob, Death Row, or L.A. Brims stopped to holler at Askari or greet one of the Bloods they knew from another time and place. Everything was cordial and on a respectful level. New Afrikans out doing their thing. Cats from the zones out on the town—out of town, mingling in a deadly atmosphere of domestic respect and wishes of well-being.

The gathering broke apart as the main event was announced. The Death Row entourage went along to their seats in a pack. It seemed as if they'd bought out the whole section of seats near the ring. They flooded the arena like locusts. Across the aisle and slightly to the back, Bingo and the Brims took their seats. Behind them, just a few rows back, sat a quadrant of Crips from Compton's south side: Lil Al, Lil Too Too, Dre, and Baby Lane. All four were infamous gunfighters who lived on the fringes of life and death. Each of them in his own way had come up on a major amount of money: robbing armored cars, dope dealing, stealing cars, and gambling. You name the activity, they had a hand in it. All were highly successful at their crafts.

"Baby Lane," spoke Lil Al, in recognition of the group of Pirus seating themselves. "Ain't that them 'Ru niggas over there?"

"Where at?" asked Baby Lane excitedly, looking around the audience wildly before being directed by Lil Al.

"Down there, near the ring. Look."

Baby Lane, tall and dark with an uncanny resemblance to Askari, followed the direction of Lil Al's point. And there, without a doubt, sat and stood a sight to behold. No less than twenty Pirus and their affiliates of Death Row Records gathered around in a nonchalant, very casual way. As if they had no enemies.

"Yeah boy," spoke Baby Lane, the young urban gunfighter, "that's them awright. Ain't that something," he added while rubbing his hands together and licking his full lips as if in line for a delicious treat.

"Ooh, they deep, too," said Dre, scoping the band of enemigos.

"Look, there go Heron, Neck Bone . . . that nigga Simon. Damn . . . ," Lil Too Too said.

"Sit down, y'all," Baby Lane ordered. "We ain't tryin' to let them see us first. Fuck them niggas. Let's watch this squabble. We'll see what's crackin' later on, you know?"

"Right, right," answered Dre. They settled back to watch the fight.

In reality, there was no fight at all. Mike Tyson made quick work of Golden. Tyson knocked his contender out cold. It was, in true Tyson fashion, a climactic letdown. One hundred and nine seconds of the first round and Golden was finished.

People didn't leave the makeshift arena quickly. They stood around and talked and flaunted their wares. Men got at women, women at men—and quiet as kept, men got at men and women at women. It was the usual exchanges of sexual undertones that accompany each such event. For Tyson fights proved to be so smashingly fast and over so quickly that folks tended to just hang out afterward to get their money's worth, in one way or another.

In clusters, people spoke in animated suggestions of Tyson's skills. People slugged the air or threw sets of punches, complete with flutters of uppercuts, in remembrance of the magic they'd just seen.

Lapeace, too, was caught up in the jousting with Sekou as he was bumped up against harshly by a passerby in the aisle. The pedestrian, Baby Lane from South Side Compton, kept walking.

"Eh," said Lapeace, catching his balance. "Eh, homeboy, you ain't gonna say nothin'—you just gon' run me over?"

With Baby Lane was Dre, Lil Al, and Lil Too Too. When Baby Lane stopped to respond, his homies did too. Sekou and Maniac stepped up to the aisle as the South Sides came to a menacing halt and turned in their direction.

"What's that?" asked Baby Lane. He stood exactly eye to eye with Lapeace. They were the same height.

"You pushed by and bumped all into me and just pushed on. What, you didn't feel that?" Lapeace's hands were out away from his body, palms open. Baby Lane looked Lapeace over and then took in Sekou and Maniac.

"Where y'all from?" he asked in his best confrontational voice, a mixture of threat and curiosity.

"Eight Tray Gangsta Crip," stressed Lapeace, expanding his chest, holding in his stomach, and feeling his nuts draw up tight to his body in preparation for a struggle. His fists began to clench.

"That's right, cuz," said Baby Lane. "My apologies, Crip. We up out the Hub. South Side Compton Crip Gang. We see y'all."

"True that, homie. This Sekou," Lapeace said by way of introduction and relief. "I'm Lapeace and this is my young homie Maniac."

Baby Lane did his intro and handshakes and hugs were done all around.

"Where y'all stayin' at?" asked Dre.

"We at the Luxor," Sekou answered.

"Right."

"Askari and a couple of them 'Ru cats over there, too," Sekou added. And then thought to remind them, "We got into it a little with them earlier."

"Yeah?" asked Lil Too Too.

"Yeah, that little nigga . . ."

"Who, Flame?" asked Baby Lane, "or Lil Tray? 'Cause if it is Lil Tray he a busta. We took his Death Row chain at the Lakewood mall."

"Naw," said Maniac. "Fool never said his name. But you probably right. One of them two."

"Fuck all them slob-ass niggas," said Lil Too Too, throwing up a big chunky Crip sign as a throng of giggling females passed by.

"I know that's right, cuz," chimed in Sekou and Maniac. Lapeace nodded his approval.

"Awright then gangstas, we fin to bounce. Y'all keep y'all heads up. And watch them dead niggas, they up here thick," said Baby Lane turning into the aisle to leave. He was joined by Dre, Lil Too Too, and Lil Al in tow.

Lapeace, Sekou, and Maniac stood for about three minutes talking before they filed out into MGM's lobby. It was in the lobby, as they walked out toward their waiting limo, that mutual sight and hateful recognition was made by Sekou, Lapeace, and Maniac with Bingo, Blister, and Blain. It was a slow-motion death reflection that flooded the space between them like raging water forced through a tube. Every movement was a lethargic and labored exertion as time, in decade-sized blocks, tumbled out between the fanned-out trios.

Anyhow and Lapeace, ever the rivals, were but the center, or the primary contenders, in the contradiction that made up the dialectical reality of the struggle in which this tragedy was being played out. The cast of characters on both sides of the competing forces grappling for supremacy were many and varied. But here, in the state of Nevada, in the city of Las Vegas, on the Strip, in the lobby of the MGM hotel, on September 20, 1996, the contradiction was again about to burst open and create a synthesis leading to a new union and thus another struggle.

Bingo looked at Lapeace and thought of his homies Lapeace had gunned down, beat up, or banged on. He looked at Sekou and thought likewise. Here were two bonafide blood killers who, by all accounts, were high-ranking members of an enemy set.

He flashed on the struggle Anyhow had raged against Lapeace as not only an enemy but a personal foe. Of how Anyhow lay at that moment in a terminal slumber due in no small part to strife caused against this man and his comrades not thirty feet away. Blain, too, was locked on to Lapeace, Sekou, and Maniac.

He knew Lapeace and Sekou intimately. He'd been acquainted with both through the mutual medium of exchange, most expressed by bangers in South Central: violence. He'd caught Lapeace dipping through his turf in a jet black 454 Chevy truck and lit him up with an MI rifle, filling the truck with holes. He'd surmised it was Lapeace and his homies who walked through Harvard Park that same night bustin' on everything moving. One of his homies was mortally wounded and two others were shot up and critically injured. He'd met Sekou in a hand-to-hand altercation inside the Slauson swap meet, when he and two of his homies were swarmed by no less than eight gangstas and pummeled to the ground and ceremoniously stomped until they were unconscious.

Blister was recognized by Maniac as a personal antagonist from youth authority where they often clashed over age-old red and blue rivalries.

Lapeace, ever vigilant, zeroed in quickly on the brown trio. He focused on Bingo, who'd gone to prison, he knew, for killing a Crip from Five One Trouble gangstas. He knew that more than likely it was Bingo now calling the shots over the Brims. He contemplated Anyhow, his archenemy, now causing him so much peril bringing his name up in the Crenshaw shoot-out. Bingo, leader, a G and a Crip killer, besides. And then in his company was Blain. A Blood par excellence. And no doubt a gunner on several missions launched by Brims against his set. Rumor had it that it was Blain who'd filled his truck full of holes one Saturday night as Lapeace crept into Brim hood on a late-night booty call. *Son of a bitch,* he thought, *damn near killed me.* The other young Damu Lapeace didn't know. But by association alone he was guilty.

Sekou knitted his brow and computed the trio of detractors among the damned. He knew Blain and Bingo as top-shelf Bloods and sworn enemies of all Crips, serious contenders in the guerrilla wars raging across the inner city of South Central. He'd seen Blain up close and personal but couldn't quite remember just where the encounter took place. He did know, however, that the exchange was in his favor.

As recognition set in among all the combatants, their strides came to a parade rest and instinctively they fanned out in battle stances and strike poses. The lobby of the MGM turned suddenly dark and foreboding. The die had been cast and the lead, no doubt, was about to fly when the loud and boisterous Death Row mob Piru crew came into the lobby. Their attention was momentarily broken by a fleeting image of Askari rushing across the lobby and running up on Baby Lane, the Compton Crip that Lapeace and his homies had just met, and knocking him to the floor with a pounding right hook. So stunned were all that, in the brief moment of indecision in which their minds tried to catch up to what their eyes were seeing, the entire Death Row mob Piru entourage was upon Baby Lane, stomping him out.

The melee brought an immediate response from MGM security and local police, which put an instantaneous damper on the brewing battle between the Lapeace and Bingo camps.

Lapeace avoided the clutches of a manic security guard by inches before spinning leftward out of the front doors and into the back of a young New Afrikan female who was also striding to evade the emerging stampede. Security guards and police were attempting to grab and take into custody any young New Afrikans who looked remotely to be involved or were potential witnesses. Most, however, escaped their net.

Lapeace, Sekou, and Maniac made it safely to their limo, as did the Brims. Inside, Lapeace spoke first.

"Man, can y'all believe that shit?"

"I told you, Peace. That nigga Askari is a Piru. *Now* you believe me?" Sekou asked in a demanding voice.

"Yeah, Peace, come on now," Maniac insisted, "you seen him rush up on cuz from South."

Lapeace was looking dejected. His brow had beads of sweat accumulated on it and his stare was fixed upon the liquor display. He was contemplating not wanting to rush his answer because this would stick. He chose his words wisely.

"What I seen was Askari rush up on Baby Lane and bomb. That don't necessarily mean he's a Piru. I don't know, and neither do y'all, what went on between them before that shit. So, me, I ain't gonna just mark him as a 'Ru. From what I hear that fat-ass nigga Simon ain't even a Piru."

Sekou and Maniac looked at Lapeace incredulously. "Oh come on with the *bullshit* Peace. Why can't you call it like you seen it?" wondered Sekou aloud.

"'Cause you should know as well as I do that it ain't that damn simple, Sekou. What did we just hear from the homie baby GC?"

"What?" Sekou asked dumbfounded.

"Baby GC told us yesterday, or was it the day before, that some cats from the South were doing some bodyguard work for Bad Boy or Biggie or some shit. That could have come out of that. We don't know, is what I'm saying."

"Naw," disagreed Maniac. "I don't think that was it, homie."

"Hold up, Yac," said Lapeace. "You ain't knowin' about this."

"Yeah, I remember that shit now. And really, on the strength of keepin' it gangsta, I'm a say you right homie. But on the same strength of keepin' it Crip, I'm a say fuck Death Row and Mob Piru!" Sekou tossed his head back in a jest of finality and reached for the dark liquor.

"I'm feelin' that," said Lapeace, "and fuck Brim too!"

"On the gang!" added Maniac, accepting both his and Lapeace's drink.

"Here's a toast to meetin' up to them Damu niggas again," Lapeace boasted, raising his glass.

"And," toasted Sekou, raising his glass to Lapeace's, "our victory over them bitch-ass slobs."

"Hold up," Maniac spoke, raising his in turn. "To all the G's on lock and in that lean!"

"*Gangstas movin'!*" they shouted in unison and clinked their glasses and threw back the XO cognac.

Lil Huck crept in stealth, enveloped in fear, along Halldale Avenue toward the corner of 70th Street. He'd made the block once in his van and was relieved to see no one hanging out in front of Lazy's house. And he was likewise consoled to see Lazy's vehicle still parked in the yard. He must still be with Tiny Monster. But now that the fight was over they could very well be on their way. He needed to perform his task with alacrity.

Lil Huck walked easily up the driveway as if going to the door to ask for Lazy. Once he was near the porch he quickly veered left and darted down the drive along the side of the house and the passenger side of the green Acura. Seeing no lights come on in either Lazy's or the house next door, he bent down around the front of the car and duck-walked to the driver's wheel well. Withdrawing the heat he laid it on the cement and pulled the duct tape from his jacket pocket. The pistol he had wrapped in a blue rag and now handled it delicately while keeping his ear peeled for sounds. He taped the weapon to the underside of the fender and replaced the tape and rag in his pocket. As he got up to leave a car turned up into the driveway. He was momentarily blinded by the headlights of the idling car. The lights shone brightly into his eyes and he shielded his vision against the glare in a futile attempt to see who it was putting him on blast.

One of the car doors opened and a detached voice spoke through the brilliant light.

"Cuz, what the fuck you doin' up in my yard, nigga?"

It was Lazy spewing hostility and venom. He'd rushed up on Lil Huck, who being no coward stood his ground.

He wasn't sure that Lazy was not going to hit him so he braced himself for a squabble.

"I came lookin' for you," Lil Huck lied. It was then that the other car door opened and Tiny Monster got out. Though he left the lights on, which illuminated the yard, the scene had an almost dreamlike feel with all the light against the deadly suspicious darkness.

"What up, Lazy?" asked Tiny Monster. "Nigga tryin' to break up in your house or what?" He was cracking his knuckles as he ambled up the drive and into the flood of lights.

"Come on, Monster, you know me better than that. I was lookin' for cuz."

"Don't come over here without callin', Huck. Ain't nothin' crackin'," said Lazy in a totally unwelcoming tone of voice, which in no uncertain way meant *leave now.*

"Aight then, cuz," said Lil Huck in a low disappointed drawl. "I'll catch you another time. I'm out."

"Yeah, that's best, *dude,*" said Tiny Monster while rubbing one knuckle into the palm of his left hand as if warming it up.

At that and under the hateful stares of Lazy and Tiny Monster, Lil Huck lumbered down the drive and started up the street.

"Eh, Huck," called Lazy after Tiny Monster had whispered something at him. "Where's your ride, how you get over here?"

"I parked on Halldale. Didn't want one time sweatin' my hoop," he half hollered back while keeping his steps steady in the opposite direction.

"That fool is shady, homie," Tiny Monster said, "better check your spot for a break-in, cameras, listenin' devices, and whatever else. Nigga foul."

"No shit," said Lazy while fumbling in his pocket for his house keys and scurrying up the steps to the door.

Lil Huck, having completed his mission and with an arrogant sense of vanity, called Sweeney from his flip phone.

"Hey, buddy," spoke Sweeney amid a wall of noise on his end, "how's it going?"

"It's *all good,*" he said, confirming their agreed-upon code for successful completion of the mission at hand.

"Oh, that's marvelous, buddy," Sweeney spoke in an obviously inebriated drawl, "just what I needed."

"Aight then, I'm gonna go. You sound like you are on a good one."

"Oh," said Sweeney, "it's more than a good one I'm on, buddy. Much more, really. Did ya see the fight, Robert?"

"Yeah, I seen it."

"Now *that* was a lesson, my friend, in pugilism. Pure and simple. Tyson is a *master pugilist*. You hear me, buddy?"

"Yep," said Lil Huck, not feeling the happiness that Sweeney felt. He had almost been caught and possibly killed minutes earlier and here this fuckin' dude was celebrating the Tyson fight at what sounded like a party. Talking about the *master of pugilism*.

"Now listen," Sweeney fumbled, "when he threw those—"

"Hey, hey buddy, I'm cool on all that. Just do what you gotta do, huh?" said Lil Huck in a blue mood, just wanting to go home and lie down.

"Oh," recognized Sweeney, "okay then, Robert." And with that he lowered the phone to its face and broke the line. He sat momentarily and thought about what was irking Robert. After telling himself it was nothing he could fix from his distance he went on back to the fight party.

Lil Huck got into his van and sat down in an exhausted heap behind the wheel. He closed his eyes and laid his head back on the rest. His repose and relaxation was disrupted by a tapping on the passenger window. A female with a hoodie sweatshirt was staring from behind a pair of thick bifocal glasses.

"Excuse me," she was tapping and mouthing. "Excuse me."

"What's up?" Lil Huck mouthed while expressing his question with his hands.

She did the *roll your window down* simulation with her hands while asking *why not?* with a slight lean of her head.

Lil Huck sighed and rolled down his window.

"What's up?"

"What you doin'?" she asked, looking up into the cab on her tiptoes.

"What you want?" Lil Huck asked.

"Got any dope?" asked the soliciting female.

"Yeah, what you need?"

"I want a dime, but I only got seven-fifty. Can I get one with that?"

"Damn bitch, you can't be comin' short like this. Next time I ain't gonna let you on. You hear me?"

"Yeah, I hear you," said the female sullenly. "Can I hit in your van?"

"You done lost your damn mind. Hell no you can't smoke in my van," Lil Huck said in instant anger. Once their transaction was over Lil Huck pulled away from the block and out of the hood.

14

In their suite Lapeace, Sekou, and Maniac changed clothes from their fight attire to casual wear. They rolled up and smoked four blunts, one apiece and one together. They contemplated their evening.

"We going to six-six-two or what?" asked Sekou to Lapeace.

"Hell," Lapeace said, rubbing his eyes, "I ain't feelin' it. What 'bout you, Yac?"

"On me, I feel like it. I want to get at them 'Ru niggas. And I want somethin' to fuck up in. Shit, a nigga horny," said Maniac, grabbing on his dick through his pants.

"Sheet," Lapeace said in remembrance of the evening activities. "Them South Side cats probably gon' heat that muthafucka up. We don't need to even be out there, really."

"Well," began Maniac, "let's at least go down to the lobby and fuck around. It'll beat being stuck up in this joint."

"I'm with that," said Sekou. Lapeace consented too and they gave themselves the once-over and started out the suite to the lobby. Having forgotten his pager, Lapeace doubled back to retrieve it. It was then he noticed the number encoded on its face: 14-1-23 (no arrest warrant).

He clipped it to his belt and joined Sekou and Maniac at the elevator. They had to wait only a moment before the golden doors opened with a muffled ring. They boarded and rode down in silence, straightening and prepping their gear.

At the lobby they fell out into a crowd of mostly female fans surrounding Askari. He'd changed as well and was wearing an Orlando Magic jersey and jeans. He looked small and vulnerable. He was flanked by two men neither Lapeace nor Sekou nor Maniac knew. Perhaps, thought Lapeace, they were his security.

"Look, there go that fool Askari," Sekou pointed out as they passed the crowd of adoring fans. "What y'all want to do, serve him or what?"

"Sekou," said Lapeace pointedly, "you still on that bullshit? We already hollered about that, let it ride, homie."

"I mean, damn, nigga standin' right there. We could just reach out and touch him with a little something, Peace."

"Sekou, you ain't stupid, homie. Why you acting like that? Cuz, you killin' me. Let's just post over here and watch the show."

"I'm a start callin' you Old Man Shakur, Peace," joked Sekou.

"Fuck you, Kou."

"Naw," Sekou said, rushing his sentence out. "Fo' real. 'Cause yo' ass done got too politically correct, serious. It's not very gangsterish of you, homie, really."

Sitting down in one of the overstuffed plush lobby sofas, Lapeace answered, "Call me what you want loc, but you'll never get to call me stupid. Let that man live and breathe. Besides, I thought you was the total Askari fan, Kou?"

"You know what, Lapeace," stated Sekou, sitting on the end of the sofa facing Lapeace over a glass coffee table, "you got me altogether twisted homie."

"Oh?" answered Lapeace with a raised eyebrow.

"Killa—yeah, you do. See, homie, I'm no 'fan' as you seem to think. I'm an admirer of his lyrics and the way he can put our lifestyle, trials, and tribulations into the art form of rap, but I'm no fan. I'm not caught up on him, or infatuated by his lifestyle. Why should I be, it's obvious from his lyrics that we are going through the same struggles. Why would I want to be infatuated with someone like me? Ah, Peace, you ain't even hearing what I'm saying."

"No, no," cautioned Lapeace with his hand raised, index finger extended, "I am. I just never heard it put like that. Which says a lot. I can both feel and appreciate that, homie."

"Well, that's how I feel. I dig the way he expresses our situations, being young, black, male, outlaws, and grinders in the west. He paints the clearest picture of our plight, to me. That's my connection. I could care less *who* speaks the truth, I want to hear it."

"Awright, awright," Maniac butted in to quake the politics, "y'all gettin' too deep into this shit. Nigga just make good music. That's it, really. Besides, the debate is over, ol' boy just walked out. Probably on his way to get some pussy, which is where *we* should be," he added in frustration.

"I got pussy in the land and can wait to get some," said Lapeace stubbornly, not liking to be interrupted nor having missed another opportunity to speak with Askari. He perhaps could have turned him on to some Panthers who knew his parents and could have taught him about their lives prior to their deaths. Goodness knew he wasn't getting that information from Aunt Pearl. And he felt a real void there in his life. He felt the emptiness there and craved some knowledge on his bloodline. This he told no one, but lived with the void daily, monthly, yearly. He felt a kindred spirit with Askari as a Shakur and he had to admit it felt good being acknowledged by him as one. It was, after all, an exclusive, almost esoteric club. A spiritual and cultural union of those women and men, boys and girls who are supposed to be totally down for fundamental social change. But he'd missed his opportunity to even get a number on Askari. For these two Shakurs had fallen, indeed been duped, into an abstract struggle that pitted one against the other for reasons so vague and inexplicable that the mere thought of *why* brought a screaming headache.

"Well, I got pussy in the land too," said Sekou getting up from his seat, "but I'm tryin' to score some in Vegas too. So I'll be back."

Sekou left, followed by Maniac, as Lapeace sat and thought over the numbers he'd observed on his pager. The numbers 14-1-23. A simple enough combination of numbers but a loaded set no less. These numbers had great significance to Lapeace. He caught up with Sekou and borrowed his cell phone. He called Tashima. She answered on the third ring.

"Hey, sexy woman."

"Hello sexy man, how are you?"

"I'm straight. Just thought I call to tell you I love you. And to relay a few other things. Like—"

"I saw the fight," interrupted Tashima. "So if that's it . . ."

"Nooo," cooed Lapeace, "that's not it."

"Oh well, *excuse* me," Shima said with feigned indignity.

"I heard from Safi about the concert," said Lapeace softly and with a sense of confidentiality.

"Uh-huh," Shima uttered in hopes of some good news. She even crossed her fingers.

"No arrest warrant was the news. That's it, that's all."

"Well, Mr. Sexy, that is the best news I've heard all day. I am relieved to hear it. I truly am." Tashima sighed her relief.

"Yeah, me too. Maybe our luck is changing. We could use it. Oh, I know what else. I met Askari—well, briefly and under less than desirable circumstances."

"Oh? What happened? Did Sekou rush up on him and start flowin' his rhymes?"

"No, nothin' of the sort. You know how I am about these phones. I'll run it all down to you tomorrow when we get back. How's A.P.?"

"Fine, laying up here asleep. She and I had a big meal of pizza from Domino's and watched the fight. I was looking for you in the audience."

"Didn't see me, huh?"

"Nope. Saw Simon, Wazuri, Askari, and a few others. But not you. And you should know I was breakin' my neck."

"We were in the cut. Good seats but obviously not like Death Row."

"Well, you had front-row seats in that section had you taken these tickets I have."

"I know, but we left in sort of a rush, you know?"

"Don't I! I barely got a kiss. But seriously, I miss you and will be glad when you are here again."

"Tomorrow, aight?"

"Aight Babes. I'll see you then, 'kay?"

"Yep. Good night, love."

"Good night."

Bingo, Blain, and Blister never went back to the Luxor. They went over to a home of one of the Pirus they'd met after they'd followed them out of the MGM's lobby once the stomping of Baby Lane had ceased. Askari entertained all with his wild antics and hyped-up demeanor. Flossing around the mansion macking on chicks and exchanging anecdotes with fellow Bloods. Nothing seemed out of the ordinary. It was just another night living the thug life. Treated as confederates they enjoyed wine, women, and song until at last they'd decided to caravan in their limo along with fourteen or so other luxury cars packed with Pirus and Death Row members to Club 662. The club was operated, indeed owned, in some part by Death Row Records CEO, Simon Knowles. So the limo carrying Bingo, Blain, and Blister fell in tow on Flamingo behind the red Lincoln Navigator carrying Lil Flame and four other gun-toting mob Pirus.

Blain sparked a blunt, Blister popped two ecstasy pills, and Bingo checked the slide on the burner. No one was paying attention to the sights when the limo slowed to a floating halt. No one paid any attention to the white Cadillac coupe as it crept up along the luxury caravan of Bloods in the gutter lane.

At the crossroads of Koval and Flamingo the white coupe came to a deadly stop. The passenger, a familiar face, peered out in stark recognition and naked aggression. Simultaneously a young female, an adoring fan, who was standing at the corner of the intersection waiting for the light to change beamed seductively at Askari over the hood of the white caddie. She could have sworn Askari was looking right at her. The woman raised her hand to wave when the first barrage of deadly bullets slammed into Askari's chest. It all happened so breathtakingly fast, yet so menacingly slow and all too clear. Askari was pounded unsympathetically against the leather seat while at the same time he attempted to shield his chest from the shots. Simon, she could see, ducked as much as his girth allowed and gunned the Beemer forward. The shots continued. The last she saw of Askari he'd either been thrown into the backseat by the force of the gunfire or attempted to climb back there to escape the rain of bullets. The Beemer limped out into the intersection smoking and resembling a wounded rhino. Both passenger-side tires were flat, the body destroyed by offending holes. She ran forward toward the car but was almost struck by the accelerating white Cadillac.

Reaching the passenger side of the car, peering in, too shocked to sense danger, she saw Askari laid out between the two front seats, torso twisted at an impossible angle on the backseat, his blood all over the beige interior. She didn't actually begin to scream until she saw that one of his fingers had been blown off. The white Cadillac turned right and disappeared into the Las Vegas night.

"What the fuck?" said Bingo, looking around in surprise.

"Somebody gettin' off!" Blain shouted in excitement. Bingo, strap in hand, stood up out of the sunroof and scanned the scene. He noticed Simon's black BMW with a flat tire on the opposite side of the street smoking badly.

"Blood, it's the homies, come on!" Bingo leaped from the limo and, followed by Blain, Blister, and a great many others, ran up to the corner. By then, as if on cue, police on bikes and undercover agents were on the scene. Askari lay in the car shot up and bleeding badly. He was unconscious as Simon began to take off his jewelry. Innocent bystanders and fans were wailing. Pirus and Bloods alike were distraught and issuing threats against the shooters—who they immediately said was Baby Lane and the South Side Compton Crips. Everyone was stunned. Soon the ambulance came and took Askari and Simon to the hospital. The caravan followed dutifully. The night's festivities celebrating Tyson's victory over Golden came to an abrupt end.

Lapeace was sitting alone in the lobby because Sekou and Maniac had scored two females and were in the suite presumably getting some, when a trio of young females came in sobbing loudly and mumbling uncontrollably about Askari just having been "shot to pieces" up the street.

Lapeace, not being able to believe what the hysterical females were babbling about, ran out of the hotel lobby and into the valet's square. There he was met by many more people who conveyed the gist of what they believed to be the shooting to pieces of Askari. His heart raced and his blood boiled so hotly his ears were flooded with the sounds of the ocean. He'd begun to trot to where the crowds seemed to be coming from. But the tide of the sentiment had grown a bit ugly as people began to utter about the Crips, that Askari and Simon had been gunned down by Crips on a drive-by. After hearing this several times and remembering that melee at the MGM, Lapeace turned back and headed for the Luxor.

Once in the lobby he used the in-house phone to call the suite. He told Sekou they had a G-3 code, meaning *drop everything,* and that he'd be up in a minute. Sekou, ever the faithful, rushed the females out against Maniac's youthful protests and got dressed. By the time Lapeace reached the suite Sekou was pacing the floor in anticipation.

Sekou let Lapeace in. Lapeace pushed past him and went straight to the remote.

"Gotta turn the news on," he said, fumbling with the buttons and surfing the channels but finding nothing.

"Why, what's up—what's the G-3?" Sekou screamed in confusion. Maniac was just coming out of Lapeace's room.

"Askari and Simon got shot up just now!" Lapeace blurted out and stunned Sekou into silence.

"You bullshittin'? How . . . I mean— Did you do it?" stammered Maniac.

"Hell naw, fool. They say some Crips did it, though."

"Oh shit," acknowledged Maniac. "Them Compton fools musta got back. Is they dead?"

"I don't know, Yac. That's why I wanted to see if it was on the news. Man, it's people all out front, up and down the streets. It's crazy."

"Man," spoke Sekou finally, as if through a fog, "is Askari dead, Lapeace? Tell me the truth."

"Sekou, you are buggin' third. I just said I don't know nothin' but what I heard in the—"

"Here it go, right here!" Maniac shouted, pointing at the news.

"*We are learning some sketchy details coming in now about the drive-by ambush of Death Row CEO Simon Knowles and the well-known rapper Askari Shakur. It is being reported at this hour that Mr. Knowles has been wounded in the head and is in stable condition. Mr. Shakur, however, is in very critical condition and is undergoing surgery right now in an all-out attempt to save his life. Again, this is all we know at this hour and will update you as we get the details. This is Shannon Wright reporting . . .*"

"Wow, this is a trip, huh?" Maniac said, staring at the screen. He'd turned the volume down but couldn't tear his eyes away. They were showing the scene.

"Yeah, really, though. I mean damn . . ." Sekou mumbled while looking into his hands in a state of near shock. His thoughts ran zigzag in no order as he attempted to organize some perspective. It was futile. He let his thoughts run wild.

"I wanna go to the hospital, Sekou."

Sekou turned and looked at Lapeace for a long moment. He was trying to measure his sanity.

"Peace, are you *mad?* Have you forgotten that Eight Tray Gangstas are a chapter of the Crips? Can you imagine what it—"

"*I am a Shakur!*" Lapeace blurted out, cutting off Sekou and again stunning his road dog into silence. Lapeace himself stood reeling from his outburst and didn't know which way to turn.

"Well, I think we should bail back to the land tonight. We should bail out as soon as possible. Them Brim cats *know* we in town. Them cats flame and that other dude, *know* we in *this* hotel, on *this* floor. We only got one gun. Think about what I'm saying, Peace!" Sekou was using a calm soothing voice.

Lapeace paced and contemplated the situation. His heart ached in a mysterious way. It hurt as it did in the late 1980s, when death was new to him. When he didn't really know how to channel the pain and frustration of having a friend, a teammate, shot up. His only recourse then, as he saw it, was revenge: my misery, he remembered, *loves company*.

"Okay, Kou, let's move back to the land. While I'm feeling a certain way, I know in my heart of hearts that what you are sayin' is right. With emotions of everyone like mines, we'd get mopped at that hospital. So let's get up out this bitch and get back on dry land."

"Now that's gangsta. Besides, we can do *whatever* better from our own turf, feel me?" Sekou said while moving toward his room to gather his belongings.

"Come on, Yac. Get your shit and let's move," Lapeace coaxed. Now that the choice had been made he was pushing the line to make it a reality. Within twenty minutes they were leaving the hotel and heading toward Cali. But in terms of exit strategies they were not alone. Lil Flame, driving the red Navigator, was ordered to leave the scene immediately and head back to Compton in order to organize a riding party against the South Side Crips. Along with him was sent Blister. Bingo lent Blister to the cause on behalf of the Brims in a show of unity. Besides, they didn't want him running around in Las Vegas on a jacking spree, especially since his energy could be better utilized in killing Crips. They'd left Las Vegas an hour before Lapeace, Sekou, and Maniac.

On Highway 15, the fastest way west to California from Nevada, Sekou drove at a moderate pace, not wanting to be pulled over by Highway Patrol officers who often lay in the cut along seemingly deserted stretches of roads hoping to catch speeders. They had Tupac on at full blast. Mirrors were vibrating both inside and out of Sekou's truck.

"Now that I'm lost and I'm weary, so many tears, I'm suicidal so don't stand near me, my every move is a calculated step to bring me closer to embrace an early death. Now there's nothin' left. There was no mercy on the streets, I couldn't rest, I'm barely standin' 'bout to go to pieces screamin' peace."

Tupac's phenomenal lyrics rained through the cab of the truck like deep gospel in a southern church at midmorning on a Sunday. No one spoke. Each let themselves be enveloped by the word. They banged the whole *Me Against the World* CD and then began *All Eyez on Me* just past Whiskey Pete's, which signaled the borderline between Cali and Nevada. Sekou could see, off to the right a half mile ahead, a pair of hazard lights blinking.

Sekou kept his same speed as the hazard lights became brighter and more pronounced. Two people were standing out behind the vehicle and one was waving his arms in an attempt to flag down some passing motorist. Their truck had a flat and on top of that the driver had locked the keys inside. Sekou slowed a bit as they passed. One of the stranded men then lit a cigarette and Sekou saw his face as clear as day, Blister from Brim.

"Whoa," Sekou said and lowered the music by remote. This broke Lapeace's and Maniac's spiritual trance. Sekou pulled over to a stop. He said nothing to either Lapeace or Maniac. He popped the stash spot, retrieved the burner, and told Lapeace and Maniac to "sit tight."

Sekou trotted back to the red Navigator with the burner held behind his right leg, finger on the trigger. Lil Flame and Blister, not knowing Sekou's truck, thanked their blessing for some help out there on that desert highway. They began to walk along the side of the road on the passenger side of the truck. Sekou met them just as they came around the front, uttering their thanks.

Neither knew what hit them as Sekou dumped them out with skill and a prejudice borne only in war. Having terminated their existence Sekou jogged back to his truck, put it in drive, and slowly pulled back out onto the two-lane highway.

"What the fuck?" questioned Lapeace, looking back over the seat, not knowing the deal.

"Blister, the Brim nigga with Bingo earlier, and that midget Piru fool, Lil Flame. Popped the Blister, blew out the Flame. *Gangsta's movin'*, end of story."

"Oh shit!" shouted Maniac in total amazement and elevated excitement. "That's what I'm talkin' 'bout, nigga. Handle that shit, fool. You did that, homie."

"Right, right," acknowledged Sekou, accepting his compliment from the young homie.

"Man," said Lapeace, eyeing Sekou with a mixture of admiration and envy. "Why you ain't let me get one, Kou?"

"Sorry, boss," feigned Sekou, "only one gun. Plus, I saw them first. Ahh, I feel so much better now." He sighed and turned the Tupac back up.

"How many brothas fell victim to the streets, rest in peace young nigga, there's a heaven for a G, be a lie if I told you that I never thought of death. My nigga we the last ones left but life goes on."

They came into the L.A. city limits at 2:45 a.m. The streets were all but deserted as they pushed up Manchester Avenue toward Denker. They made their right and took Denker to 71st and dropped off Maniac. He promised to holler at them the following morning. Sekou insisted that Lapeace drop him off since they were already in the hood, keep his truck, and scoop him up the following morning. Having done that, Lapeace pushed his way up to Tashima's and pulled the Explorer all the way to the back just behind her Lexus.

Hearing the truck, Tashima rushed out onto the porch in her robe and hugged Lapeace fiercely when he stepped up to her. He held her firmly too and put his head into her tangle of braids and breathed her scent in deeply.

"Damn, I'm so relieved you all right."

"Yeah," sighed Lapeace, "me too, Babes. Me, too."

"Let's get our asses inside before we freeze to death."

Lapeace looked in on Aunt Pearl and Ramona, who was lodged in the service porch area. He and Tashima then retired to her room and he filled her in on all the Las Vegas activity. That is, with the exception of the roadside assistance that was provided on the way back.

They made serious, desperate love with every limb and appendage of their bodies. It was a needed remedy against a reality now fraught with so much uncertainty that each moment seemed borrowed against bad credit. Time seemed a stalking reaper.

It was 8:15 a.m. Thursday morning when Lazy pulled out of his yard and came to a halt at the corner of 70th and Denker. He looked both ways and pushed across 70th and up to Harvard and turned left. There, in the middle of the block, he saw Tiny Outlaw, Nutt Case, and Lil Sodici. They were walking at a brisk pace toward Florence Avenue. He blew his horn three times in acknowledgment and kept it moving. The black-and-white CRASH unit patrol car came down 71st and made a right turn directly behind Lazy's Acura. Seeing the action, he swore to himself but felt no immediate threat since he wasn't riding dirty. He was on his way, actually, to Tiny Monster's house so they could go to breakfast. He had nothing on him but cash.

The patrol officers lit him up with their flashers beckoning him to pull over. He pushed across Florence and came to rest just before an alleyway backing a vacant lot. He sat idle while they did their usual thing. One approached the car on the driver's side while his partner hung back on the passenger side, hand on his service weapon, eyes watching the driver.

"What's happening?" the lead officer spoke to Lazy. He acted as if the stop was nothing more than a routine attitude check.

"What you stop me for?" asked Lazy in an offended tone, knowing his registration, insurance, and license were all current and up to par. No dope, no burner, no warrants. Not even another gangster in the car with him. They had to treat him like a normal citizen.

"Let me see your license and registration, please, sir."

"Yeah, I got all that," Lazy said while reaching for his wallet and taking out his license. "But why was I pulled over?"

"Registration, please," said the Amerikan without answering Lazy's question.

"Thank you," the CRASH cop said when Lazy handed him the registration. The registration was not really needed since before they'd come to a complete stop they'd already run his plates. They even knew that he had a current license.

"Sir, it'll just be a minute while I run your name for wants and warrants. Relax and I'll be back in a minute." At that the officer walked back to his patrol unit and sat behind the wheel. Instead of punching in Lazy's info on the unit computer, the officer dialed Sweeney's cell number from his own.

"We got your boy over here on Florence and Harvard. Southwest corner. What's your ETA?"

"Good. Um, seven minutes, I'm en route," said Sweeney, clicking his tongue and winking over at Mendoza.

"We're on our way to a traffic stop on Florence. They've stopped a member of the Eight Trays and this same guy, I was given a tip about, who they've stopped, is supposed to be armed," Sweeney spoke while speeding up Florence Avenue westward.

"I don't get it, though, John. Why are we going to a traffic stop for an ordinary armed banger?" asked Mendoza while beginning his left-side tug on his mustache.

"Help," said Sweeney. "This same guy is supposed to have pertinent information on the Cren mass. He's supposed to be one of the few who's actually seen the tape."

"Oh yeah?" asked Mendoza, a bit perplexed about the perfect fitting of circumstances.

"Yep," Sweeney gloated, "here we are." Sweeney maneuvered the Crown Victoria up behind the patrol unit.

"Let's see what we got," said Mendoza as they exited their vehicle. The lead patrol officer greeted the pair, gave Sweeney Lazy's license and registration, and told them he was clean.

"Have you conducted a vehicle search?" asked Sweeney, peering at Lazy watching them in his side rearview.

"No. Stopped him, ran him—which as I stated was clean—and called you as I was ordered."

"Good. We'll need your backup as we conduct a search of the vehicle."

"But sir," objected the CRASH officer. "We actually have no probable cause to do a search of the vehicle."

"This guy is a known gang member, right?" asked Sweeney, a bit perturbed by the patrolman's line of questioning.

"Yeah, right. He is in Cal-Gangs index," answered the patrolman.

"That there, buddy, is quite enough. Gang members are known to carry guns and drugs. Plus—"

"Sir, this man has a valid driver's license and was not—"

"Look here you damn softy," threatened Sweeney through clenched teeth. "Whose fucking side are you on mister? I don't give a fuck if he has a note from Chief Willie Williams. You pull him out of that damn car and put him in cuffs while my partner and I conduct a fucking search. Is that clear?"

"Okay," sighed the patrolman. He turned to leave and added, "your balls in court, not mine."

"Can you believe this guy?" Sweeney asked Mendoza, who chose not to answer at that point. The patrolman asked Lazy to exit the vehicle. He did so with some profane protests and some deadly eye contact with Sweeney and Mendoza.

First they searched the interior, which turned up zilch. The patrolman looked on at the odd spectacle of two gold shield homicide detectives conducting a vehicle search during an ordinary traffic stop, which itself was questionable. Then they popped the trunk and found nothing but athletic equipment, including a basketball and an athletic supporter.

Having come up empty, which began to irritate Mendoza, Sweeney suggested they search under the car. He'd take the passenger side and Mendoza would take the driver's side. They began at the rear, down on their knees. Lazy stood in cuffs on the sidewalk and looked on in mild amusement as they crawled their way along the undercarriage of his car. He knew he wasn't burning, so why sweat it. He just watched their antics.

"Hey, partner," said Sweeney. "I got nothing over here." He was standing up, brushing off his clothes.

"Holy shit," exclaimed Mendoza. "Gun!" Things flew into motion then. Mendoza bent farther to retrieve the gun. Lazy rushed forward in an attempt to kick Sweeney but the patrolman next to him grabbed his cuffs in one hand and the back of his neck in one swift motion and slammed Lazy hard to the concrete.

"Man, hell naw," he protested through blood and pain, "that ain't my muthafuckin' gun. Fuck y'all. Y'all set me up."

"You shut the fuck up, Dawson," Sweeney threatened, standing over Lazy proudly. "We got your ass now. What's this, your third strike?"

"Fuck you racist-ass dogs. You set me up."

Mendoza showed the weapon to the others and then cleared the chamber, locked back the slide, and stuck a pencil in the breach. He then secured the pistol in the trunk of his car and helped Sweeney to load the prisoner into the unmarked Crown Victoria. Seeing that he'd be transported to 77th Division in the detective's car, Lazy ceased to protest. He figured that if they'd set him up with a heat they'd very well conduct a way to kill him. He held his tongue.

"Have the vehicle impounded and held for investigation," ordered Sweeney before climbing into the driver's side.

"Sure thing," said the patrolman and then more to himself, "fuckin' asshole."

Sweeney and Mendoza said nothing to Lazy as they traversed northward on Western Avenue to the makeshift trailers that served as their station house while the new, fortresslike 77th Division station prison was being constructed on the original site. They pulled into the lot and unloaded the prisoner.

15

Lazy sat cuffed to a chair in the interview room. Corked paneling decorated the walls on all sides. This was used as soundproofing against the possible beating of unruly or uncooperative prisoners. He pretty much knew the drill. *Fuckin' pigs,* he thought looking around, *set me up.*

In walked Sweeney and Mendoza, holding notepads and steaming coffee in Styrofoam cups.

"Hey Lazy, can we get you anything?" asked Mendoza.

"Naw, I'm straight," mumbled Lazy with a "fuck you" attitude.

"Oh, is that right? Well, by the time you're released you may be gay," said Sweeney disrespectfully.

"Man," responded Lazy, "I ain't trying to hear that ol' shit."

"Okay then," Mendoza interviewed, playing the good cop, "let's see . . . Well, you know your situation. I mean you are aware of the charge. It's a firearms possession charge. And with your record, it's likely that you won't be able to bargain your way out of this one."

"Where's my car?" asked Lazy.

"We are holding it for investigation. It's here at the station," noted Mendoza.

"Man that's bullshit and y'all know it. What kind of fool carries a gun taped under the wheel well?"

"Okay," said Sweeney, writing on his pad. "So, you *did* know where the gun was, huh?"

"I saw him," indicating Mendoza, "bring it from there."

"Look," said Sweeney, putting his pen down, "we could care less about a rat-ass gun charge, really. You can help yourself, really, by helping us. We need some information and no one has to know it came from you. It's just something we need corroborated. We can make this little gun charge disappear. You can be back on the street today."

"Man, you're not telling me the truth," Lazy prodded.

"No, we are. But you see, the deal is this. You'll have to agree to help us *before* we tell you what it is. It's sort of like a blind trust thing. You see, we don't want it to get out about what we're working on. So the choice is yours. Three strikes or a hot meal at home tonight. Sleeping in your own bed tonight or on the floor in county intake. What's it going to be?"

"That's not my gun, man. Y'all know that, too," Lazy pleaded, trying to hold on to his last vestiges of strength, but he felt himself giving way. A dead bang gun charge was a definite three strikes.

"*Fuck man . . .*," Lazy said, rolling his eyes toward the ceiling. "Aight, man, what is it?"

"Do we have a deal? You help us, we make your problems go away. Deal?" Sweeney asked.

"I said yes, man, yes," exerted Lazy, but his steam was losing pressure fast.

"Here's the thing. We are investigating the big shooting last month on Crenshaw. We believe we know the principal players but we need some substantiation. We were lead to believe that you were there."

"There, how? I ain't do no shootin', if that's what you heard?"

"No, that's not what we are saying we heard. We believe you were there with your car club. Is that right?" Mendoza asked.

"Yep, that's right. So?"

"Well, did anything happen?" Sweeney asked, poised to write.

"Our cars were shot up by them bitch-ass Brims, that's what."

"Anything else . . . something of greater importance?"

"Oh, that shit between Anyhow and Lapeace?"

Sweeney almost dropped his pen. Beads of sweat formed immediately over the top of his head. Mendoza tugged with abandon on his mustache.

"Hold on a minute, Greg. I'm going to tape this. All right, go ahead," cajoled Sweeney, turning the tape recorder toward Lazy.

"Well, I mean, everybody saw it. They both came up in the muscle cars. Lapeace was in his black SS Monte Carlo. Anyhow—"

"You're talking about Alvin Harper, right?"

"Yeah."

"And Lapeace is Lapeace Shakur. Is that right?"

"Yes."

"Go on," coached Sweeney, "you're doing good."

"Anyhow was in a green Grand National. They started bustin' at each other. And then all hell broke loose. Explosions and shit."

"Okay, now we have been led to believe that there is some sort of tape showing some people?" Mendoza asked anxiously.

"Yep, that's the truth. I seen it."

Lapeace, Aunt Pearl, and Tashima sat at the kitchen table enjoying a late breakfast. The news was on and inadvertent pieces of info were being transmitted about the medical condition of Askari. Various speculations as to who may have been responsible peppered most broadcasts. Each time an update came on Lapeace was especially attentive. He sat stoically through the reporters' comments and speculations.

"You want more eggs, Babes?" Tashima asked, seeing he'd demolished his pile of scrambled eggs.

"No, love," Lapeace answered, "I'm good, thank you."

"Aunt Pearl, can I get you anthing?"

Lapeace looked across the table at Aunt Pearl and hoped she wasn't going to ask for a drink. She looked up from her plate and into the eyes of Lapeace.

"Yes, thank you darling, I'll have some more orange juice. I've forgotten how good it tastes straight." She smiled coyly across at Lapeace. He smiled broadly back at her. Tashima felt the moment and smiled down into her plate.

"Aunt Pearl," Lapeace began polishing off his potatoes, "I met Askari while I was up there in Vegas yesterday."

"Oh?"

"Yeah. He asked me a curious thing when I told him my name. Well, at first there was a bit of static . . ."

"What do you mean by *static?*" Aunt Pearl asked probingly.

"Aw, nothin' much," Lapeace began evasively. "You know, some young black male stuff."

"Confusion, you mean?"

"Pretty much. Well, it wasn't goin' too good, right?"

"Uh-huh."

"And then when I said my name, my *whole* name, he seemed to change a bit. Almost like I'd hit a nerve."

"Hmm," Aunt Pearl sighed, nervously busying herself with her plate and silverware, and she wouldn't make eye contact with Lapeace.

"Yeah, and then, as if nothing or no one else mattered he focused his attention on me and then—and check this out Aunt Pearl—he asked me *who* my people were. And, really, I didn't know what he meant. I mean, I was standin' there with Sekou and another homie of mine, who, to me, were *my people,* you know?"

"Uh-huh," Aunt Pearl acknowledged but still refused to look at Lapeace, who by now in his narrative was standing up and getting excited.

"So then . . . well, he asked me who my bloodline was. That's what he was askin'. And I just told him about Mom and Dad, you know, about the things you've taught me about their affiliation with politics, Black Panthers and stuff. I told him . . . and all this tumbled out, that Dad was BLA, Moms was a Panther. Dad died while a prisoner of war. Moms died during my birth. And I told him about what I knew of his bloodline. I don't know . . ." He trailed off.

"What is it, Lapi?" Aunt Pearl questioned.

"Well, it's just when he, at the end, he . . . he called me 'Shakur.' It felt different. Not like when a teacher in school or even a police in the street would say my name. I felt a connection with him, Aunt Pearl. I felt, like . . ."

"You belonged to something deep?" said Aunt Pearl looking up into Lapeace's brown eyes and holding his stare.

"Yeah, Aunt Pearl, just like that. At the same time, I felt lost in a sea of mystery and a spiritual . . . *hole.* I mean, it's hard to explain. It's just a feelin' I know, but it felt strange and exciting and—"

"Scary?" she offered.

"Oh, you felt this way before?" he asked Aunt Pearl. His eyes were pleading for acknowledgment. He needed to be consoled and in some way confirmed. He was speaking now from his heart.

"Lately in my . . . my *condition,* yes I feel like that *all* the time, Lapi. And I'm so sorry that you are experiencing this, baby." Aunt Pearl's eyes began to water and overflow.

"But it's not a sad feeling to me. It's a need to know sort of feeling. Like a piece of me is missing. Aunt Pearl," Lapeace turned his chair backward, sat down near Aunt Pearl, and leaned toward her, "I need you to help me on this. Teach me what I am supposed to know . . . please?"

"Your legacy, you mean?"

"All that. I need to know, please."

"Why don't we go into the living room where we can sit comfortably," offered Tashima while scooping up the plates and moving them to the side of the sink.

"Shakur . . . ," began Aunt Pearl, seated comfortably on the couch, a cup of hot coffee balanced on her thigh, "means 'the thankful.' The line begins with Baba Shakur, who was blind. He lived in New York. The name came from the East Coast."

"What language is it?" asked Lapeace on the edge of his seat.

"It is of Arabic origin, but has Afrikan roots. The Arabs, no great friends of ours, usually spell theirs S-H-A-K-O-O-R. Baba Shakur had two sons, Lumumba and Zayd, who started the New York Panthers. They took in as a family member Mutulu."

"Askari's stepfather?"

"Yes. When the civil rights movement gave way to the Black Liberation movement, Lumumba, Zayd, and Mutulu were leading figures. Black Panther Party members first and then fighters in the clandestine ranks of the Amistad collective of the Black Liberation Army.

"Mutulu dated Amira and she became a Shakur. Zayd was with Assata and she became Shakur. Mutulu begot Sekina and Mooreme. And Askari, whose father was a non-Panther named Gaisi, became a Shakur. Zayd was killed in action during a police action in 1973. Assata and Sundiata Acoli were also there and were captured. Assata Shakur was liberated from a New Jersey prison by Mutulu and his Revolutionary Armed Task Force on November 2, 1979."

"Damn, they was puttin' it down, huh?"

"Baby, you don't know the half," said Aunt Pearl with a wave of her hand and a roll of her eyes. Shima too, was amazed at the pedigree.

"Your father, Tafuta, was a fierce combatant too. He and your mother, Asali, became Shakurs through me." Aunt Pearl took a deep sip of coffee.

"You?" asked Lapeace, confounded, eyes wide open.

"Hell yes, me. What you thought, Lapi? I was always like . . . like this?"

"Well . . . I just never thought you were a Shakur. I always saw Jackson on the mail. On school papers and stuff."

"That's my *slave* name. But baby I am a *Shakur*. I ain't have to go to no Amerikan court to ask them if I can change my name. Ask them if I can be Afrikan. They didn't ask us if we wanted to be a *Jackson* or *Williams,* you hear me?"

"Yeah, that's pretty slick."

"Not slick—right. A birthright. It is a *human right*."

"Go on, Aunt Pearl!" Tashima coached.

"No, I'm serious, Amerikans got their nerve on this name thing, really."

"Aunt Pearl, do you have a first name, too?"

"No, my mother named me Pearl and I'm satisfied with that. Anyway, in 1981 Lumumba was assassinated in New Orleans. Assata went to Cuba in 1986 and Mutulu was captured here in L.A. by the Joint Terrorist Task Force. He was given sixty years for a one-point-six-million-dollar Brinks expropriation in Nyack, New York. And the liberation of Assata. Things got real hot for the movement around this time. But the Shakurs continued to prosper. Talib, Abdul, Sanyika, and Askari all out and about writing, rapping, moving, and shaking. But without a movement our young soldiers are swimming against the current in blood alley."

"Oh, hold on," said Tashima turning up the television.

". . . has undergone an operation to remove a lung and is currently on a respirator to aid his breathing. It is being reported at this hour that a vigil is being held around Shakur's bedside as he struggles to hold on to his life. Reporting live, I'm Gina Gideon."

"Poor baby. This is so sad. I don't know what the hell to think about any of this."

"It's gonna be all right, Aunt Pearl. Finish telling me about . . . *us,*" Lapeace said quickly, anxious to hear connecting historical threads about his bloodline.

Sweeney and Mendoza sat in familiar seats in front of Captain Killingsworth. He was leaning back in his chair, both hands clasped behind his bald head, eyes glued to the ceiling. They were listening to Lazy's taped conversation.

"Yep, that's the truth. I seen it."

"And what did you see on the tape?"

"I saw the whole thing. Lapeace shootin' at Anyhow and Anyhow shootin' at Lapeace."

"Is either one of the shooters' faces clear on the tape?"

"Both of 'em. I could see both clearly."

"Do you recognize anyone on this six-pack photo lineup?"

"Number four is Lapeace."

"And on this one here?"

"Number two is Anyhow."

"You are pointing at Alvin Harper, number two?"

"Yes."

Sweeney switched off the recorder. Captain Killingsworth leaned up to the desk, the chair squeaking in protest.

"You two think this Dawson character is reliable?"

"Well, he *has* substantiated the existence of the tape. *Has,* unlike the other CI, seen the tape. He claims to be able to actually identify Shakur and Harper on the tape. Sir, this is a corroborating direct link. This is an actual eyewitness."

"Hmmm." Captain Killingsworth pondered. "Okay, bring this dirtbag in. We'll hold a press conference at four should your efforts prove futile. Well, go on out there and round him up,"

Killingsworth said while shooing Sweeney and Mendoza out of his office.

"Oh and Sweeney, Mendoza?" he called in afterthought.

"Yeah captain," they said in unison.

"Good job."

"Thank you sir," they responded in unison again.

From Century Boulevard to 66th Street, from Van Ness to Vermont, the entire Eight Tray Gangster hood was saturated with patrol units combing the streets for Lapeace. Black-and-white unmarked cars, homicide and CRASH. Anyone on the streets within this radius was stopped, shown a picture of Lapeace, and asked a series of questions. All movement was either harassed or suppressed.

With this sort of heat on the hood it didn't take long for Lapeace's pager to go off. Having learned the police were looking for him, he immediately called his attorney Safi. He was instructed to lay low until he could find out what the situation was. Lapeace took a call from Sekou, who was distraught over the prowling police. Lapeace replaced the phone and fell back onto the couch. He'd have to tell Aunt Pearl about the situation eventually. He'd just learned of his legacy, was just brought up to speed on his folks, and now this. He decided to ask Shima her advice. Just yesterday he had no warrant; today he was a wanted man. Fuck.

"Tashima," Lapeace called down the hall.

"Yeah love," she answered, fastening the last rubber band on Aunt Pearl's hair. "Come up here a minute, will you?"

"Here I come."

Lapeace led her to the black sofa. She knew something was wrong by the pinched look on his face.

"I need to tell Aunt Pearl the deal on this case, Shima."

"Why you calling it a 'case' now? You acting like . . ." She faltered in her speech. She'd stumbled because in his eyes she could see it. His pupils had turned to bars.

"Noooo," she said and turned away. "Not this, Lapeace. Not now."

"They all in the hood showing my picture, jackin' everything movin.' I talked to Safi and he's going to get back to me when he sees what's up."

"This ain't right, Babes. Hey, why don't you go to Cuba like Assata? I can settle my business affairs and join you later. We could live free over there. I didn't want to leave before but now we may have to."

"Naw, remember what Aunt Pearl said, Assata is a *political* exile. She was in an organized formation, which was at war with the U.S. government. My shit is criminal. Fidel ain't gonna let no criminals come over there. That's dead. Besides, I ain't tryin' to run. I was defending myself."

"Yeah, I know, but I just can't stand the thought of you being in jail. Have you ever even been in jail?"

"A few times. Just the county, then I bailed out. I ain't no jailbird, though. What time is it?"

"Two-forty-seven, why?" Shima asked.

"Just wanna keep up on the time."

Shima's phone rang again and it was Sekou. He gave Lapeace a number of a little homie who wanted Lapeace to call him. It was important, the homie had said. So Lapeace took the number and found it was to Tiny Outlaw, one of his favorite little North Side soldiers.

"What's up, Outlaw, how you doin' homie?"

"I'm straight, cuz. Thanks for callin'."

"No doubt. What's crackin'?"

"Eh look, I know you know they on you, right?"

"Yeah, I'm up."

"Well, I don't know if this is anything, but early this mornin' me, Lil Sodi, and Nutt Case was movin' on foot through the North and saw one time pull over the homie Lazy, who live on Seventieth, right?"

"Right."

"And we just laid in the cut and watched. Well after CRASH had him fo' a minute, another one time pull up, a narc car, like homicide or some shit."

"Yeah?"

"Hell yeah, but check it: they then pull cuz out the hoop, cuff him, and begin to search the hoop."

"Which car, the lolo?"

"Naw, the green AC. Anyway, cuz, one time the detective, a bald-headed fat-ass white boy and I think a hat dancer, lookin' all through cuz shit, but find nothing. Then, the hat dancer fool reach under the front fender and, cuz, on me, pull out a burner cuz . . ."

"Like that?" Lapeace asked.

"Like *that!* Pulled it out of the part where the wheel at. Look like that bitch was taped up under there. Anyway, the homie see that shit, cuz, and try to rush the white boy detective, but the CRASH fool slam the homie on the ground."

"Damn, that's crazy. But Outlaw, why you telling me this? I mean, what this gotta do with me?"

"Well, here's the thing. Cuz ain't see us, right?"

"Right."

"And we seen the burner and the detectives. Seen cuz go to jail. Now the one time looking for you and guess what?"

"What?"

"I *just* seen that nigga Lazy mashin' through the turf in the green Acura!"

"No shit?" Lapeace asked incredulously.

"On *me,* homie! So I'm just lettin' you know the business, cuz. Shit don't seem right to me."

"Hell naw and that's good lookin' out, Outlaw. I appreciate that."

"You know how we do it, big homie."

"Look, swing by Sekou's, he got a stack for you, homie."

"That's gangsta, Peace. Thanks."

"No problem, Crip. Keep it movin'."

Lapeace depressed the phone button and called Sekou. He conveyed the info and Sekou swore to get on top of it. "Also," Lapeace advised, "slide the homie Outlaw—T.T.—a grand for me. I'll tighten you up when you swing by for the truck."

"I got that, don't trip."

"Thanks."

Lapeace needed to go on and let Aunt Pearl in on the goings-on. She'd not asked him nothing. Which was not inordinate. Aunt Pearl was like that.

"What is it?" asked Shima still sitting there, which caused Lapeace to be slightly startled.

"Oh shit, I forgot you was sitting here. You heard all that, huh?"

"Yeah," Shima said sadly, "I heard all of that. Now what?"

"Wait on Safi. See what the situation is."

"Hey, Peace?"

"Yeah."

"I'm in love with you. I want you to know that. I'll never let you go. No matter what."

"Come here you incredibly sexy specimen, you." Lapeace engulfed Shima in his powerful arms and hugged her to his body tightly. She stepped up on his feet and he danced her around like that for a few circles. Shima laid her head against his chest and closed her eyes, never wanting to lose this loving feeling. Lapeace held her to him and they swayed to a rhythm only their hearts could hear and feel. It was peaceful.

They were interrupted by the screaming of the phone. It was Safi. Shima sighed heavily before giving him the phone. She braced herself for the bad news.

Lapeace listened intently, eyes darting around the room, foot tapping lightly on the carpet. Shima studied him closely, hands under her chin, propping up her head like a child.

"I'll have to think about that, Safi. I'll let you know one way or another tomorrow. Okay, man, I really appreciate your work. Yeah, I'll call you tomorrow. Sure. Later."

Lapeace hung up the phone and looked at Shima.

"Should I get Aunt Pearl, Babes?" Shima asked sadly.

"Yeah, I think that'll be best. At four o'clock they're having a press conference on me."

"Did Safi tell you that?"

"Yeah." Lapeace walked to the window.

The press conference was being set up in front of Parker Center, the Los Angeles Police Department's headquarters. A desk was set up with a bank of microphones representing all television, electronic, and print media in L.A. and their affiliates across the nation. News reporters of every stripe stood fanned out from the podium and desk with recorders and stenopads ready. Camera crews were set up from network vans, trucks, and mobile homes.

The entire lawn and cement walkways in front of Parker Center were densely packed with curious onlookers and media hounds.

On cue at 4:00 p.m. sharp the chief of police Willie Williams wobbled his girth out into the L.A. sunlight in a dark blue Brooks Brothers suit. He was flanked by associate chiefs, captains, and a lesser degree of lieutenants. Sweeney and Mendoza were some paces behind him but nevertheless there.

The microphone closest to the chief bled a piercing scream until it was adjusted just so by a minion of the chief. That having been done, the chief cleared his throat and spoke to the barrage of cameras.

"Thank you all for coming. I am happy to announce today a break in the horrific case that we've all come to know as the Crenshaw massacre. The terrible circumstances, which caused the deaths of eight innocent people on the evening of August third, have crystallized under the highly specialized investigative services of LAPD personnel. To give you our findings to date is Detective John Sweeney."

Chief Williams moved his mass aside to allow for Sweeney to stand in front of the podium.

"Thank you, Chief Williams. As the chief said, we've been able to make a break in this horrendous case. We now know who both gunmen are. This is a good day for law enforcement. Next to me here is a chart showing the death flow as it occurred."

Sweeney took the cloth off the chart. At the top there were the words CRENSHAW MASSACRE. Under that were two pictures.

"The picture to the left there is of suspect Alvin Harper. He is also known as Anyhow, a known gang member of the Bloods gang. He is in custody. The second photo here to the right is the second suspect, Lapeace Shakur. He is a known Crips gang member. Mr. Shakur, we have determined, is the principal shooter who is responsible for the melee on Crenshaw last month. Mr. Shakur is being sought as we speak and is believed to be here in the Los Angeles area. We are asking for the community's help in apprehending this suspect. Please take a good look at his picture. Be advised he is considered armed and very dangerous. That is all for now, thank you."

Sweeney and Mendoza shook hands with the chief and his entourage and then left the crowd. They went through headquarters and down the elevator to the parking garage. Once inside the car Mendoza spoke frankly to Sweeney.

"You know, John. As I'm pondering things I'm beginning to smell a rat here."

"Oh yeah," answered Sweeney, maneuvering the powerful Crown Vic through the congested downtown traffic. "What's that supposed to mean?"

"Well, it's just that I was noticing the convenience of the gun on Dawson. The cozy nature of you with the rampart cowboys. Just a series of good luck breaks we've been getting here lately. I just have come to know how these cases come together and it's not at all like this."

"Jess, I don't know what to tell you. I mean—"

"Tell me the fuckin' *truth!* That's what you tell me. I'm your *fuckin' partner* for chrissakes!" Mendoza shouted and pulled furiously on his mustache.

"You need to calm down, Jess. Relax. There's nothing wrong going on. You're uptight about nothing, really. Hell, you're the one always barking about these criminals getting away with bargains for pleas—what the fuck?"

"You know damn well what I mean. Yes, fuck letting these parasites take deals on dead bang cases. I am one hundred percent against that. But also, I am a sworn public servant of this city. And what's more, John, I am a minority. And I've grown up with racism and abuses of power, wealth, and privilege perpetrated against minorities. And I may be an officer of the law, but I will not bend that law to fit a profile. I won't be a part of anything like that. You know and I know those cowboys at Rampart are filthy. And the shit going to come down on them. I don't want it to fall this way."

"Yeah, well, I don't know anything about that, Jess. I have a job to do and I am going to do that job. I am on the side of law and order. If in my capacity I have to bend a law to maintain order for the betterment of this city and its taxpaying citizens, I'm very well going to do that. Not saying I have in this case or ever before, but my goodness I will." Sweeney wiped his sweating brow.

"Well I am telling you, John, I won't." Mendoza threw a handful of ranch corn nuts into his mouth and crunched loudly.

Lapeace pressed the MUTE button on the remote and sat back on the sofa. No one said a thing. Tashima had her eyes closed but her bare foot was rubbing up and down Lapeace's lower leg. It was a good feeling, a loving touch of support and affection. Aunt Pearl had her legs crossed at the ankles and was rocking to and fro. She looked worried.

"So," Lapeace spoke and broke the awful silence, "you've heard my side and that, my dear ladies, was their side! I am, to them, a one-dimensional 'gang member.' A 'principal shooter.' Even when they say 'mister,' it's like a mockery. I was defending my life," he concluded with some determination.

"You don't have to convince us of that, Lapi. I know you are not some mad dog killer. Come here." Aunt Pearl had her arms open wide and Lapeace leaned over into her warm embrace and closed his eyes tight.

"Don't you worry 'bout them filthy ol' pigs. They've been castigatin' us since 332 B.C. Ain't nobody worried 'bout them." Aunt Pearl soothed him against her bosom.

"Peace, why don't you call Safi back and see what he says about this?"

"It'll be the same thing from earlier. He told me not to get caught up in the sensationalism of the press conference. The press conference is one thing, a court of law is another. What they ain't say is that Anyhow is brain dead . . ."

"What?" Aunt Pearl asked confounded.

"Yep, he cut his wrist in a suicide attempt and lost so much blood, he had some kind of stroke. He's messed up. He's no suspect, he told them *I* was tryin' to kill *him*."

"What . . . how do you know this?" asked Aunt Pearl.

"Safi told me. Anyhow is a vegetable right now. They'll need to manufacture some witnesses. Either that or . . . " Lapeace tore off the ending of his sentence but it didn't go unnoticed by Aunt Pearl's astuteness.

"Or what, Lapi? Huh, you better go on and tell me the whole truth, baby. Or what?" she demanded

"Keep it clean, Peace," Shima counseled, looking directly at him.

"Naw, it's just that durin' the . . . course of me defending myself, some of the homies, cats from my squad, were video-filmin' the whole thing."

"Oh my goodness," gasped Aunt Pearl, "ancestors help me!"

"No, it's not *that* bad. Aunt Pearl, listen," Lapeace cautioned. "I have the tape. Nobody got it. I sent it away to a squad member in the sticks."

"The sticks?" she asked.

"Down south, Mississippi."

"The *National Territory, New Afrika,*" Aunt Pearl corrected him. She spoke with dignity.

"Yes," Lapeace conceded. "New Afrika."

"Very good. Now, what does your attorney, this Safi character, have to say?"

"He suggests I turn myself in."

"He *what?*" shouted both Tashim and Aunt Pearl in unison.

"He says it'll be better to get this on and over with. We have good grounds, he says, and plus it's best to go in on my own than to risk them killing or injuring me in a hunt. Plus, I wouldn't want to contaminate you two with all this. Goodness knows I'm going to need y'all."

"So you're actually thinking about turning yourself in, Babes? I mean, you've come to a conclusion already?" Shima asked, a bit alarmed and perturbed.

"I *am* thinkin' 'bout it, yes. I don't want to live on the run. I have a life. I don't want Bob Hope freezin' my accounts, doin' no-knock raids on your house, sweatin' your company. I can't live like that. I like to be outside in the sun. I wanna hold my children. I need to be free. Or none of this will mean shi . . . nothing."

"Damn, this is all so crazy." Tashima felt depressed.

"I know . . . I know."

Lapeace got up early on Friday. He needed to tie up all the loose ends and put his business affairs in order. Sekou came over early and they held counsel. He'd be Lapeace's go-to man in his absence. He spoke at length with his accountant and broker. He conveyed to Sekou all that needed attention. Sekou left, taking Aunt Pearl with him, against her mighty protests. It was best this way. She'd stay at his house during Lapeace's stay in the county. He'd been told by Safi not to expect a bail. Sekou had left him with a "survival kit" to take along with him. With things squared in his favor he united with Tashima in her room.

They held each other for a long, long time. Lapeace held her face in his big hands and kissed her full, delicious lips. Their tongues played lightly in each other's mouths and Lapeace's right hand rested at the curve of her neck. He manipulated her silky skin softly. They each moaned their lustful excitement. Tashima's little manicured hands found his zipper and fumbled to undo his fly. They broke their embrace and began to disrobe quickly, Lapeace down to his bare essence and Shima down to a matching pink panty and bra set. They hugged again and spoke their love for each other.

Lapeace's erection was up between Shima's breasts as she closed them together and masturbated him warmly. He grinded against her and she held her breast's tight against his swollen shaft. Unable to last much longer, Lapeace broke the embrace and peeled her out of her dainty little pink panties. He took his time over her voluptuous ass and thick, shapely legs. At her gorgeous feet she stepped out of them. He laid her on the bed and began at her feet and licked and nibbled his way up to her knees. He licked and nibbled all around her legs, paying special attention to the area behind her knees. She moaned and sighed in lust and ecstasy.

He licked her inner thighs and kissed her wonderful black skin. Before reaching her secret garden, he rolled her over and lavishly licked her shapeful cheeks. He took his time as if attempting to taste every inch of her body. He pulled apart her lovely gluts and licked and nibbled her nether world. She tasted delightful and moaned exquisitely against his magic touches. Having left a saliva trail all over her, he went for her temple, exploring gently with his sensitive tongue. Shima delighted in his technique and awareness. He was so gentle that she could not believe it. She felt his love with every touch, lick, nibble, and bite.

They made love slowly and easily. Wild and open, free and gentle. Then hard and rough, deep and strong, over and over and then over again.

At 3:45 p.m., Lapeace and Tashima laid closely in her bed. She'd not been to work in four days. So what. They touched and listened to Ramona and Kody play together outside under the window. It was quiet and peaceful. Lapeace suggested they watch the news at 4:00 p.m.

Shima got up to get refreshments and Lapeace turned to Channel 7's *Eyewitness News.* The broadcaster came on with a solemn face.

"We are getting breaking news at this hour from Las Vegas, Nevada, that rapper Askari Shakur, shot in Wednesday's drive-by ambush, has died. Doctors, it's reported, did all they could to save the injured rap star, but today their efforts were not enough. Again, actor and rapper Askari Shakur is dead at twenty-five."

Tashima came padding in and found Lapeace sitting up on the end of her bed with a steady flow of tears streaming down his dark face. His eyes were wet and sad. Putting down the lemonade on the nightstand, she rushed to his side.

"What is it, baby? Why are you cryin'?"

"Askari died today, they said. That's *fucked* up . . ."

"Oh no," Shima cried and felt the tears wall up in her eyes. "Oh, this is *so* sad. Such a loss for us. I'm so sorry, Lapeace, I really am." She held his head to hers and they cried together.

"Yeah," he said, wiping away his tears with the back of his hand, "I know . . ."

"In related news, authorities out of Devore are investigating the shooting deaths of two Bloods members along Highway Fifteen. Police say the shootings appear to be somehow related with the shooting of rapper Askari Shakur, though they refuse to say how. These deaths are also believed to be connected to a string of shootings in Compton that since the Las Vegas shooting of Shakur have left more than twelve people dead."

"Damn, a lot of people are dying behind this shit. Whew," said Tashima.

"Yeah, it's a mess."

"You are going in, aren't you, Babes? Tell me."

"Yeah, I am. I feel it's best. The sooner begun, the sooner done. I just want this over. And then, I want to get my sons back. So much to do."

Sweeney thought he was dreaming when Mendoza brought him the news.

"You're shitting me, right?" he asked, jumping out of his seat.

"No, man, I'm not. The captain just told me he and his attorney are supposed to be en route now to Parker Center. Can you believe that?"

"To surrender?"

"Yep."

"Un-fucking-believable. This is a first, huh? I mean, what banger turns himself in?"

"Either a rich and confident one or a stupid and scared one. By all accounts Shakur doesn't appear to be the latter."

"Shit, I don't care. I just want to clear this case. We'd better get on down to headquarters, huh?"

"You bet, partner. You bet."

16

As soon as Safi and Lapeace pulled to a stop in front of Parker Center the black 600 Benz was swarmed with reporters jockeying for a word from Lapeace or his attorney. It was a virtual stampede as reporters and journalists alike literally ran over one another in expectation of a word or an interview.

"Did you kill eight people on Crenshaw?"

"Are you remorseful for the lost lives?"

"Is it true you are admitting to being involved in the Crenshaw massacre?"

"Are you a leader of the Eight Tray Gangster Crips?"

On and on the questions came from men and women, black and white. "No comment. My client has no comment, thank you," Safi informed the jostling crowd of rude reporters. Still, they harassed the pair all the way to the front doors of the jail. There, two patrol officers took control of Lapeace and walked him, holding his arms, to booking front. Other officers, detectives, and jailers stood lining the hallway gawking at him and Safi.

They were led down a corridor and Safi was asked to stay put in an anteroom while Lapeace was taken through the rigors of booking. Fingerprints, photos, and questions about his birthdate, address, sexual preference, and if he had any safety concerns while in the county. He was fitted with a red wristband with "K-10," his name, and the county jail number typed on it. He was not treated roughly. He was allowed to keep his own clothes and shoes, though he knew this would change once he got to L.A. County jail. Parker Center, while headquarters for the LAPD, is also the L.A. city jail. All departments around L.A. were substations. Parker Center was also called the Glass House because of all the windows with the mirror tints facing the streets.

Once booking was done and he was officially charged with murder—eight counts—he was led down a corridor and posited in an interview room. He was soon joined by Safi. The door opened again and in came Mendoza, chewing corn nuts and carrying his black leather notebook. He was followed by Sweeney, bald head glistening, a sinister smile painted on his pasty face.

"Good evening men," Sweeney said, pulling his chair out and sitting down.

"Hello," said Safi. Lapeace said nothing. Mendoza stared across the steel table at Lapeace. Lapeace, not batting an eye, stared back.

"Okay," sighed Sweeney with a huge exhale of air. "Well, I am John Sweeney and this is my partner, Jesse Mendoza." Mendoza nodded his greetings.

"We are the detectives on this case. We'd like to ask you, Mr. Shakur, for a statement regarding these charges." Sweeney sat poised with his pen ready to write.

"I am exercising my right to remain silent," Lapeace stated. He said it evenly and clearly.

"Hmmm, well, is there anything you want to get off your chest or . . ."

"I am exercising my right to remain silent," Lapeace repeated.

"Well," Sweeney began, switching tactics, "some of your homeboys have sung a sweet song against you. Yep," he said, trying to make it sound really awful, "we have a couple of corroborating witnesses who are putting you at the scene as the shooter. What have you to say for yourself?"

"I am exercising my right to remain silent," Lapeace repeated again.

"Well, then, you will be happy to know—"

"This interview is over, gentlemen," said Safi. "I'd like to have my client lodged in his sleeping quarter, please."

Sweeney sat in stunned silence against the interruption and nerve of this pompous attorney. He'd never been talked to like this. But there was little he could do because, by law, the accused had the due process rights to terminate an interview with the exercising of his right to remain silent. Sweeney slapped his notepad shut and scooted his chair back loudly. He drilled a hole through Lapeace with his eyes.

"We'll see you in court, *Mister* Shakur."

Sweeney and Mendoza left the room and Safi patted Lapeace lightly on the arm. "You did good, brother. You did good. Now, keep that same attitude. Don't speak to no one about your case at County. Don't write any letters except to me. You write your letters and send them to me in legal mail. I'll send them where they need to go. Trust no one. Keep your nose clean. I'll be down to see you on a legal visit Monday. I'll let you know where we stand. You'll more than likely go to court Tuesday. We'll talk Monday, okay?"

"Aight, Safi. I'm with you. I just want it to be over with. Can you find out who that is he's talking about singin' on me?"

"Sure. We'll file for discovery and all that. Sit tight, Lapeace. We'll win."

"I believe that, man. That's why I'm here."

"All right, I'll go. I'll have this five hunderd dollars deposited in your account tonight. You have all my numbers?"

"Yes."

"Good night, then, Lapeace. See you Monday."

Safi left and Lapeace was momentarily alone in the interview room. Surprisingly he didn't feel bad for turning himself in. He had a top-flight attorney and he was sitting on $350,000. All legal. And this was just what was in his savings account. He had bonds, blue chips, IRAs, and property. What he didn't have was his freedom. That was the struggle now.

Two officers came and retrieved Lapeace. They took him out the back of the jail to a waiting unmarked vehicle and seated him inside. The officers fell into a police caravan of some four cars and an SUV. They pulled away from Parker Center and headed toward the Los Angeles County jail. Lapeace rested his head against the backseat and closed his eyes.

He thought about Askari. So much wasted energy. He thought about Sekou. So much vested loyalty. He thought about Tashima. Such a reservoir of love. He thought about Aunt Pearl. Such a strong soul. He thought about himself. Such a rebel spirit with a curious mind. He needed to find his niche. He had an uphill battle, but he had faith that his mission was bigger than this. This was not his destiny. Somehow in his heart of hearts he knew this.

The caravan of police vehicles turned onto Bauchet Street heading for the County's intake area. At an electric chain-link fence marked AUTHORIZED PERSONNEL ONLY, they sat idle while their ID was checked. The gate opened at a snail's pace before the space was big enough for a car to pass through.

Inside he was put into a cold, dingy holding cell. He'd been handed off to the custody of the Los Angeles sheriff's department a half hour earlier.

"Shakur. Inmate Shakur. Last three four-six-seven. Where are you?"

"Over here," Lapeace yelled. "Over here."

The voice came from a speaker mounted against the wall in the hall outside the cell.

"Where?" said the metallic, detached voice through the speaker.

"Over here!" Lapeace was at the cell gate hollering through the bars.

"Well that's where your black ass will stay. Just checking."

The prisoners in the adjoining cells all roared with laughter at the little joke made by the deputies in the intake booth. Lapeace walked to the back of the dirty holding cell and brooded in silence. *Here we go,* he thought to himself, *games being played at my expense.* He steeled himself against such foolishness but was human nonetheless. With the loss of his individual freedom he knew he'd also lost much of his strength to affect any meaningful change. His care and welfare largely depended on the mental health of his captors. Some in law enforcement came equipped with a cold reptilian blood flow and used the philosophy of white supremacy as a sword and shield against any perceived threat, real or imagined. He knew he'd need to grow a thick layer of armor to withstand any transgressions. An hour passed and he was escorted to a rectangular glassed-in space with about twenty other prisoners. All were Mexicano and New Afrikan.

"Take off your shoes and socks, put your feet on the yellow line in front of you, place your shoes and socks behind you," barked a tall, muscular deputy who had a high and tight military haircut.

"No talking, gentlemen. The faster we get through this process the sooner you'll get to your housing units. Let's go!"

The smell in the strip space immediately assaulted Lapeace's nose. Funk from what seemed a hundred years whirled up and slapped him several times across the face.

"Take everything out of your pockets. Place it on the yellow line. Strip down and place your clothing on the yellow line. Do it *now!*" shouted the deputy. And then the funk from several unwashed and jaundiced bodies put Lapeace in a terrible headlock. The prisoners, being searched like so many more before and to come, were from the dregs of society. Not all, but most. Drug addicts, homeless, derelicts—the hopeless. Prisoners of America's class wars. The stench was just about overwhelming because most had been in substations for two days without showers, just sweating, kicking dope, worrying about their cases. Fear and neglect and apathy stinks.

"Don't look down. Look straight ahead. If I catch you looking down you'll be sent back into the holding cells to be processed tomorrow. Let's do this quick, gentlemen. Hold out your palms, lift up your arms. Lift up your nut sack, turn, bend at the waist, crack a smile, cough three times. Lift up your left foot, let me see the bottom, now your right. Okay, don't put nothing on. Grab your clothes and come this way. Quickly!"

The naked group, including Lapeace, was led to a communal shower and told to stand against the tiled wall. Standing naked and barefoot on the cold tile was a torture all its own. In came another deputy with a hose and opened up on the group with a milky-white antiseptic-smelling substance that was supposed to kill lice. The hair, armpits, and crotch areas were sprayed at length. They were made to shower next. Their clothes were taken and bagged and stored. And they were dressed out in county blues. Those with non–steel toed shoes were allowed to keep their own. Lapeace had on white and blue leather Nike Cortez. After having an X-ray, blood drawn, and a brief medical exam they were guided to yet another holding cell. Because Lapeace was classified "K-10," special handling, he'd be spared another extended stay in the holding cells.

He was plucked out of the bunch and escorted by two deputies through the jail and into K-10 module 1750. He came onto the narrow tier at 11:35 p.m. Lights were out but ever vigilant prisoners who were in tune to the slightest movement and sound gave off a warning to others as soon as the deputies' keys were put into the lock to open the tier gate.

"Front to back," a prisoner yelled. And seeing Lapeace in cuffs carrying a bedroll, the prisoner added, "New arrival."

From the back of the tier came an acknowledgment, "Asante." It sounded far away.

Lapeace could feel eyes upon him as he passed cell after cell, but he kept his vision straight. He noticed that the bars were painted a forest green, the floor was a light brown, and mirrors lined the whole tier across from the cells.

"Open eighteen, on Denver row."

One of the escorting deputies spoke into his walkie-talkie. The trio came to a stop in front of cell 18. The numbers were painted above the cell.

"Step in," Lapeace was ordered. He flung his bedroll onto the steel bed and backed up to the food-tray slot to get uncuffed. Without a word the deputies left. The cell was a tiny, one-occupant deal. Steel bed, steel combination toilet and sink. Paper thin, two-piece mat to serve as a mattress. It was freezing.

"Hey Eighteen," someone hissed from an adjoining cell.

"Yeah," Lapeace answered.

"What's your name?"

By the tone, timber, and dialect, Lapeace could easily tell it was a New Afrikan speaking to him.

"Lapeace," he answered.

"Aight then. I'm Lil Blue Ragg, South Side Compton Crips."

"Right," said Lapeace. "I'm from North Side Eight Tray Gangstas."

"Aight, look. It's late right now but I'll holler at you in the mornin', huh?"

"Okay, I'll be here, don't look like I'll be goin' anywhere," sighed Lapeace looking around the pathetic little steel cage. Even the walls were steel.

"And that's fo' sho," said Lil Blue Ragg.

Lapeace spread out his bedding and laid on his back in the dark. In what seemed like an hour's time, the lights came on and down the tier rattled a dilapidated food cart. He'd been sleeping hard and struggled to get up on his feet. What startled him out of his daze was looking out of his bars and seeing himself locked in. For a fleeting moment he'd forgotten about the mirrored windows facing all the cells. Not only could he see himself but he could see other prisoners too, both to the left and to the right of him, for at least four cells in both directions. He stood at the bars as he saw the other prisoners near him doing.

"What up, homie?" greeted Lil Blue Ragg from next door. He was a tall, thin youth, trapped and held for a triple murder charge. A young gunfighter.

"Hey, aight now. Damn, what time is it? Seem like it's three in the morning."

"It's about five-thirty or six. They feed late on Saturdays. It's all garbage, though. After they feed I'll lace you on the tier."

"Thank you."

The trustee, a Mexican, passed out the paper plate meal of cold scrambled powdered eggs and green potatoes, a milk, and a juice. Lapeace could see that hardly anyone ate. He paced his space and thought of his situation. Lil Blue Ragg finished his morning constitution and came close to the bars so he wouldn't have to talk loud and be overheard.

"On this tier it's twenty-four cells. As far as Crips, there's me, Silk from East Side Nine One Hustler, D-Rocc from DuRocc, and you. There's a black dude from Tiny Rascal gang in the back. His name is Loki, he's straight. There's a couple others, Bennie, Free, and Thai: all nonaffiliates. The rest on this tier are southern Mexicans, Surenos. Your homeboy Chico is on the other side."

"Right. But what am I doing in this module?"

"This is High Power. People with big cases, media cases, multiple murders, prison gang members, and shit like that are kept down here. They keep us locked down all day. Every other day for thirty minutes we can come out on the tier, one at a time, to shower or use the phone or just bullshit. Even and odd numbers. Today's the fourteenth, so even numbers come out today. Here you go, Lapeace."

Lil Blue Ragg handed him a plastic bag with soap, deodorant, toothpaste, lotion, shower shoes, and coffee in it.

"Thank you," said Lapeace with gratitude.

"Aw, that's just a little care package, homie, don't even trip. They start tier time from front to back. You'll probably be coming out around two-thirty or so. I'm a holler at Chico to let him know you here, awright?"

"Yeah, I appreciate that. Hey, but look here, I, um, brought a little something with me—if you know what I mean?"

"Oh? Yeah, well if you tryin' to get something over to Chico I can swing that. What you workin' with?" Lil Blue Ragg asked in the strictest confidence.

"Black, white, and green," whispered Lapeace. He had two handcuff keys too. But he didn't want to reveal that.

"You tryin' to do what, slang it?" asked Lil Blue Ragg.

"The black and white, yeah. But I'm a blow the green."

"Me, I don't get down, but I know you can do your thang here. The Mexicans is on that black, the woods is on that white. I'll shoot a barua up the tier to see what's crackin'. Give me a minute."

Lapeace met his other neighbor in cell 17. He was an Amerikan named Ray. Ray had a New Afrikan wife and wasn't of the Nazi persuasion. He'd been snatched out of the U.S. Army and charged with a murder. Like everyone else he was innocent. Lapeace and Lil Blue Ragg became tight over the weekend. He told Ragg about his homies he'd met in Las Vegas just the week before. About his girl, about his cars and his bike. Ragg did the same. Lapeace spoke to the other Crips but really didn't trust them. Besides, they acted funny and it wasn't a damn thing funny about High Power.

Lapeace kept his dealings between he and Lil Blue Ragg. He communicated with Chico on the down low and otherwise kept it low. Safi pulled him out Monday for an attorney visit and prepped him on what to expect on the next day's court proceeding. Tashima and Aunt Pearl sat stoically on the benches of the big courtroom while other prisoners were arraigned on a dizzying array of charges. They grew bored by noon. With no sign of Lapeace they went to lunch. On the way back in they met up with Safi.

"We've been here all morning," protested Aunt Pearl, looking pensively at Safi.

"Oh, well, I guess I should have explained this, but with big cases like Lapeace's they tend to arraign them at the end of the day because of media coverage and all that. When you see reporters flocking you'll know he's about to come out. I'm going to make a couple of calls."

"Ain't that nothin'? Shit, how were we supposed to know that, huh?" Aunt Pearl was growing indignant. She sighed and sucked her teeth and straightened her dress.

"Don't let it bother you, Aunt Pearl. We don't have long to wait now. Half the day is already over," Shima said soothingly while rubbing Aunt Pearl's arm.

The media came out of the woodwork with quickness. Following Safi's advice and his lead, Aunt Pearl and Tashima filed into court and took a seat. Media were fanned out throughout the courtroom talking among themselves excitedly. After ten minutes of them setting up and bullshitting, the judge rapped his gavel and the order to quiet down was followed.

Lapeace was brought out of a side door in a blue two-piece county jail uniform, locked in waist and leg chains. He moved like a turtle. Every step was labored and looked to be painful.

Lapeace was guided by a deputy to a table and stood next to Safi.

The judge spoke with a dry nasal effect, looking at the court over the rim of his glasses. "This is the arraignment in the matter of the people of the State of California versus Lapeace Shakur. For the people?"

The D.A. cleared her throat and said, "Yes, your honor. For the people, Katy Lake."

She was an attractive New Afrikan woman with shoulder-length hair and glasses, which only added to her attraction.

"And counsel for the defendant?" asked the judge.

"Yes, your honor, Safi Wazir, private counsel for the defendant, Lapeace Shakur."

"Thank you Mr. Baraka. Ms. Lake, now I will read the charges. Well," said the judge, almost balking at the litany of charges in front of him, "let me see. Your client can enter his plea at the close of my reading.

"*Murder* in the first degree. Eight counts, special circumstances.

"*Attempted murder,* twelve counts.

"*Assault with intent to cause great bodily injury,* twelve counts.

"*Shooting into an inhabited vehicle,* five counts.

"*Mayhem, causing great bodily injury,* seven counts.

"*Possession of a firearm,* one count.

"And one count of a *gang allegation.*

"As to these charges, Mister Shakur, how do you plead?" asked the judge against the backdrop of a courtroom so quiet a mouse could be heard pissing on cotton.

"Not guilty," Lapeace said, loud and with conviction. Safi leaned over in support and whispered, "It's all bullshit, stand firm."

"Okay, is there anything from the people, Ms. Lake?"

"No your honor, not at this time."

"Defense?"

"Ah, yes your honor, the defense moves to have a gag order and a media restriction placed on this case and all proceedings to follow," Safi said.

"People?" asked the judge to see if there was any resistance to this.

"The people have no objections at this time, your honor." Ms. Lake was quite gracious.

"The matter is," the judge began, pulling his glasses off and chewing on the arms' ear piece, "that this is a free country. And this is a newsworthy item that has attracted the attention of a community overrun with violence of this kind."

"Be that as it may, your honor, my client has the constitutional right to a fair trial. And I'd not like to contaminate a potential jury pool with media visions of Mr. Shakur dressed in chains as if he were a convicted felon, because he is not. So this issue goes to that matter, your honor."

The judge thought on it for a moment and raised up in his chair. "I'm going to grant that, Mr. Baraka. Should it be challenged later on by the people it can be discussed."

"Thank you, your honor."

Lapeace was tapped on the elbow by a deputy and then led out of the courtroom through the same door from which he had been led in.

He'd been given a copy of his charges and looked them over when he was alone in the court holding cell. It was enough to make him nauseated. At this rate he'd be given five death penalties and fifty years.

Back at the county jail he was in a foul mood. In his cell he had to listen to stupid-ass conversations going on over the tier. Lapeace would just stand at the bars and look at the clowns around him. Big mouths with nothing to show. Sitting up in jail bragging about what they had, where they'd been, and what they were going to do when they got out. If it wasn't so sad it would all be amusing, but it was profoundly real and terribly nerve-wracking.

High Power had one amenity that Lapeace could appreciate: television. Behind the mirrored windows in front of every other cell were twenty-five-inch color televisions. When anyone went to court his case usually was shown that night on the tiers. So it wasn't a surprise that at ten o'clock on Channel 11 Lapeace's arraignment was shown at length. There were ohs and ahs up and down the tier. And another curious thing happened—a switch was thrown in the mind of Bennie Weems. It dawned on him that it was Lapeace, in cell 18, that Sweeney had told him about and who he was supposed to try and get information from regarding the Cren mass. Bennie decided to sleep on it and approach Lapeace in the morning.

17

After morning roll call, Bennie called over to Lapeace and had him retrieve a brief note off the tier.

It read: *Brotha, I just wanted to let you know that I am in a similar situation as you. And if you ever feel like having a mature conversation, I'm here. A true brotha, Bennie.*

Lapeace read the kite a couple of times and paced his cell. He looked over at Bennie's cell and saw him sitting at his steel desk reading. Lil Blue Ragg said he was all right, but sort of a braggard. He was from New Orleans. Lapeace didn't really know what he meant by a "mature conversation" or by his being in a "similar situation." From what Lil Blue Ragg said, Bennie was in jail for burglary.

A curious thing happens to people when incarcerated. When not in the presence of their attorneys, where it's best to ask questions and seek advice, they feel a lonesome need to question their case factors vis-à-vis their imprisonment. This is especially so when in the throes of High Power custody. Because the prisoner is in the company of people with heavy cases who are going to trial and coming back guilty 99 percent of the time, where one is laden with shackles and chains *every time* one leaves the cell—whether it's to a visit, court, or the shower—a permanent sense of doom hovers over the High Power module like a virulent strain of deadly ebola.

This state of dread causes most to reach out to fellow prisoners and seek some form of solace in the face of all the dread. When in doubt and raging against the cacophony of guilt, one seeks and reaches out for that whisper in the storm. It is a soft spot, a chink in the armor, of every prisoner held.

It was this chink that Bennie was knocking against and attempting to lay open for entry.

"Hey Bennie," Lapeace spoke over the space of Ray's cell, "I got that and I appreciate your offer. I guess I could use some decent conversation. Basically it's me and Lil Blue Ragg over here choppin' it."

"Yeah, well you know, I pretty much know a little somethin' about most things. You into sports?"

"Naw. Takes too much attention and time. I'm into business ventures, music, and I guess some politics. You got anything to read?"

"I got some law books, that's about it. I be studying the law. I'm trying to get up outta here," Bennie said, standing on one foot then the other and resembling a person with the hot foot.

"Yeah, I hear that, me too," confirmed Lapeace. "I got a question. How can they charge me with all the things they have when it's just me?"

"Well," began Bennie, licking his pink and brown lips and squinting his eyes in anticipation, "I don't know anything about your case except what we saw on the news last night."

"I've been advised by my attorney not to talk about my case with anyone. Not even the media can come in my court anymore," Lapeace conveyed, keeping his voice low. And while the television didn't come on until noon, which would somewhat mask any conversations, it wasn't a fail-safe against hungry ears or recordings.

Lapeace told Bennie he'd write his points and seek his counsel on paper. This, of course, was perhaps the worst, because words spoken evaporated into the atmosphere. Words written, however, remained in existence. They'd stay in this world for any to see as long as the material the words were written on stayed intact. Therefore, this was perhaps the worst Lapeace could have decided to do. Bennie, no dummy, exploited this chink to his advantage. He'd let Lapeace lead with a vague question concerning the merits of witness testimony and then feign ignorance, causing Lapeace to have to go deeper into his case for examples and thus giving Bennie more information. Lapeace made another poor choice in his secret communications with Bennie. He failed to ask for his communiqués back. Therefore his thoughts, questions, and fears were piled up in the cell of this unsavory character Bennie.

They exchanged kites most of the week, Lapeace writing furiously regarding his case. With each kite and response he grew more bold and comfortable. And Bennie feigned greater ignorance, thus inspiring Lapeace to venture more clarity, rendering greater exposure. Bennie reveled in his manipulative ability. He was a hater of the highest degree. A festering fool trapped by a seething hate for himself and anyone who looked like him. Though he was well camouflaged by the cultural trappings of "blackness," he wore dreadlocks and prefaced his sentences with "brother" and delighted in disrespecting Amerikan people on television. It was all a play and front. The man was poison.

The following week, after an army of communication was exchanged between the two, Bennie made his call to Sweeney. He and Mendoza rushed down to the jail. Bennie, under the guise of an attorney visit, went out to give them Lapeace's thoughts, questions, and fears. None of the other prisoners ever stopped to question the contradiction of him going to an "attorney visit" when he'd gone *pro-per* on his case. He acted as his *own* attorney. He had no counsel. But this was the level of preoccupation with their own cases, drugs, and a protective layer of desensitization that most prisoners wore like a thick layer of fat. "Ain't got nothing to do with me." An informant anywhere is a threat to criminality everywhere. Still, ignorance is as ignorance does, and Bennie walked out of 1750 with a pocket full of damage.

Sekou pulled his truck into the parking lot of Saint Andrew's park and scoped the scene. Over seventy-five members of the Eight Tray gangstas were in attendance. It was a Sunday and while it wasn't a "hood meeting" in the strict sense, it was a hopeful gathering of young men and women who shared a particular worldview. They stood around in clusters, trios, quads, and groups of fives, but never six. The Eight Trays triangulated on the "three." While some sets rotated on the "zero," the "five," or the "deuce," gangstas kept it on the three, or the third. Blue and gray, the gangsta colors, were draped on most in some way or another. Beer, hard liquor, and weed were passed around with all the abandonment of cigarettes. As Sekou walked up to a trio of youths he was quickly entertained by a lively conversation.

"Naw, I'm a tell y'all like this," bragged one tall youth to his homies, who listened with rapt attention. "I don't wanna get old. Fuck that, nigga, I'm *real* gangsta. On my C-Day after fifty-nine, fool, I'm a stand on the Tray line and blow my own brains out so I won't turn sixty. Fuck sixty."

"On *me,*" came the response in unison from the two listening. Sekou gave his greetings and pushed to another group where another animated conversation was in progress.

"We all know why the sky is blue, homie."

"Why is that?" asked a young home girl.

"Fool, cause God is a Crip! Dang, you ain't know that?"

"I guess I do now." She looked down bashfully, ashamed for not knowing common knowledge.

Seeing who he came to speak with, Sekou scattered his love and respect and strolled over to Tiny Monster, who sat in a triangle with Flip and Baby Hunchy. When they saw Sekou coming their way they ceased their conversation and gave shakes, greetings, and hugs all around. He congratulated Flip on the bowling championship he'd just won and Baby Hunchy on the college degree he'd just earned. Not to be outdone, Tiny Monster wanted his props on winning ten stacks (thousand) at the casino the night before.

"Yeah, you got that TM. Congratulations, homie."

"Well, damn. It's about *time*. I mean, it was only ten *thousand* dollars!" TM said, mimicking Thurston Howell III on

Gilligan's Island. Everyone laughed and patted him reassuringly on the back. Sekou, knowing he was in the company of the trustful, breached the subject.

"Monster, was you with Lazy the night of the fight?" Sekou asked, putting his Chuck Taylor'd foot up on the bench.

"Yeah, we watched the fight at my spot on the big screen," TM said easily.

"Was y'all in his car or . . ."

"Naw, we was in my Lex. Cuz shit was parked in his yard," TM answered.

"Why?" asked Flip, always sharp on his feet. "What's crackin' with cuz?"

"No shit," chimed in Baby Hunch, curious as to the line of questioning. "What's up?"

"Lazy got cracked the next mornin' with a burner," Sekou told the trio.

"Naw, that ain't true," responded TM. "I spoke with him Friday. The day Askari died."

Everyone looked at Sekou for some clarity. Both Flip and Baby Hunchy had seen Lazy since his supposed arrest.

"One time found a burner taped to his wheel well on Thursday morning. Took him to jail, two detectives, then the same day he was seen in the turf. Tiny Outlaw saw cuz being arrested. Saw Bob Hope find the strap, too."

"Damn . . . ," pondered Flip, "that ain't gangsta right there. Ain't nobody gettin' caught with a heat and gettin' out the same day. Eh Monster, ain't cuz on probation already fo' a strap?"

"Yep," TM answered, recollecting that Thursday morning. "Matter of fact, we was supposed to go to breakfast that Thursday at the Serving Spoon, but he never showed up. He called and said he was on his way, but I ain't seen him yet." Tiny Monster spoke looking around the park as if expecting to see Lazy. But he was also thinking about that night. About what Sekou said about a gun taped to the wheel well.

"Hold up, homie. I remember the night of the fight. I was bringin' Lazy back home. We pull up into his driveway and out from the back, on the side of the house where cuz car is, Lil Huck came out."

"What?" everyone said at the same time in disbelief.

"Yeah," Tiny Monster continued. "It was *crazy*. We pull up, right? And I got my lights on when we turn up in the driveway. All of a sudden, there go cuz, lookin' all suspicious and shit. Lazy went off, jumps out, runs up on him, and checks him hard. Cuz say he there to see Lazy. But earlier, before the fight, he walked right past us and barely spoke. Nigga know we don't fuck with him like that. That shit was sideways," TM concluded with finality. Sekou cleared his throat and spoke.

"Well, here's the thing. Y'all see Lil Huck and Lazy gets caught up, an arrest warrant gets issued on Peace, and his face is all over the news. What that sound like?"

"Sound sideways all around to me, Sekou," Flip acknowledged.

"Me, too," confirmed Baby Hunchy.

"Now Lapeace is sittin' in the funky-ass county jail fighting for his life. While these paper-thin-ass niggas runnin' round out here doin' one-and-a-half backflips for Bob Hope!" Sekou hissed in anger.

"That's real," howled Tiny Monster,

"Keep this between just us, cuz. Y'all let me know *whenever* y'all see Lazy. Call me on my cell. I need to get to the bottom of this fo' my nigga. Shit ain't gangsta."

"Fo' sho," they acknowledged and Sekou pushed off and

out of the park. He left his homies as he'd found them, gathered around discussing, promoting, and confirming their worldview and way of life.

Tashima sat behind her huge desk in her office doing absolutely nothing. She went over a few contracts and talked with her VP of A & R. Now she sat watching the clock. Her life with Lapeace, gone, was a prison within itself. She sat alone most of the time and watched the clock like a prisoner would. Her days revolved around Lapeace's calls. It was this time that her heart would feel light and whole and she'd get that warm, gooey feeling of real love. The calls were always too short, too monitored, and too far apart. Fifteen minutes every other day, always at a different time. Then it would be so much noise in the background and he'd be so distracted by whatever was going on there he could hardly concentrate on their conversations. It was a mess. The visits, twice a week, were for a pitiful twenty minutes behind some old scratched-up, dirty-ass Plexi-glas window. The conversations, even then, were clipped, tore in parts, jagged, and stilted innuendo helped along by hand signs and facial expressions. It was so hard for Tashima to see Lapeace locked up like that. He'd lost all of his natural, sun-given color and was an almost sickly looking gray. His eyes had sunken somewhat into their sockets and taken on a vacant look that tended to mystify Tashima. She'd have to tear herself away from his gaze when the deputies came to chain him up and haul him back to his cell. Each would hold a hand over the other's in lieu of a hug and she'd just die inside twice a week seeing him so subdued. She was doing time too.

Of course, Lapeace could not see that. He couldn't overstand it. He felt that only he was locked up, that he alone was in a steel cage, under surveillance, and facing the death penalty. He had no way of actually feeling that Tashima, too, was under hatches, the caught, the pained. Her love was so complete, deep, and pure that it wasn't a waking minute she didn't feel his pain. She'd slacked in the running of her company and her employees were beginning to chafe under her attitude and snaps. Tension was at an all-time high at RapLife. The boss, it was whispered, was on the rag—heavy.

At 3:57 p.m., her office phone rang.

"This is AT and T with a collect call from Lapeace. If you wish to accept this call press three. If you wish to deny this call press six."

Elated, Tashima quickly pressed three.

"Thank you for using AT and T."

"Hey, Babes, how you doing?" Lapeace said into the phone.

"I'm fine," Tashima lied, not wanting to put a damper on the conversation, "waiting for you to call."

They spoke for their allotted fifteen minutes and then sadly, as always, Lapeace had to go. He'd called to tell her that Thursday he'd not be allowed a visit because he had court. He wanted to be sure that she'd attend. Of course she would, his court appearances were hers, too. Their lives were inextricably bound by love, hate, and Amerikan law. They hung up and again Tashima sat alone in her office. She looked around and she mourned. She needed her some Lapeace—bad.

Damn, she cursed the day she met Lapeace. Her feelings, her reasoning rebelled against the pain and wished it wasn't real. But who was she fooling? Like a heroin addict cursing the use of its magic poison while it coursed lovingly through the body, her addiction was little different. She was a full-blown addict.

* * *

Working on a call from Tiny Monster, Sekou cornered Lazy at the spot on 80th. He and the homie Baby Stagalee rushed him into a waiting van. From there they took him to a safe house and rustled him inside. He struggled against the ties that bound him, but it was no use.

Inside the house they lodged him roughly in a vacant room. He was thrown violently onto the carpeted floor. A burlap bag was tied around his neck, covering his head. His hands were clasped tightly behind his back by a plastic tie. His legs were tied at the knees and at the ankles. Sekou, calm as ever, stood over the wiggling body. He had little sympathy for Lazy. He'd lost his road dog to this rat-ass bastard. Fuck that. Fool gotta come clean and then he gotta pay.

Sekou went and retrieved the butcher knife. But before leaving the kitchen, he laid it on a burner on the stove. He allowed it to heat until it was red hot. Without the wooden handle, he'd not have been able to even hold the knife. Back in the room, Baby Stag had sat Lazy up into a chair and tied him to it.

"Lazy," began Sekou, "I need some information from you. I am not in the mood to play. I don't have any patience or love for you. I want you to know this off the top. So to show my seriousness, I'm taking a finger now!"

At that Sekou sliced off Lazy's baby finger. He screamed like a woman in labor.

"Now," Sekou began again, "I'm goin' to ask you some questions. You got nineteen more fingers and toes to tell me the truth. Every time you lie you lose one. Now, were you arrested Thursday?"

"No, man, I don't know what you talkin' bout," Lazy lied against Sekou's threat. "Please, no, I was not arrested."

Sekou reached down and sliced off Lazy's ring finger. Lazy howled with pain and struggled against his ties. All to no avail.

"You can lie all you want, Lazy. But I already know the answers to the questions I'm asking."

"Who are you? Who's that?" Lazy demanded through his tears and pain.

"Were you arrested Thursday?" Sekou asked, poised to cut off his middle digit.

"Yes," Lazy consented. "Yes, okay, I was arrested." He sounded defeated, resigned, hopeless.

"Who arrested you?" demanded Sekou.

"Two detectives," squealed Lazy, crying now against the interrogation.

"Names. What were their names?"

"I don't know. I . . . ahh, okay, okay," Lazy cried. Another finger hit the floor.

Sekou had sliced off the middle finger. He wasn't up for no shit. He had no time for games.

"Names, nigga, names," threatened Sekou.

"Aight," gasped Lazy, realizing now he had no more choices. "Sweeney and a Mex named Mendoza."

"You tell on Lapeace?" Baby Stag asked with menace stepping up to Lazy.

"What?" Lazy asked in disbelief. "Ahhh!"

Sekou sliced off Lazy's index finger.

"Aight, please, just stop," Lazy begged. "Okay. Yes, they asked me about Lapeace. They asked if I was on Crenshaw on August third. I said yes. They asked what happened. I said I saw Lapeace and Anyhow shootin' it out. Told 'em I saw the tape. That's it, I swear. Please, that's it. Please let me go, *please!*" he whimpered.

"Handle that," Sekou nodded his head toward Lazy. Baby Stag stepped up with no hesitation and put a .25 automatic beside Lazy's head and squeezed the trigger. The *poof* sound was a quick snap and then there was silence.

"Get some trustworthy North Siders to help you clean this mess up, huh?"

"Fo' sho, homie," Baby Stag acknowledged.

Sekou had one more fish to fry. One more rat to capture. He left but in motion he called Shima and through codes told her what to tell Lapeace.

He then called the Big Homie to let him know the score.

Across the city, in a plush four-bedroom house, laid deep in the cut like germs, sat Sista Monster and Poppa North. They sat stoically on either side of a magnificently made chess set pondering their next moves. Well, actually, it was Sista Monster, with her brow knitted tight, who contemplated the next move. Poppa North, ever the strategist, considered his moves two, three moves ahead. She was a good chess player, but against Poppa North she had little chance. They played to strengthen her game. And not just at chess. He was also teaching her patience, perseverance, and offensive and defensive strategy. The skill of the setup, the layout, and the takedown. What Poppa North taught Sista Monster was the philosophy of Thick Face, Black Heart. Watch *all* pieces in the game 'cause everyone is a potential threat. The cell phone used for interhood communication rang and broke Sista Monster's concentration. She reached across her plate of salad and picked up the phone.

"Yeah?" Her voice was familiar, but Sekou couldn't pin it down.

"Who's this?"

"You called *this* number and you wanna know who *this* is? Come again."

"Sista Monster?" Sekou ventured.

"Maybe, who wants to know?" she said slowly.

"This is Sekou. Let me holla at Poppa North." The phone was passed.

"What's up?"

"Done dada on one, in search of the other." Sekou spoke the code fluently. "The G's are strong, the world is weak. All day."

"Good lookin,' third. Keep me abreast of how you movin'."

"Aight, G."

"Movin'," Poppa North said and broke the connection. Sista Monster swung her knight up and over into Poppa North's bishop. Poppa North stared across the expansive board at Sista Monster. She was satisfied with her move. A look of triumph on her pretty face. She pursed her lips and sat back taking her eyes off the board. Poppa North, ever the drama king, rubbed his jeweled hands together. He then ran his queen from the back field straight up into her bishop, killed him, and smothered the king.

"Checkmate, homie."

Lil Huck parked his van on Raymond Avenue. He walked around the block and onto 71st. He posted up against his better judgment in front of a vacant house. He had a few cocaine rocks left that he needed to get off in order to recoup. He quickly sold a few and began to feel better. Against the nagging rumors about his collusion with the police, he soldiered on with some reserve. He tried to reason as he went about his days along the line that Sweeney had once told him: No one knows everything about any of us. If anyone knew everything about us, no one would talk to anyone.

The night had fallen and 71st Street, being the low end, was also a hangout spot for gangstas. Lil Huck knew this but still pressed his luck. He'd felt the vibe for over a month but still stubbornly clung to the notion that no one knew. Or better yet, because he was big Huck's brother, no one would push up on him. No one would actually take his wind.

A few homies pulled up—youngsters: Baby China, Sista Sodi, and Tray Star I-Rocc. They greeted Lil Huck, smoked some weed, shot the shit, and moved on. Lil Huck was down to his last two stones, milling around, watching the block.

From between the houses, behind his back, crept a silent assailant in a dark-hooded sweatshirt, black pants, and black shoes. His face was shaded over by the enormous size of the hoodie. His steps were slow and measured, both hands buried into the pocket of the dark hoodie. Coming to a standstill in the middle of the driveway, the assailant scanned the street. When he looked left, a pair of parking lights came on from half a block away.

Lil Huck saw the lights activate but brushed it off as insignificant. When the lights went out the assailant stepped forward with two long strides and filled Lil Huck's head full of holes. Four direct shots found their mark and extinguished his life in an instant. Stepping over the lifeless body, the assailant was met at the curb by a black Suburban from down the street. They pulled off from the curb at a normal pace. A night's work well done.

* * *

On October 3, Lapeace went to his preliminary hearing, a minitrial where the prosecution presents the state's evidence and the judge alone must determine if there is enough evidence to bind the defendant over for trial in a superior court. Lapeace's counsel had already filed a motion to override Prop. 115, which allows for a police officer to simply read the police report and from this scintilla of "evidence" bind a defendant for trial. He also filed a 995 Motion to Dismiss on the grounds of no eyewitnesses and no evidence (gun, tape, etc.).

Sweeney's notes, given by jailhouse rat Bennie Weems, were resoundingly rejected by the judge, who said they were "scandalously gathered."

"After careful observation of the factors presented before this court today, I am not convinced that there is enough evidence presented by the state to determine beyond a reasonable doubt that Mr. Shakur is complicit in the crimes charged. Therefore, I am granting the defense motion to dismiss."

The judge cleared his throat, shuffled some papers, and that was it. The courtroom buzzed with disbelief. Lapeace stood motionless for several seconds before looking back at Tashima and Aunt Pearl and mouthing *I love you*. He was then led out of the courtroom by a deputy.

Lapeace was driven quickly back to the jail in a sheriff's van. The sunshine outside, as the van moved through downtown L.A., never seemed so bright. His heart was light as a feather. At the jail, even the old filthy holding tank he had to wait in pending an escort back to High Power didn't phase him. He paced the small space to and fro while thinking of all the things he needed to do. Especially follow up on the bloodline issue. His interest had been piqued and nothing was going to deter that. His sons were uppermost in his mind. Certainly he didn't want them to grow up like him, not knowing. So that and their parental custody was his main priority.

Back in the module he conveyed to Lil Blue Ragg his good fortune.

"That's the shit right there," exclaimed Lil Ragg, smiling in spite of himself through the bars at Lapeace.

"Hell yeah it is."

"Eh, Peace, what you gonna do when you touch down? I mean, like what you gon' eat?" asked Lil Ragg, serious as hell about it.

Lapeace at first thought the question odd and curious. He would think that most long-term prisoners thought about sex, about running up in something. But here was Lil Blue Ragg asking about food. And then it dawned on him about the actual length of time that Lil Ragg had been down in the county: four years. He could with just his month or so truly empathize with him. So why not indulge Lil Blue Ragg's fancy?

"Well, my girl—I gotta get out of that habit—my *lady* can cook like a champ, you know? So, it's all about the green, red, and yellow stuffed bell peppers. Ground beef, turkey, and more ground beef. Seasoned with onions, tomato sauce, cheese, the works."

"Hell yeah!"

"Then, I want some potatoes. French fries made from whole potatoes with the skin still on 'em. You feel me?"

"Man, like a muthafucka. What you gonna be drinkin' on, Peace?" asked Lil Blue Ragg, sounding like a starving man. He was holding on to the bars for dear life.

"With my food, I'll be sippin' on some cherry soda. You know, that's my favorite soda. But then after that, it's blunts and booze, you know?"

"Yeah," said Lil Ragg, "but I don't drink or smoke. I'll knock a hole in some food, though."

Both Lapeace and Lil Ragg got a good laugh out of that. They chatted on until Lapeace remembered about the business at hand. He was so caught up in the revelry regarding his pending release that it had totally slipped his mind. Safi had confided to Lapeace that the district attorney had revealed that he was in possession of handwritten letters from Lapeace supposedly regarding the generals of the case. Lapeace knew immediately where those letters had come from. Luckily the kites gathered by Bennie were ruled inadmissible evidence by the judge. Still, he was in major violation, use or no use. He scribbled a quick note to Lil Blue Ragg. Having learned his lesson, he asked for the kites back once Lil Ragg had finished. Lil Ragg nodded his acknowledgment and sent the kite back. Lapeace tore it up and flushed it.

"Shakur, roll your property up, you're being released," resounded the deputy's metallic voice through the speaker system on the narrow tier.

Lapeace said his so longs and was cuffed up by deputy Madrid to be escorted to booking front for release. As he passed Bennie Weems's cell Lapeace looked in but Weems wouldn't even venture a glance. His head was down as he pretended to busy himself with an imaginary task. No matter, his goose was cooked.

Lapeace went through the tedious waiting process—the rigorous criminal index code searches for wants or warrants and then the degrading strip search before finally, some eleven hours later, he walked through the electronically operated door leading out onto Bauchet Street and Freedom. Ever the faithful, Tashima was parked right outside the door. When she saw Lapeace making his long strides up the sidewalk she bolted from the Lexus and started screaming Lapeace's name. They embraced tightly, Shima up on her tiptoes, Lapeace bending forward to finish the embrace. Neither spoke. Shima had her face buried in Lapeace's muscular neck. His face hung over her back.

"Let's get up outta here before they change their minds, huh?"

"Yeah, you right about that big head," Tashima chided, "but they gonna have to kill me to get you away from me again."

"I know that's right. Let's bounce."

After the meal and the wine and weed, the lovemaking came easy. No awkwardness or neglect. There was total involvement—complete satisfaction. To Lapeace, Tashima was as lovely as ever. Her body was voluptuous, tight, and inviting. His to her was strong, muscular, and enduring. They lay spent, listening to *(It's the Way) Nature Planned It* by the Four Tops.

Lapeace spoke first.

"Shima, I love you. I don't want to live in this life without you. I need you. And you know I think, or rather I feel, we should get married. I mean, it's just that . . . well, will you marry me, Tashima?"

Tashima pulled herself up on her elbows to stare down into Lapeace's face. She pulled back her tangle of braids.

"Love, of course I'll marry you. I am in love with you. But look, I don't want to be married and registered with the state like a car. Or possessed like a thing."

"Do I treat you like that?" Lapeace quickly asked.

"No, you don't. But that's how society tends to regard it. Which is why I want to have a private, personal wedding exclusively engineered by us."

"Okaaaaay . . ." Lapeace answered, indicating he was lost a bit.

"What I mean is, we write our own vows, we have just our family there, and we jump the broom like our ancestors used to. What do you think about this?"

"That sounds like a winner, love. But can we do it soon?"

"How about this weekend?" Shima asked excitedly, breasts jiggling seductively.

"Yes, this weekend will be just right. Sekou can come, right?"

"You know Kou family."

"Cool."

On Saturday, October 5, another bright, sunny day in California, Lapeace and Tashima stood facing each other in Tashima's backyard. They were dressed in ordinary clothes, those they'd wear every day—just like their love. Two exceptions: they both wore crowns and they both were barefooted. The crowns symbolized their Afrikan heritage, the bare feet their connection to Mother Earth. Aunt Pearl was the flower woman who spread red and white rose petals around lavishly. Sober and with a healthy sheen to her, Aunt Pearl beamed with pride and love. Sekou, their best friend, stood with his chest out, hands clasped right over left delighting in Lapeace's freedom and happiness. His brown eyes sparkled with respect and admiration. Lapeace had shown him so many things—had given him such an example to follow that he could never not stand firm under any circumstances.

Tafuta and Sundiata, ever the little child soldiers, were chain boys. After Tashima and Lapeace had read to each other their handwritten vows, the boys stepped up and handed over two chains—a bracelet for Lapeace with Tashima's name on it and an anklet for Tashima with "Lapeace" written on a small tag.

Kody and Ramona stood as sentries. After Lapeace and Shima jumped the broom, Aunt Pearl walked up to both and planted kisses on their cheeks. She smiled pleasantly and then without warning jumped the broom. This prompted Tafuta and Sundiata to jump the broom. Kody and Ramona needed little encouragement. They sauntered up side by side and stepped all fours over the broom. Not to be left out Sekou, with his cool ass, strolled over to the broom and hopped over smiling. Everyone clapped and said "right on!"

"Now," Aunt Pearl said, "we are family for real. Let us rebuild and free the land!"

Anyhow's life hung dolefully in the balance at General Hospital. He was alive but not conscious. He could breath, but not on his own accord. He'd wasted away. He was not even a shell of his former self. And so it was that on that Saturday morning, October 5, Bingo, accompanied by Blain, came to visit their old friend one last time. They stood on opposite sides of the hospital bed staring down at the emaciated remains of their comrade. It had all come out that what the murdered messenger in the park had said about Any being tortured and then telling was true. Anyhow, a trusted member of their chapter of the Damu Nation had broken his oath and informed on a rival street combatant. Enemy or not, that was not the business. True to the game, Damu Ridahs didn't swing it like that. Nor could they tolerate such weakness.

Bingo pulled his red flag from his right back pocket and wrapped it twice around his right hand. Blain went to stand watch at the door. Bingo quickly smothered the little remaining life out of Anyhow's wasted body. There was no struggle, no resistance. Bingo uttered a small final prayer to Satan as he folded and retucked his nation's flag.

Out in the noonday sun Bingo and Blain headed toward the San Fernando Valley. They caught the westbound Santa Monica out to the 405 North and exited at Palm and hung a right. At Orchard Street they slowed in the middle of a residential block momentarily and then came to a gliding stop. They quickly strapped up and exited the black Nissan Maxima.

They approached the well-manicured house as if they'd been there before, walked up the flagstone walk to the potted porch, and rang the bell.

"Just a minute," intoned a masculine voice from within the dwelling. Moments later the door was pulled open and the look was truly a Kodak moment.

"What . . . ?"

Bingo and Blain rushed forward like Lawrence Taylor used to in his prime. They bumrushed Sweeney to his carpeted floor, beat him into submission, and bound him with duct tape. Sweeney kept crying and trying to bargain for his life, so Blain taped his mouth shut tight. He offered them drugs and money, guns and immunity—all to no avail. The Damus came for blood and soul. But first, they wanted to introduce him to a close friend of theirs called pain. Once Sweeney had met pain—unlike any he'd ever felt—he longed to embrace death. Though death was never to be rushed. So Blain and Bingo, knowing his fate, left Sweeney there in his bathtub dying an agonizing death—conscious the whole time.

Mendoza sat in the same diner, at the same table he and Sweeney had always sat at, reading the morning paper. He sipped his strong coffee and tugged absentmindedly on his mustache.

The main item was still the shocking discovery of homicide detective John Sweeney having been discovered murdered in his San Fernando Valley home the previous week. Though little was being said in print it was stated that the murder appeared to be the work of a deranged group of devil worshippers. The slaying appeared to be ritualistic.

Mendoza tipped his coffee cup, drained the last bit, folded his paper, and readied himself to leave. His new partner, Michell Anderson, an African American, stood and folded her arms into her coat.

"You know, partner," mused Mendoza, "this life is often what we make it to be."

ACKNOWLEDGMENTS

Bulletproof Love is extended to the Monster Nation (Lil, Tiny, Sista, and Young); China, Erica, and Tray; Omar (Chico) Dent; Lil Sidewinder, Big Skull, Lil Cavey, Water, Tybud, Boom and Young Quentin; Big Flip; the Dog Fam; the Menace Crew; Big, Lil, Baby, and Sista Sodi; the Stag-Nation; Big and Lil GC; Big, Lil, Baby, and Tiny Diamond. The West, North, Bacc, South, Far, Deep, and Hanford.

Bulletproof Unity is extended to the Provisional Government-Republic of New Afrika; the Spear and Shield Collective/ Crossroads Support Network; the Black August Kollective and All New Afrikan Political Prisoners and Prisoners of War. The August Third Collective and all other forces active in the New Afrikan Independence Movement. Free the Land!

Bulletproof Appreciation is extended to Thomas Lee Wright —Friend Extraordinaire (Thanx for everything); Jay-Z (you shot that homie!); Willie D, Scarface, Bushwick (good lookin'); Nutty Brain, Lil Mad Dog, Garland, Shaggy (Keep it Moving!); my editor Andrew Robinton (the smooth operator!); my publisher Morgan (thanks for having faith in a cat); Danny Osborn (South Bay's finest); Teri Woods (my favorite writer). My attornies H. Russell and Stacie of Halpern and Halpern (the Dream Team—thanx). D-Rocc from DuRocc (Eternal Love); Snoop Dogg, Tray Deee, Goldie Loc, C-Style (i Love Your Life). Antoine Fuqua (a true friend, thank you!) Nitra (thanx for the three-way calls), Big Oso Azusa (Right on for the "you know"), and my dearest Comrad-Sista Thandisizwe Chimurenga—perfect love.